BOOK BOYFRIEND BUILDERS

RATING THE BOOK BOYFRIEND

JADE DOLLSTON

Dedication

To my BBB girlies - AK, L.A., and Carolina - you sexy bitches! You three mean the world to me, and I'm so happy we did this project together. Especially because it gave us an excuse to have an "author retreat" and practice our hawk-tuahs.
Also, I'm still not sure I used the right font. Can someone check that for me? K'thanks.

To Doreen, whose information about Port Saint Joe and Mexico Beach, Florida was invaluable while writing this book. Thank you for running around, taking pics, and completely schooling me… oh and I guess Mike is pretty cool too. I love you, sis!

Prologue ~ Libby

"This bra has got to go," Ava proclaims before the door to the hotel suite we're sharing has even shut behind us.

She does that magical bra-removal trick, pulling it through the sleeves of her emerald-green sweater and flinging it across the room.

"Ow!" JoJo yells, yanking the lacy black garment from her head where it landed. "I think you gave me a concussion with your boulder holder, woman."

"Sorry," she shoots back, shimmying her boobs. "The old bacon hangers need room to breathe."

I choke on my own saliva, and Gemma smacks me on the back. "Jesus, Ava. You're a romance author, and the best description you can come up with for your breasts is *bacon hangers*?"

She giggles, her sapphire-blue eyes sparkling. "My grandma used to say that, and I always thought it was hilarious."

Gemma tucks a lock of her dark-brown hair behind her ear and begins tapping in her notes app, something she does about a hundred times a day. "I like it. You care if I use that in my next book? I have a character that loves to say outlandish shit."

"Be my guest," Ava tells her, grabbing the handle of her cart.

"Let's put our stuff in our rooms and then order something to eat."

"Yessss," I agree, practically feral for some food at this point in the evening. "I didn't think there was any way someone could screw up a turkey sandwich, but that hockey puck they served for lunch proved me wrong."

"And all for the low, low price of forty-nine dollars!" JoJo replies with her trademark sarcasm.

"Other than the food, this was the best book signing event I've been to," Gemma says.

"Yeah," I say quietly as we head to the bedroom of our suite with our carts in tow.

"What's wrong?" she demands as soon as we're inside.

"Nothing."

"Liar." Her pale green eyes narrow. "How many books did you sell?"

"Forty-nine," I sigh.

"Ah. One short of your goal."

She knows me so well. I'm very target-oriented, and when I don't reach my goals, I get disappointed in myself.

"It's fine. It was only one book. I probably expected too much of myself."

Gemma marches over to my portable cart and rummages through the books I have left. "This one," she announces, holding up my latest release, *Rolling the Dice*.

"Gem, you really don't—"

"Psssh. Stop talking. I buy every one of your paperbacks, just like you buy mine. Now sign it."

"Bossy ass," I say with all the affection in the world for my best friend, taking the purple Sharpie from her hand and signing *Libby Cox* on the title page. I notice Gemma stuff a twenty into my money pouch on top of the contents of my cart.

I hand the spicy romance novel over, and her beautiful face creases into a smile as she stares at the words. "Ahh, the fabulous Libby Cocks."

My eyes roll to the top of my head. "Don't think I don't hear you pronouncing the *cks*, you perv. It's Cox with an *x*."

"You'll always be Libby Cocks to me," she informs me as she places the book neatly in her suitcase.

"Well, since cocks are your favorite thing, I'll take that as a compliment."

"You should," she agrees, stripping off her raspberry off-the-shoulder top and tossing it haphazardly onto the bed on her way to the bathroom. I immediately grab it and begin folding it precisely as she calls, "And stop folding my shit. It's going in the laundry bag anyway."

"Sorry," I call back, "I don't know why I'm like this."

Gemma pops her head around the doorframe and lifts a perfectly arched eyebrow. "We both know why you're like this, Libs, and it's okay. It's the same reason you're a spreadsheet whore."

I giggle. "I thought I was the banter queen." That's the nickname she'd given me after reading my first book three years ago.

My friend retreats back into the bathroom. "You're both." I finish folding her shirt that doesn't need to be folded before pulling my cozy ivory sweater and lounge pant outfit from the dresser drawer.

Gemma returns to the bedroom wearing a magenta satin pajama set with her initials monogrammed on the breast pocket, her hair up in an elegant bun. I shake my head.

"Why do you look like a supermodel in pj's?"

"I like nice things," she says, her eyes flicking to the shirt I'd folded before picking it up and tossing it unceremoniously into her laundry bag in the corner. "Now get dressed so we can eat."

After pulling my long blonde hair up into a ponytail and donning my comfy clothes in the bathroom, I find Gemma unloading her cart and plopping the swag container and books in her spare suitcase.

"I'll pack that properly for you tomorrow," I say.

"I'm sure you will, doll. Let's go."

Ava and JoJo emerge from their room at the same time as us, and we move as a group into the living area. We'd booked a two-bedroom suite at the Colorado Springs Hotel and Convention Center for one of the biggest book signings in the romance world. We were completely exhausted.

"Chinese or pizza?" JoJo asks, sifting through the takeout menus on the dark wood desk as the rest of us sink onto the cushy furniture.

"Chinese," we all call simultaneously.

After placing our orders on the online app, she heads to the kitchenette and returns with two bottles of white wine, a bottle of vodka, and four stemmed glasses on a tray.

"Let's get our drink on, ladies."

"I'll have wine," I announce.

"We're all having wine… with a booster," JoJo says, wiggling her eyebrows at me as she pours four glasses of wine and then adds a healthy shot of vodka on top.

"What the hell?" Ava asks. "Are you trying to kill us?" She twirls a lock of her reddish brown hair around one finger, her brow furrowing with concern.

"We need to relax," JoJo replies with a casual shrug of her shoulders.

As we each lift our glasses of *boosted* wine to our lips, Ava yells, "Wait! All four of us haven't been together for six months, so we have to do toasts." She bites her bottom lip and thinks for a second. "Here's to love, laughter, and happily ever after."

"Aww, that's sweet," Gemma says. "How about this one? Here's to staying positive and testing negative."

I snort out a laugh as everyone looks to me. "Here's to women and horses… and the men who ride them."

"Amen," JoJo crows. Her lips curve into a smirk as she lifts her glass. "I would rather be with the people in this room than with the finest people I know."

We all roar with laughter before taking our first of many drinks. "Holy hell, that's strong," Ava coughs.

"But it's not half bad," Gemma comments, "if you like drinking fruity kerosene."

My throat burns, but I take another sip. "This'll definitely put hair on your chest."

Ava pulls the top of her pink floral sleep shirt away from her body and peers down into it. "Nope, no hair yet. Better drink a little more."

JoJo and I share an amused look. Ava is a wine connoisseur and doesn't drink hard liquor often. She's probably already tipsy. This is going to be fun.

"I'm so glad we all decided to stay an extra day. That will give us time to unwind after an entire day of smiling and talking," Gemma comments, curling her legs beneath her on the cushy taupe armchair. "And since JoJo lives in Colorado, she can take us sightseeing."

"I can show you the bars where all the hot guys hang out," our friend offers, checking something on her phone. "Uh-oh. It looks like there's a storm moving in Monday afternoon. You're all flying out that morning, right?"

We all nod before Ava meets my eyes and lifts an eyebrow, a silent gesture of encouragement—and maybe a tiny prod. Taking another fortifying gulp of my vodka wine, I blurt out, "Logan and I broke up two weeks ago."

Gemma cranes her neck forward, green eyes wide, and JoJo's mouth gapes open. Ava is the only one who doesn't look surprised because I'd called her the day after the breakup. She's the most empathetic person I know, and I'd needed that during my post-breakup pity party.

"I'm sorry I didn't tell you guys yet, but I needed time to process."

"What happened?" JoJo asks, topping off my glass with a little bit of wine and a whole lot of vodka.

"He said he didn't, and I quote, *see a future with me.*" The bitterness rang true in my tone.

"That fuckwad," Gemma snaps. "You moved from Texas to

Florida to be with him. He should have thought about *the future* before dragging you away from your home."

"I didn't have much left there anyway since my cousin, Gianna, moved to New York," I reason lamely, and everyone's faces soften with sympathy. "To be honest, it wasn't that much of a surprise, and I'm more pissed than heartbroken. Does that make me sound bad?"

Gemma nudges me with her foot. "Not at all. You told me a few months ago that things had cooled off for you and prickface. You don't need to be with someone that doesn't know your worth and treat you accordingly, so maybe this is a positive thing."

The other girls nod in agreement, and I fucking love these women.

I force a brightness into my tone. "Ya know, it's cool. I'm moving to Port Saint Joe, which is a little over an hour away from Panama City Beach. It's a small, cozy town, so I'm really excited. PCB is popular with the tourists and can get really crowded, so I'm looking forward to the slowed-down pace."

"I know it sucks, but I'm happy you'll be in a small town now," Ava says, wrapping an arm around my shoulder and squeezing.

Needing a change of subject, I ask, "So what's up with you, A? You heard from your man-child ex-husband recently?"

She takes a long pull of her boosted wine and barely winces this time. "Ohhh, yes. Zach called me the other day because his electricity got turned off. He didn't know how to pay his electric bill online, so I had to walk him through it."

We all burst into laughter. Fucking Zach. He's lovable but has never grown up, and I'm glad Ava is no longer responsible for raising him—I mean isn't married to him anymore.

A knock sounds at the door, and JoJo rises to answer it. "That must be the food."

For the next thirty minutes we eat, drink, and laugh. It's so good to be back with my girls again. We'd met in an author group on Facebook a few years ago and instantly hit it off. Though we only see each other in person a couple times a year, we text every day and talk often.

Gemma claims that if anyone ever got hold of our text threads, we'd either be arrested or declared clinically insane, and she's probably right. It gets pretty crazy sometimes when four romance authors enter brainstorming mode.

After we clear our food away, I wash my hands, feeling the roughness of my skin beneath the foamy soap. "Anyone have lotion? The dry Colorado air is wreaking havoc on my skin."

"I have some in our bathroom," Gemma says, storing the left-overs in the fridge. "It's in the hot-pink tube."

Heading into the bathroom, I pick up a pink tube and carry it back into the living room, squirting a healthy dollop onto my palm.

"What kind of lotion is this, Gem? It's really sticky," I call out, settling onto the couch as I spread the goop between my fingers and up onto my forearms.

She walks in from the kitchenette and stares at the lotion I'd placed on the coffee table. Her eyes flick to my hands, which are covered in the thick, clear substance, and back to the tube.

"I said the *hot-pink* tube. That one is *fuchsia*."

Lord, I hope I didn't use one of her very expensive hair products. "Oh crap, sorry. Is this your hair gel or something?"

She picks up the *fuchsia* container and holds it a couple inches from my face. I read the words.

Loob in a Toob.

"Oh my gawd!" I yell, jumping up and holding my arms out to the side like they're covered in a hazardous material. "I just rubbed your pussy lube all over me!"

Everyone else is in hysterics. JoJo has fallen onto the floor and is holding her stomach, and Ava has tears streaming down her pretty face as I flail my goo-covered hands around wildly.

My eyes widen as a thought occurs to me. "Please tell me it's not your butt lube. For the love of all that's good and holy, *please*, Gemma!"

She's not even trying to hide her laughter as she shakes her head. "No, this is the front door one. The back door stuff is in a coral tube."

"Coral! Fuchsia! Pink!" I holler. "Why are they all so close? Haven't these people ever heard of blue? Or yellow? Fuck!"

I sprint to the kitchen, hearing the hilarity continue behind me as I turn on the hot water. After scrubbing my hands and arms until they're red and raw, I stomp back into the living area to find my crazy friends still chuckling.

"This. Never. Happened," I demand, pointing a stern finger at each of them.

Everyone is silent for a few beats before Gemma pipes up with, "But we've shared something special here tonight. I feel so close to you right now, Libs."

JoJo covers her mouth and then snorts behind her hand. "Yeah, I think you two may actually be married in some third-world countries."

I scowl, and Ava pats my arm. "Don't be mad. We're just teasing you." And then under her breath mumbles, "Lubey Libby."

"Ha ha, fuckers," I say, a giggle bubbling up from my throat. There's always extreme ridiculousness when we get together.

JoJo refills our glasses once more, and her pour is becoming increasingly heavy on the vodka.

She lifts her glass again. "Here's to alcohol, which makes us see double and feel single."

Ava giggles as we drink. "We are all single now."

My nose scrunches up. "I'm not sure how I feel about getting back into the dating scene."

JoJo leans her head against the back of her chair and stares at the ceiling. "It's horrible. Men are intolerable. I suggest you forget about dating and orbit your own Venus, if you know what

I mean. Stock up on vibrators. You can borrow some lube from Gemma."

I take a healthy swallow of the vodka with a splash of wine, my limbs feeling loose and soft. "You're never going to let me live that down, are you?"

"No, Lubey Libby. We're not," Gemma replies. "And back to the subject at hand, JoJo is right. Dating sucks. Why can't we find men like the ones we write about in our books?"

"Fuck if I know," JoJo wails. "Is it too much to ask to have a man with a big, hard body, some well-placed tats, and a mouth that would make a hooker blush?"

"One with an actual job and a maturity level that's a few notches higher than a prepubescent chimpanzee," Ava adds.

"Someone who is honest and *loyal*," I mutter, thinking of Logan.

Gemma rings her finger around the rim of her wine glass. "There needs to be some kind of boot camp for guys where they're trained to be book boyfriends."

Everyone giggles at the thought, and I stand, my back ramrod straight as I take on the demeanor of a drill sergeant. Picking up a forgotten chopstick from the coffee table, I march behind the couch and tap JoJo on the top of the head.

"You! Lean against that door frame and look longingly at me. And make it sexy!"

She grins as she hops up and hurries over to the door of the small kitchen, lifting her arms over her head to grasp the top of the entrance. Her eyelids drop, and she licks her lips and flashes me a sultry look.

"Excellent, recruit. I can tell you've been practicing that." I point my chopstick at Ava. "You, there! Tell me I'm a good girl."

She fights a smile and says, "You're such a good girl, Libby."

"No, no, no!" I bark. "That was weak, Costa! You have to growwwwl! Make me feel it!"

When she starts laughing, I give her my best glare, hands on hips until she schools her expression. With her voice as low as she can make it, she growls, "You are such a good… fucking… girl, Libby."

"By damn," I drawl, "that was pretty impressive, Costa. You almost made my panties wet."

She splutters out a laugh, and I whirl around to Gemma, brandishing my stick. "Fairchild, give me a pet name. Now!"

"Ahhh, la mia piccola tigre," she purrs before translating. "That's *my little tiger* in Italian."

I give a curt nod, keeping in character. "I like it. Bonus points for using a foreign language. I'd totally fuck you at this point."

She gnaws on her bottom lip to keep from laughing as I stroll back over to JoJo and demand, "Estes, what's my coffee order?"

"Macchiato with one cream and two-and-a-half sugars, ma'am."

"Favorite flower?" I ask Ava.

"Anything yellow," she replies, bobbing her eyebrows at me. "Uh-huh."

I stomp around the room and manage to stay in character the entire time while barking out more and more outlandish commands, and my crazy friends play along.

Then I approach Ava and poke her in the chest with my weapon. "Say something inspiring, Costa."

And then Ava—dear, sweet, shy Ava—wraps her small, pale hand around my throat and squeezes slightly before growling, "You are mine, Libby, and if anyone lays a finger on you, I'll paint the earth with their blood." My eyes almost bug out of my head in surprise as her blue ones darken. "Am I understood?"

I'm unable to speak for several long seconds before I croak out, "Well. I suppose that's acceptable."

"Christ, Ava," Gemma says from behind me. "I think I just had a spontaneous orgasm. Who knew you had that in you?"

Our friend releases my throat and brushes non-existent lint from her shoulder as she smirks. "Maybe I'm not as sweet as you all think I am."

JoJo skips over and tugs Ava's dark ponytail. "I think we've learned a lot here tonight. Ava is a secret domme, and Libby would be a superb man trainer."

We all laugh and plop back down onto our respective seats for more drinks. The bottle of vodka is emptied, and words begin to slur over the next hour.

"I got to meet Riggs Romero today," JoJo announces. "He's even more impressive in person." A ping of jealousy shoots down my spine.

"Oh, that book cover model? He's soooo hot," Ava agrees.

"Libs has a huge crush on him," Gemma adds. "Look, she's blushing just thinking about him."

My face is indeed heated, but I demur. "It's just the alcohol."

"Whatever. Your eyes were like saucers today when he was walking around in our area."

"He's nice to look at," I allow, and Gemma lifts an unimpressed eyebrow at me. "Okay, fine. I want to lick every book cover that man graces. Are you happy now?"

"Ecstatic," she replies smugly. "I was watching him, and he was definitely eyeballing you today."

"He was not!" *Has someone turned on the heater in here?*

"Was too. I think he was headed to your table next when the director pulled him away for that industry panel. Otherwise, he would have hopped on the Libby Cocks train."

"Mmmm, a train. Can you just imagine a whole line of Riggs Romeros waiting to take their turn with you?" JoJo mused.

I squeeze my thighs together and squirm in my seat on the couch. Gemma's correct. I have a huge crush on a man I've never met in person.

Riggs was the muse for every single male main character I'd ever written. Even the ones that didn't have jet-black hair and sexy tattoos had some piece of the stunning man in them. His ice-blue eyes. His sharp, square jawline. His chiseled abs. His parts I could only dream about…

Luckily, my condition goes unnoticed by my best friends as JoJo brings up the subject of book sales.

"My sales have been in the tank the past month," she laments. "I've been busy writing and preparing for this book signing, and I haven't had much time to market on social media."

"It's hard to keep up with everything," Ava agrees.

"Mine have picked up, but they always do around release time. It's helped a lot since I'll have moving expenses now."

"Still no luck finding a job?" JoJo asks, tilting her head so her blonde hair falls over one shoulder.

"Not since leaving Texas. I'm doing some freelance web designing, but no one wants to hire a full-time designer. Apparently, twenty-seven is ancient in my industry. But added to my book sales, the jobs I have picked up are enough to pay my rent and utilities. Luckily I already had this trip paid for."

We continue drinking as we talk about our respective book sales, and I'm pretty sure I'm completely drunk. My fingers and toes have gone numb, and my words come slower and with more effort. I become aware that Gemma has been silent for quite a while.

"Gem, you're quiet. Everything okay?"

"Ya know, it's not that bad of an idea."

I exchange amused glances with JoJo and Ava. We're used to this. Gemma often has entire conversations going on inside her head and forgets that the rest of us are not privy to what she's thinking.

"What's not a bad idea?"

She refills her glass from the new bottle of vodka JoJo produced from seemingly out of nowhere. After taking a long slug, she taps a perfectly manicured finger against her full lips, her eyes thoughtful.

"Training men to become book boyfriends."

JoJo's eyebrows lift to her hairline. "Well, yeah. That would be nice. Someone needs to do something with the current dating pool. It's abysmal."

Gemma's eyes meet each of ours. "Just hear me out. What if *we* started a business to do that?"

Ava giggles. "You want to turn Drill Sergeant Libby loose on the men of America?" Her eyes widen in excitement. "Ooh! Can we get her a whip?"

We all laugh at that. Except for Gemma. I can practically see her mind spinning as her teeth work back and forth against her bottom lip.

"Maybe not boot camp style—though I would love to see Libs wield a whip on some clueless sap—but why couldn't we be consultants? We write the kind of men that women want, so why couldn't we be hired to… *educate* guys?"

My pink lips twist to the side as I sit there stunned at what our friend is proposing. "But then some poor girl gets stuck with a man who's just pretending."

Gemma shakes her head back and forth, her bun bobbing from side to side. "No, not like that. We'd want them to be their authentic selves but just a better version. Teach them how to be more thoughtful." Her finger wags back and forth between me and JoJo. "Like when Libby asked you for her coffee order earlier. You knew the answer immediately. I dated Aiden for years, and he was still clueless about my favorite coffee. And I order the same damn thing every time."

"Sooo you want to help men learn their woman's coffee orders?" I ask, skepticism coloring my tone.

"Among other things. I think there are a lot of good men out there, but some are clueless about a lot of things. They just need to *pay attention* to their woman's needs. We could give them the tools they need to do that. To read verbal and non-verbal clues."

JoJo's dark-green eyes brighten. "You know, that might actually work. It's definitely an untapped market with lots of potential."

"I have a friend who reads my books with her boyfriend," Ava tells us. "She said their relationship has really improved a lot since they started, and not just in the bedroom. She thinks it inspired him or something."

I mull that over in my fuzzy brain. "So we could sell our books as instructional manuals? If we marketed to men as well as women, that might boost sales." *And the extra money couldn't hurt.*

Gemma's shrewd gaze meets mine. "Not exactly what I was thinking. We should provide an actual service to clients who are interested."

"And charge people for it?" I ask incredulously.

"Yeahhh," JoJo breathes, seeming to warm up to the idea even more. "I imagine a lot of women would enroll their boyfriends in the… what would it be? An online course?"

Ava shakes her head. "It would be more personal if we met the clients face-to-face."

I wave a hand at the insane people in front of me. "Y'all are talking like we're actually going to do this."

JoJo turns to me in challenge. "Why shouldn't we? Who better to help men become book boyfriends than romance authors? We know all the tricks. And just think about how many women it would help. It could turn their man into their *dream man* with a little advice from four authors who know a thing or two about what women want."

Okay, I like that idea… Helping women by guiding their men into the book-boyfriend domain.

"True," I said slowly. "We all get tons of messages and reviews from readers saying they wish they could find a man like the ones in our books."

"And though we write our men as uber attractive, I guarantee ninety percent of those women are more interested in how the book boyfriends *act* than their physical appearance." Gemma stares down at her hands in her lap, and her voice softens. "Every woman wants to be treated with the respect she deserves."

My heart breaks a little for her, and I stand before nudging her over and squeezing into the chair beside her so I can wrap her in a hug. Gemma Fairchild is a badass lawyer and as tough as nails, but I know her breakup with Aiden cut her deeply.

"You really think we can do it?" I ask.

Her lips curl up into a smile as she blinks away her emotions. "Fuck yeah, we can. I think it could be something really great."

For the next three hours, we brainstorm. Some of the ideas are silly as fuck because we're all pretty much trashed on vodka wine— which at some point had become vodka vodka—and we laugh hysterically until the wee hours.

We also make lots of promotional videos, and at some point Gemma spanks me with a hairbrush and calls me a good girl. *So many shenanigans.*

Eventually, we come up with a name and a game plan.

While I design an engaging website, Ava, the marketing genius of the bunch, makes us a gorgeous logo.

"Okay, Gemma. You're the lawyer. Make sure this client contract is how you want it." I pass her my laptop.

She squints drunkenly at the screen before closing one eye and slanting her head to the side. Approximately twelve seconds later, she nods her head. "Yup. Looks good to me."

"All set then. Activate the website," JoJo instructs, and I do. "We made some graphics and reels, and Gemma wrote a script. Sending it to your phones now."

Everyone's devices ping, and we pick them up. "This looks soooo good," Ava drawls, tipping over sideways against me. "Can we share to our social media accounts now?"

"Let the marketing commence," I yell, and Ava startles.

"Shit, you get loud when you're drunk," she complains as we all begin posting on Facebook, Instagram, and TikTok.

When we're done, four sets of eyes find each other, and we burst into spontaneous laughter.

"That may have been the most idiotic thing we've ever done," Gemma crows, swiping tears of mirth from her bottom lids with her thumbs.

"It was your idea," I point out.

"We're business owners," Ava says, her drink-flushed face beaming with pride. Then her eyes round, and she slides dramatically to the floor. "Oh my god! We're business owners!"

"Don't start freaking out," JoJo warns.

"But what if everyone thinks it's stupid?"

"Then we say it was just a joke… an early April Fool's gag." It's currently October, but whatever. "I can delete the website like it never happened." My shoulders lift and fall in a shrug.

"We probably need to do that anyway," Gemma slurs. "In the morning. This was a dumbass idea."

"And it was yours," I remind her again.

"Yeah, well I'm hammered, babes. You shouldn't listen to a thing I say when I've been drinking."

JoJo lifts her almost empty glass. "Well, for the next few hours anyway, we own a business like the boss bitches we are. More toasts!"

"Here's to the floor. It'll hold you when no one else will," Ava calls from her position on the rug.

"Here's to being naughty and saving Santa a trip," I say before turning to JoJo.

"Here's to all the liquor we drank tonight and the Advil we'll swallow tomorrow."

"That's probably the most accurate toast of the evening." Gemma's face softens as she raises her glass. "Here's to the nights we'll never remember with the friends we'll never forget."

"Hear, hear!" Ava says, snagging her drink and spilling half of it on her head.

A sloppy grin overtakes my face when we all clink glasses and yell, "To the Book Boyfriend Builders!"

CHAPTER 1

Libby

"Gem…"

I hear movement from the bed beside me. "What the fuck is that?"

"Gemmmmm…"

"Libby?" Her voice is muffled. "Why does your voice sound like my Uncle Louie? He smoked three packs a day and has one of those voice box thingies. Did you get one of those implanted?"

My brain aches. *Did I?* "Not that I can recall."

"Well, stop talking. Your voice is freaking me the fuck out. It's like you swallowed about thirty frogs while you were asleep."

Still not opening my eyes, I call out, "JoJo, is there a frog epidemic in Colorado?"

"No. Shut the fuck up! I'm trying to die in peace," comes a voice from the other room.

Convinced I hadn't inhaled any amphibians, I rest my head back on my pillow and hear Gemma groan.

"Who are all these people in our room?"

"That's what I was trying to ask you a few minutes ago when you started talking about frogs and Uncle Louie. They seem to be members of a demonic marching band."

"Uncle Louie is a demon?"

I huff out a sigh of frustration as my head pounds. "No, the ones playing the bass drums in our room."

"And cymbals. So many fucking cymbals," she whines. "It sounds like they're inside my head."

"Literally the worst marching band ever."

"They're demons. What did you expect?"

I lay silent for a few seconds as the booms and crashes escalate, making my head hurt even worse. "We should try to get rid of the evil drummers," I suggest. "We need to do one of those things like in that movie."

"An exorcism?"

"Yeah, that."

"Mmkay, go ahead."

"Okay, here goes." I clear my throat and struggle to remember the words the movie priest used to expel the demons. "By the power vested in me, stop fucking playing percussion," I call out. Gemma laughs, and our noise prompts another response from JoJo through the wall.

"I swear to god, I'm going to stab you both if you don't shut up."

"Libby is getting rid of the demonic marching band," Gemma calls back.

"You bitches are still drunk. That's not a marching band; it's the vodka pounding your pointed little heads."

"Huh," Gemma muses. "That actually makes more sense."

"I'm going to open my eyes and check for evil fiends anyway," I say, creaking open one reluctant eyelid and then the other. The room is mostly dark, but I can see a bit of light peeking through the floral drapes.

"Anything?"

"Nothing except those hideous curtains. Who thought it was a good idea to combine orange and chartreuse?"

"Oh, your ass knows chartreuse but can't tell the difference between hot-pink and fuchsia?"

An image of me with sex lube on my arms and hands somehow filters through the Jell-O mold that is my brain, and I giggle through the throbbing pain in my head.

"Chartreuse should seriously be banned from the color wheel. It serves no purpose and reminds me of vomit."

As soon as that last word passes my lips, my stomach does a backflip, and I slam my hand over my mouth. *Oh shit!* Scrambling from the bed, I sprint to the bathroom, wobbling a little until I fall to my knees in front of the toilet.

I lean against the cool wall and watch as Gemma enters the room, looking more disheveled than I've ever seen her. Her silky top is mis-buttoned, and for some reason, she's wearing Ava's floral shorts, one thigh-high stocking, and some kind of odd belt. Dark strands stick out of a raggedy bun on one side of her head, and the other half of her hair is fashioned in a french braid.

"You done calling Uncle Ralph?" she asks, wetting a white washcloth and handing it to me.

I wipe my face and nod. "Are you feeling sick?"

Gem's face crunches into a look of misery. "Yes, but I'm trying to hold it in."

Pressing the cloth against the back of my neck, I say, "Get it over with. I feel better already, and you look like shit."

"You're one to talk. What is that hat you're wearing?"

Rising up on my knees, I look in the mirror. Some kind of pillbox hat with multicolored feathers is sitting askew on my blonde head. "Where the fuck did I get this hat? Is it yours?"

Gemma throws me a flat look. "As fetching as it is, no. Also, your breath smells like ostrich ass."

"How do you know what ostrich ass smells like?"

"Long story. Don't ask," she mutters.

JoJo stumbles in, and we both gape at her. She's wearing a bright-orange construction vest. "What in god's name is that?" I ask.

She shrugs. "You gave it to me. You went downstairs about two in the morning to get a bag of Doritos, and you came back with that hat and this vest." She points at me and then herself.

"What the hell happened last night?" Gemma whispers.

"We drank all the alcohol in Colorado," Ava moans, stumbling into the room, and we all burst out laughing. Her hair is done in Pippi Longstocking braids. She holds up her middle finger and waggles it at all of us.

"Did you get sick too, Ava?" Gemma asks, and our friend nods.

"Yes, I just tossed my fortune cookies, and I feel a little better."

I frown. "Isn't the phrase *tossing your cookies*?"

"Yes, but we had Chinese food, so I improvised." Ava flaps her hand. "Stop overanalyzing my euphemism. I'm trying to remember what we did all night. Something with our computers, I think. I definitely remember that."

"Writing exercises?" Gem suggests. "Can you just imagine what we wrote while drunk off our asses?"

The hair on the back of my neck stands up as vague images flash through my mind. "Umm, I think we started some kind of website. Like, a business or something?"

JoJo's eyes widen. "We did. The thing where we decided to help guys be more like the men in our books." She stares up at the corner of the room in thought. "What did we name it?"

"The uhhh..." Gemma scratches the back of her neck. "Wasn't it The Man-Training Book Sluts?"

I shake my head. "That was Ava's suggestion, and we were so drunk, we actually considered it for a few minutes."

"I still think it's a solid business name. Very descriptive," our friend argues.

"Book Boyfriend Builders!" JoJo crows, scrolling through her phone, and we all wince at her volume.

For a long moment, four sets of eyes dart to and from each other in a bit of panic as the memories truly begin to sink in. "Shit, we were going to delete it," Ava reminds us, "before too many people saw it."

"Libby needs to do that. She set up the website," Gemma says quickly, reaching out a hand to help me off the floor.

"Crap," JoJo spits out, staring at her phone. "I hate to tell you this, but I just got an alert that the winter storm is moving in faster than anticipated. You ladies need to try and move your flights to today unless you want to be stuck here for a week."

"Libs, I'll work on your flight. You just get that fucking website taken down. JoJo and Ava, find us Advil, lots of water, and something to eat that will absorb all this damn liquor." Gemma is now in full crisis-management mode as I run for my laptop in the living room.

"Fuck! It's dead," I curse, scrambling around on the floor, searching for my charger. I look under the coffee table and scoot the couch over, but it's nowhere to be found.

"Yes, my name is Liberty Hill," Gemma says, zooming past me, as she pretends to be me on the phone. "I don't care what you have to do. Get me on a flight *today*."

JoJo hands me a bottle of water and three tablets as I move things around on the desk against the wall.

Where the fuck is my laptop charger?

Gemma paces back the other direction, doing that fast-walk thing she usually reserves for work at her law firm. And that's when I see it. *Her "belt."*

Stopping her with my hands on her shoulders, I untie my charging cord from around her waist, earning me a confused look before she begins barking into the phone again.

Once I get my laptop plugged in, I wait impatiently as it powers on. Quickly pulling up the Book Boyfriend Builders website, I take a second to admire the setup, logo, and graphics. It really does look wonderful.

That's when my eyes drop to the counter at the bottom of the page.

What the ding-dong hell? Almost half a million hits? In only a few hours?

Navigating to the sales page, I'm surprised once again.

Payment received.

Payment received.

Payment received.

Those words are repeated hundreds of times. Hundreds! I check the accounting numbers and almost fall off the damn couch. The balance is $8550. And that's just the deposits people paid to retain our services. It doesn't include the exorbitant fees we planned to charge once we begin with a client.

Apparently, vodka gives you a false sense of confidence that you can actually pull off a man-training business. But… these numbers…

Excitement bubbles in my stomach. Or maybe that's still the vodka talking.

"Y'all, I think you need to come look at this," I call, and everyone wanders over to look at my screen.

"Holy shit," JoJo whispers as Gemma and Ava shake their heads in awe.

Gem says something into the phone and hangs up, jamming her hands on her hips as her green eyes sparkle. Then a crafty smile curls her lips upward, and she points a finger at the screen.

"Liberty Hill, don't you dare fucking delete that website. We've got some book boyfriends to build."

CHAPTER 2

Libby

I settle into seat 2A and smile at the luxurious feel of the leather window seat. The only seat left on this plane was in first class, and with bossy-ass Gemma's help, I was assigned here without any additional cost due to the weather situation.

I could get used to this shit, I think as I stretch my long legs and pull out my laptop. Opening it up, I begin organizing, making spreadsheet after spreadsheet of BBB stuff.

I still can't believe we're going for this, but after looking at the numbers in the light of day—and with most of the alcohol expelled from our systems—my friends and I decided that this untapped market had so much potential, and we were going to tap it.

"Hi, I'm Cara. Can I get you something to drink before take-off?" someone asks, and I look up to find a pretty flight attendant with her brunette hair in a tidy french twist smiling down at me.

What the hell? They're still boarding the plane. Is this normal for first class?

"Just a water, please," I say, "with lots of ice." *Because I'm never drinking alcohol again. Ever.*

"My pleasure." She returns moments later with a real glass—not one of those plastic ones—filled to the brim with ice and cold water. "Would you like a snack?"

She presents me with a basket of goodies, and I quickly latch onto a bag of Skinny Pop, my body still craving salt even after eating the bacon sandwich JoJo ordered from room service this morning.

"As soon as we're done boarding, you'll have to stow your laptop until we get in the air," the woman says.

"Of course." I save the spreadsheets into my newly designated BBB folder and put the device away in my backpack. JoJo's newest paperback is right on top, and I pull it out before stuffing my bag beneath the seat in front of me.

Riggs fucking Romero. The man's light-blue eyes seem to stare directly into my soul from the cover, and I draw a heart around his face with my fingertip.

"You actually like that ugly mug?" a deep voice says from beside me, and I look up with a frown, ready to tell off this asshole who dares to judge me.

And my mouth drops open. Ice-blue eyes and a face full of designer stubble meet my gaze, and an amused smirk splays across those perfectly kissable pink lips. No, not pink, they're really more of a mauve color, to be precise.

I wonder if any of Gemma's lubes come in mauve containers?

Not that I'd need any lubrication at this point. My vagina is doing just fine on its own at the sight of *Riggs fucking Romero* standing in the aisle beside me.

Did I conjure him by merely touching his face on the cover of the book?

The man is simply delicious, from the top of his jet-black hair down his six-foot-four frame and to the tips of his... *holy fuck! What size shoe does he wear?*

My gaze lifts to see if the goods behind his zipper match the ginormous feet the man is sporting. *Wow.* The bulge behind those pale-gray dress pants tells me the *big feet, big dick myth* is most decidedly not a myth.

"Um, are you okay?"

I'd like to say the sound of that deep, raspy voice pulled me from my awkward admiration of his family jewels, but that would be a lie. It's like my eyeballs are magnets, and his penis is made of reinforced steel, the attraction between the two naturally unbreakable.

You're staring at his dick. Stop staring at his dick. Why for the love of all that's good and holy are you still. Staring. At. His. Dick?

With the force of a thousand horses trying to pull my eyeballs upward, I comfort myself with the thought that at least he has no idea who I am. He can go back to his friends and tell the story of some kooky, crotch-gazing weirdo he'd seen on the plane. They'd laugh and then forget about it within a few days.

But that little comfort bubble I'd wrapped around myself bursts spectacularly when he holds out a hand. "You're Libby Cox, right?"

Oh-shit-oh-shit-oh-shit, I chant in my head as I look up into his eyes and shake his hand. They're almost as mesmerizing as that well-defined ridge his pants neglected to hide. And the way he said my last name invoked all kinds of dirty thoughts.

"No," I lie, "my name is J. Estes."

He laughs and breaks eye contact, lifting a small suitcase into the overhead compartment and giving me a bird's eye view of his delectable abs when his sky-blue henley lifts a little.

"I think we both know that's not true," he says, tapping JoJo's pen name on the book cover as he takes the seat beside me. "I met her yesterday, and you're definitely not her."

Why is he sitting here? And why the hell does he smell like the very essence of masculine sin?

I down the rest of my water, resisting the urge to tip the contents over my head to cool myself down. The flight attendant approaches.

"Mister Romero, can I get you a drink?"

He stretches out his mile-long legs and makes himself at home in what is apparently his seat. "Bourbon, please. McKenna's if you have it; if not, whatever you have will be fine."

"And Ms. Hill?"

"I'll have a bloody mary, extra spicy," I croak.

Fuck my ban on drinking liquor. I'm gonna need it all for this flight.

CHAPTER 3

I s Libby Cox staring at my dick? I beg the fucker not to put on a show for her as I stow my bag and sit down.

She's stunning. I'd never met the woman in person, though I saw her yesterday at the book signing and noticed how attractive she was. Today her long hair is wavier, and she's not wearing a bit of makeup, but I think I prefer her this way.

The flight attendant brings our drinks, and I smile when Libby thanks her and calls her by name. She seems really sweet and treats people with respect, unlike…

Fuck. I rub a hand over my face and lean my head back, staring at the round air vents above me. I've really got to do something about this situation with Lucinda. It's becoming untenable.

The flight attendants begin their safety talk, and I prepare myself to zone out like I usually do. But the woman beside me is listening attentively, nodding and smiling at Cara as she goes through all the motions that I'm sure she gets bored with after doing it numerous times a day.

When she's done and picking up the glasses from the first-class passengers in preparation for takeoff, Libby reaches out and touches the woman's hand.

"Cara, I'm in awe of how you buckle that safety vest around your waist during your presentation without even looking. I'd look like a bumbling fool."

Cara literally beams at the praise. "Thank you, Ms. Hill. I feel like no one even pays attention anymore." *Yeah, dickheads like me.* "It's nice to know someone does."

"No problem. I just wanted to make sure you know how much I appreciate you and the crew. I know it's a hard job."

Jesus, who is this woman? She's got a face and body that won't quit, *and* she's kindhearted?

"Did she call you Ms. Hill?" I ask, turning to look at Libby.

She blinks a few times with those hazel eyes before speaking. "Oh, yes. That's my real surname. Libby Cox is my pen name."

"And is Libby your real first name?" I ask and then catch myself. "Sorry, that's a bit personal."

"No, it's okay," she says, tilting her head and allowing all those wavy locks to spill over the shoulder of the sunshine-yellow sweater she's wearing. "My full name is Liberty Hill, but most everyone calls me Libby, in real life and in the book world."

"Liberty Hill." I let the name slip from my tongue. "I like it."

She rolls her eyes and giggles, and I'm captivated by the sound. "It sounds like somewhere Custer would surrender the troops."

A rush of laughter bursts from my lips as she joins my hilarity in a completely self-deprecating way. I adore a woman with a sense of humor, but I don't have many of them in my life.

Except for my sister, Silvia, and my grandma, who are my two favorite people in the world.

I smile just thinking about my grandmother. Viviana Romero was a renowned ballbuster in her day, breaking through glass ceilings and running my grandfather's business with an iron fist after he passed away at age forty. But to me, she's just Nana Viv, the woman with a wicked sense of humor and a deep love of family.

"What about you?" Libby asks, smiling at me with brilliant

white teeth surrounded by full pink lips. "Is Riggs Romero your real name?"

"Yes, though when I started doing cover modeling, my sister, Silvia, decided to try and come up with a *stage name,* as she called it."

"You didn't like any of her suggestions?"

Closing my eyes, I shake my head. "Nope. We couldn't get on the same page, so I decided to just use my real name."

Libby's eyes sparkle with excitement. "What were some of the names Silvia came up with?"

"She wanted the first name to start with an R like my last name. Said she liked the alliteration." I pull out my phone and scroll to my notes app before lifting a challenging eyebrow her way. "I have a list, if you'd really like to hear some."

"Ooh, I love lists," she says with an enthusiasm that makes me laugh. "And I'd love to hear."

"Okay, here we go. Prepare yourself, Liberty Hill. Some of these are doozies, but I'll start you off easy."

She points a finger gun at me. "Shoot. I can take it."

"Remus."

Her nose scrunches adorably. "All I can think of is Professor Lupin from *Harry Potter.* You'd need a sketchy porn star mustache to pull off that name."

A snort escapes from my throat. "These next ones aren't too bad. Roman, Rufus, and Rogue."

"Rogue is trying too hard, and Rufus is a hard no, but Roman is nice. Not as sexy as Riggs Romero though."

Her eyes widen, and she smashes her lips together while red spots darken her tan cheeks, as if she's embarrassed she said that out loud. Meanwhile, I'm trying not to preen like a fucking peacock that she thinks my name is sexy.

"All right, we're about to dive into the deep end, Libster. Hang on tight." She makes a show of clenching the armrests of her seat, and I lean forward to whisper, "Romeo."

Her eyes go skyward as she mouths, "Romeo Romero." Then

she shakes her head and tosses a piece of popcorn into her mouth. "Not terrible, but with your last name, it's too busy. What else ya got?"

"Rocco."

Libby inhales a wheezing breath and holds it, and I become concerned that she's sucked a piece of popcorn down her throat. Just as I'm about to pound her on the back or perform the Heimlich maneuver, she expels the air with a cackling *hahaha* sound, and I'm pretty sure it's the weirdest—and cutest—laugh I've ever heard.

"Oh. My. God. Does your sister think you're a meathead?"

"Apparently," I chuckle, still amused at her exuberant laugh and wanting to hear it again. "You ready for the final and most ridiculous one?"

"Hang on." She holds up her hand and takes a long swig of her drink. "I have a feeling I'm going to need alcohol to hear this one."

"Wise choice," I say before spreading my hands dramatically. "Rocket."

Libby freezes for a long beat, and then she does that completely adorable wheezing laugh again, waving one hand at me. "Oh shit," she gasps when she's finally able to speak again. "That's classic. Can you just imagine the pocket rocket jokes?"

Her laughter is contagious, and I join in... until the flight attendant walks over. "S-sorry, Cara," I stammer through my chuckles. "Are we being too loud?"

She smiles. "Not at all. I wanted to see if you two needed more beverages."

Noticing both our drinks, as well as Libby's popcorn bag, are empty, I circle my finger in the air. "Bring us another round, and can you hook Liberty up with more popcorn?"

"Certainly. It would be my pleasure," she says, returning a few minutes later with two full glasses and another bag of Skinny Pop.

"Jackpot," Libby whispers, holding her bag toward me, and I take a couple fluffy kernels.

"Not terrible, but not as good as movie theater corn drenched in butter."

"Agreed," Libby says. "Did you give your sister atomic wedgies or something when she was a kid? Is that why she hates you?"

I chuckle yet again. *What is it about this woman that makes me want to laugh constantly?* "No, she actually adores her older brother. She honestly thought she was being helpful, though I think she threw a few of those names in there just to fuck with me."

"What's your age difference?"

"Six years. I'm thirty-three, and she's twenty-seven."

"Oh, I'm the same age as your sister. Where did you get the name Riggs?"

"My mother was a big fan of Mel Gibson when *Lethal Weapon* came out. How did you get the name Liberty? It's very unique."

"You should meet my sister, Freedom, and my brother, Second Amendment."

I literally choke on my bourbon, covering my mouth to keep from spewing the dark liquid against the back of the seat in front of me. "Seriously?" I cough out, and her wide grin tells me she's joking.

"No, I'm an only child. I honestly don't know where the name came from. I was adopted. My birth mom and I were in a car accident when I was only two years old, and she didn't survive."

"Libby, I'm so sorry. That must have been hard."

She shrugs but never quite loses her smile. "It's okay. I went into the foster care system and then was adopted by the Hills when I was eight. They were unable to have children, so they doted on me."

I want to ask why someone as charming as her wasn't

adopted before age eight, but that seems awfully personal, so I veer the conversation a bit.

"And where did you come up with your pen name?"

"Cox was my birth mother's last name. I guess she and my sperm donor weren't together because I never found out who he was.

"I'm sorry. That must have been hard."

"Not really. My adoptive parents were awesome." Libby holds out the popcorn bag, and I absently reach for another bite, fascinated with her story. "I did find some family on my mother's side though, after going through her things when I was a teenager. Like her sister, Nancy."

"And you've met her?"

"Yes, I met Aunt Nancy. She was a sweetheart."

"Was?"

"She recently passed away."

"Damn, I'm sorry. Are your parents still alive?"

Her smile turns sad for the first time, and I mentally kick my own ass for prying. "They were a little older when they adopted me, almost in their fifties, though you'd never know it because they were as active as the twenty-something parents. They both died when I was twenty."

"Shit," I huff out, "so you had no one?"

Her full-wattage smile returns. "No, Aunt Nancy had a daughter named Gianna."

"So, your cousin?"

"Yes, we're super close. She and Aunt Nancy actually lived only a few miles from me when we found each other, though Gia recently moved to New York."

I feel the plane begin its descent, and Cara comes by to pick up our glasses and trash. *Where the hell did the time go?*

As soon as we land at DFW airport, Libby checks her phone. "It's been so nice talking to you, Rocket Romero, but I have a connecting flight to catch from Terminal E in less than an hour."

I laugh at her Rocket joke. "You're not getting rid of me that easily, Libby. My flight leaves from E as well."

Her smile is brilliant. "Okay, I've never had to switch terminals in this airport. What's the fastest way there?"

"Stick with me, Lib. We'll take the Sky Tram."

We walk swiftly down the concourse, and I notice her long legs have no trouble keeping up with mine, even though she's around six inches shorter than me. "I didn't realize you had a connecting flight. I just assumed by your accent that you live in Texas."

"I used to," she says, but doesn't expound on that.

Libby checks her phone again. "I'm at gate thirty-three. Where are you?"

My heart thumps in my chest. I can't believe this. "I'm at thirty-three as well."

Her eyebrows lift in surprise. "Oh, you're going to Northwest Florida Beaches International?"

I'm as surprised as she is. NFBIA isn't a huge airport like Miami or Orlando, mostly serving the Panama City area.

"That's exactly where I'm going. Do you live in Panama City?"

She hesitates, and I mentally kick myself. *Of course she wouldn't tell a virtual stranger where she lives, doofus. She's smarter than that.*

"Sorry, that was rude of me to ask. You don't have to answer."

Libby shakes her head. "No, it's okay. It's just… complicated. I'm in the process of moving."

"Oh, gotcha." We start walking again and finally reach our gate. The sign over the counter informs us that boarding will begin in eleven minutes. "We made it," I say, finding two chairs beside each other, and we sit.

My phone pings, and I check it to find a text from Lucinda, my girlfriend.

> Lucinda: I signed you up for this. I think it will
> really help you.

There's a link attached, and I click on it and begin reading. Before I reach the bottom, I scroll back to the top and start again because I absolutely can't believe what I'm seeing.

"She has got to be fucking kidding me," I mutter, and Libby looks at me with concern.

"Is everything okay?"

"No, it's not. My girlfriend has signed me up for… something. I don't even know what the fuck this is. It's the most bizarre thing I've ever heard of."

"Like the Pickle of the Month Club? Because a friend of mine bought me a subscription for that once, and I actually enjoyed it."

My laughter breaks free and soothes a little bit of the anger that's boiling in my veins. "No, not the Pickle of the Month Club. I would like that a lot better than this bullshit. It's called the…"

I look down to see the name again and shake my head in disgust. "The Book Boyfriend Builders. Isn't that the most ridiculous thing you've ever heard?"

CHAPTER 4
Riggs

I go off on an anger-fueled rant. "I can't believe this shit. Book Boyfriend Builders." That comes out as a sneer. "Who the hell ever thought that was a good idea? It's honestly probably the dumbest business I've heard of since that social media network for imaginary friends."

Tapping on the *About Us* page, I glance up at Libby to see if she's going to crack a well-deserved joke about this idiocy. Her face looks stricken, her normally almond-shaped eyes going round, and I scramble back in my brain to see what I possibly could have said to upset her.

"Oh my god, do you have imaginary friends? Because, you know, that's totally cool if you do. I had one when I was little. He was a mouse named Carbonara."

She swallows hard and shakes her head vigorously. "No, no imaginary friends."

Something on my phone screen seems to have some kind of magnetic pull that forces me to look down. And I see a face. I look back up at Libby and see the same face. My eyes flicker so quickly I'm afraid I may give myself a seizure. Phone… Libby… phone… Libby.

I repeat that cycle about forty-seven times in the five seconds it takes for reality to click into place.

Well. Fuck.

"Libby, I'm so sorry. I didn't… I didn't mean what I said. That was just the surprise talking."

The smile she puts on her face looks completely forced, her lips trembling a bit, and I feel like the biggest asshole on the planet. "No, it's okay. It is a pretty dumb idea."

I have to agree, but fuck. She looks like she's about to cry. "No, it's really not. It's… unique. I just… I'm sorry. I think I was reacting poorly because maybe I was a little offended that my girlfriend thinks I'm not a good boyfriend."

"That's understandable," she says sweetly, though the look on her face makes me want to rip out my own tongue. "We were drunk when we came up with the idea, and it's… you know what? I think I'll go to the restroom before we board."

And with that, she hops up and practically sprints to the restroom across from our gate.

Well, Riggs. You fucked that up.

Taking a deep breath, I look back down at my phone and begin reading about the business. As I let my mind process it, I can kinda see where they're coming from.

I mean, it's still the wackiest damn thing I've ever heard of, but I'm ashamed I hurt Libby's feelings. She's so funny and has such a kind heart.

So I do the only thing I can. I click on the *Select Your Coach* button and choose Libby Cox.

Libby is quiet when she returns from the restroom and loops her backpack straps over her shoulders.

"Thanks for talking with me on the plane. It was really nice to meet you, Riggs." Her smile is tight and doesn't reach her eyes. I hate that.

"Libby," I say, wrapping my hand gently around her wrist as she turns to walk off. "Please sit. I wasn't done groveling."

She cracks a small smile. "It's okay. You don't have to grovel.

Like I said, we were snockered when we set all that up. I don't blame you for thinking it's crazy."

"No, really. I read more about it, and I've changed my opinion."

"In the five minutes I was in the restroom?" she asks flatly, and I nod.

"I chose you as my coach."

Her hand covers her face, and she sinks into the chair beside me. *At least she's not leaving. Yet.* "Nooo, please tell me you didn't do that."

"I did. Liberty, can you please uncover your eyes and look at me?"

"The magic eight-ball says *not at this time.*"

God, she's fucking funny.

"Okay, just listen then. I've read all your books, and the way you write your male characters… I don't know… it just speaks to me. I've always thought I would love to be the kind of man you write about."

She separates two fingers and peeps through them with one eye. "You've read my books?"

"I have. And now I have the chance to improve myself, to be a better boyfriend. I mean, I do my best, but no one is perfect. I'm hoping you can help me."

Pulling her hand away, she wrinkles her brow. "Are you trying to become the teacher's pet?"

"Most definitely," I assure her. "I will be your most dedicated student, and I plan to earn all the gold stars you'll give me."

Her genuine smile makes an appearance, and the tension in my shoulders relaxes.

An announcement is made for first-class passengers to board. Once on the plane, I assist a tiny elderly lady—who informs me her name is Tillie—with getting her bag into the overhead compartment.

Tillie has the aisle seat beside Libby, but when she catches me staring at the pretty blonde, she whispers, "Would you like to switch seats with me?"

"Yes, please," I say gratefully, and she pats my chest.

"Good luck, handsome. That young lady is very lucky. If I were ten years younger, I'd throat punch someone to sit beside a big hunk like you."

I chuckle and thank her, neglecting to mention that she'd have to be closer to *forty* years younger before we'd even be close to an appropriate match. Feeling happier than I have any right to be, I settle in beside Libby for the two-and-a-half-hour flight.

"I guess since we'll be working together, I probably need to ask where you live," Libby says, working on her third packet of cookies.

How the hell does she stay in such good shape with the way she eats? Not that I'm complaining. I love seeing a woman enjoy her food.

"I live in Mexico Beach."

"Oh. That's not far from Port Saint Joe."

My heart rate picks up a notch. "You live in PSJ? That's only twelve miles from me."

"No. Well, yes, I guess. I'm in Panama City Beach now, but as of tomorrow, I'm moving to Port Saint Joe." She sets down her empty cookie package and picks up her phone. "That reminds me. I need to rent a U-Haul. I keep forgetting to do that."

She taps around on her phone for a minute and then scowls. "Why isn't this stupid wi-fi working?"

"I have a truck," I blurt out. "How much stuff do you have?"

"Um, I have a couch and some boxes. I plan to shop for more stuff once I get settled in a bit."

"I'll come help you." I'm not sure why I say that. It just flies out of my mouth.

"You don't have to do that, Riggs."

"I know I don't, but I already have the day off work because I was planning to travel home tomorrow."

"Are you sure?"

"Positive," I say definitively. "We can probably make it in one trip."

With that decided, she gives me her address in Panama City Beach, and I tap it into my phone.

By the time we arrive at the airport in Florida, I'm utterly charmed by Liberty Hill. She's funny, sweet, and obviously beautiful.

I only wish my life was different.

CHAPTER 5

I hang around a coffee shop until after eleven, which is when Logan goes to bed, and then make my way to the house that will be my home for one more night.

Yes, I still live with my ex-boyfriend, which is just as awkward as it sounds, but I've gotten into the routine of not coming home until he's asleep to avoid having to see him. The upside is that I've gotten a shit-ton of writing done while sitting in the coffee shop around the corner.

Pulling my suitcase into the living room, I don't even bother to unpack. I'm moving tomorrow anyway.

Things haven't been great between Logan and me since we moved to Florida a year ago; I felt us growing apart and didn't know what the hell to do about it. But since he broke up with me two weeks ago, I felt like an unwelcome visitor in the place that was supposed to be my home.

A sense of relief trickles down my body like a warm shower at the thought of moving out of here. I unfold the blanket that's waiting for me at the end of the couch and smile when my thoughts wander to Riggs.

He's such a sweet guy, and it was really nice of him to offer to help me move. As I lay down on the couch with the flat, lumpy pillow Logan so graciously offered to let me use, I cover my body with the blanket and drift off to sleep with one thought in my head.

Too bad a nice guy like Riggs is already taken.

"Libby."

I jerk awake at the sound of my name and look up to see Logan standing beside my makeshift bed, thumbs tucked into the pockets of his jeans.

"Yeah?" My voice is scratchy with sleep.

"You'll be gone by the time I get home?"

I squint at his tall form, topped with sandy blond hair that I used to love running my fingers through. I should probably feel sad at the loss of our relationship, but all I can muster is disdain.

"Yes," I sigh, sitting up and rubbing my hands over my face. "I'm going to my new place today."

He just stands there without moving, eyebrows raised as if he's waiting on something. When I lift one in return, he asks, "Aren't you going to thank me for letting you stay here?"

With an incredulous gape of my mouth, I stare back for a long moment before gathering all the sarcasm in my chest. "Yes, Logan, thank you for allowing me the privilege of sleeping on *my* couch after you broke up with me without warning. Even though I paid my half of the rent, it was astoundingly kind of you to pretend to be a decent human being."

His jaw tightens, and his eyes dart away for a few seconds, possibly due to guilt, if he's even capable of that emotion. "You can leave the couch if you want, since you can't move it by your-self." I can hear the hope in his voice.

Oh, this fucker. The couch, which is the only piece of furniture I actually want from this house, is freaking gorgeous. The burgundy cushions are deep and soft but not squishy, and the surface is like butter on velvet, making it incredibly comfortable. It's literally the most perfect couch I've ever seen.

There's no way in hell Logan is getting my couch. Even if I didn't have Riggs's help, I would carry the damn thing on my back before I'd leave it here with this asshole.

"It's no problem. Since you refused to help me move, I have someone else coming to help me."

His brow furrows. "Who?"

"None of your business."

"A guy?" I stand and begin folding the blanket, ignoring his question, and I can feel his indignation rising. "Are you dating someone?"

"Also under the heading of *none of your business,*" I retort mildly. "Go to work, Logan."

His annoyance is palpable, but I make a little shooing motion with one hand, and he finally exits through the front door without another word.

Asshole.

As I'm getting ready, I wonder, not for the first time, what's wrong with Riggs Romero. Why did his girlfriend feel the need to sign him up for the Book Boyfriend Builders?

Aside from sticking his foot in his mouth about the BBB business, he was perfectly sweet and very easy to talk to yesterday. And I can't see where any woman would have a single complaint about the man's looks. He's completely drool-worthy. There's got to be something I'm missing.

After dressing, I pack up my toiletries and stow them in the box labeled *bathroom* before sealing it up. I still have about fifteen minutes before Riggs is scheduled to arrive, and I pull out my laptop and create a spreadsheet titled "Book Boyfriend Ratings."

Hmmm, what should I put in each column? A few are obvious: attentiveness, sensitivity, flirting, protectiveness, romantic, complimentary, thoughtfulness, honesty. Tapping my lips with an index finger, I envision what I would like to have in a man, and then I smile and add two more columns: dirty talk and generous in bed.

Seriously, what kind of book boyfriend would he be if he didn't have a mouth on him? I was tempted to add penis size, but I was pretty sure that wouldn't be very professional.

Excuse me, sir, but I'm going to need you to drop your pants so I can rate your penis on a scale of one to ten. Or if your girlfriend is really lucky, on a scale of six to twelve.

Yeah, probably not the best idea.

Hearing a knock, I cross to the door and open it, trying to hold back my giddy smile when I find Riggs Romero standing there. With his jet-black hair, straight Roman nose, and piercing blue eyes, the man looks like a god among humans.

He's tall, with broad shoulders and a trim waist, and his legs seem to go on for days. Muscular arms and legs are shown off by a tight white tank top and black athletic shorts with a white stripe down the sides. I do my best not to drool at the tattoos that cover his upper arms.

Riggs has the dark Italian looks of a wealthy mafia don, which is why most of the covers he graces are mafia or billionaire romances. He's got brooding down to a science, but when he smiles like he's doing right now? Good lord almighty, I'm not sure how my clothes haven't completely melted from my body.

"Libby, you look great," he says, glancing down at my butter-yellow tank and black Nike Pros. "Yellow is definitely your color."

Well, he gets a ten so far in the compliments category.

"Come on in, and thanks for doing this. I can't tell you how much I appreciate you spending your day off helping some crazy lady you met on a plane."

His laugh is low and deep and makes me have tingles in places I ought not think about. "Definitely better than going to work," he says, entering the living room.

"You said you work for Mercato?" I ask, remembering our conversation from yesterday.

Riggs nods. "Yes, my grandfather, Luca, and his best friend, Salvatore Farina, emigrated to the U.S. in the sixties and started a single grocery store in Tallahassee. Then it grew into a chain from there. Sal's son is currently the president of the company, and I'm the VP."

"Oooh, look at you being all corporate," I say, poking his bicep and practically breaking my finger in the process. *Damn, that's hard. I wonder what else is—*

Stop it, Liberty Hill! He has a girlfriend!

His smile doesn't quite meet his eyes as he runs a large hand through black hair that's so thick, it should have its own zip code. "Yeah, it's great." He takes in the room, squinting at the light neon-green walls. "This is… lovely."

"Oh, don't even try to be nice. I wanted to paint the walls a kind of airy blue, but Logan insisted on green. I thought maybe a soft sage green wouldn't be too bad, but then I came home to this." I wave my hand around. "It's like living in a giant Gatorade bottle."

That makes him smile even wider, his straight, white teeth shining between lips most women would kill for. "It's definitely bright. I'm pretty sure I now have retina damage," he remarks before clapping his hands once. "So, put me to work, Liberty."

For some reason, I like when he calls me that.

Gesturing toward the couch, I say, "Well, this is the only big thing. Everything else is packed in boxes."

He bobs his head up and down, surveying the couch. "Okay, probably best to put this in the truck first, and then we can fit the boxes around it and in the back seat."

"Sounds like a plan," I say cheerily, picking up the blanket and pillow. "Let me just move my bedding."

I carry it to the bedroom, and when I return, Riggs has a scowl on his face. "Did you sleep on the couch last night?"

"Yes, for the past two weeks, actually. I told you Logan and I broke up."

Ice forms in his narrowed eyes. "He makes you sleep on the couch?"

"Well, I certainly wasn't sleeping in the bed with his stupid ass," I retort.

Riggs shakes his head in disgust. "Then he should have taken the couch."

Patting his arm, I say, "That's one of many reasons he's a complete prick."

We work together to get the couch into the back of the truck, and I almost trip over my own feet several times because I can't stop ogling his bulging muscles. Then we begin loading the stuff I stored in the garage. After placing a heavy box of books in his backseat, Riggs lifts his shirt to swipe the perspiration beading on his forehead, and *dear god in heaven!*

I'm blessed with a full view of his torso, those tight, cut abs taking center stage. He has the perfect amount of dark hair, which tapers between his V lines and directly into the waistband of his shorts.

"Jesus, Riggs. Were you born or manufactured?" I ask, losing all filters at the sight of the most perfect male specimen I'd ever seen in person.

He chuckles and pats his flat stomach. "I try to keep in shape. No one wants a pot belly on their book covers."

Movement catches my eye and pulls my pervy gaze from Riggs's body.

Oh for Pete's sake…

Logan's white Prius pulls up at the curb, and my idiot ex steps out, his eyes darting from Riggs to his big, red Chevy truck in the driveway.

"What the hell is Logan doing here?" I mutter.

"Your ex?" Riggs asks in a low voice, and I nod.

"Hey, Libby. Who's your friend?" Logan asks, strolling toward us with faux casualness. *Why is he here? He never comes home for lunch.*

As I open my mouth to speak, Riggs steps forward, extending a large hand. "Hi, I'm Cobra."

Wait. What?

Logan's forehead looks like fault lines are forming on his skin. "C-cobra?"

Riggs puts on a winning smile. "Yeah, Cobra McSnugglebuns."

I have to slap my hand over my mouth and turn away to keep from laughing out loud.

Oh, but he's not done. "Libby and I met at a club where I dance. We had a drink afterward, and she mentioned she was moving and didn't have a man in her life who's strong enough to move furniture, so I naturally volunteered." He shoots me an affectionate smile that makes my vagina almost choke on thin air.

Seriously, how is he this hot *and* funny?

And taken, my mind reminds me.

"Cobra?" Logan repeats stupidly.

"Well, that's my stage name. The manager of the club gave me the name after my audition." Then he winks, and it takes the strength of a thousand men to keep me from doubling over with laughter.

After blowing out a stream of air through pursed lips, I manage to get hold of myself and ask, "Did you forget something, Logan?"

He finally seems to remember I'm there and turns his attention on me. "Yeah. No. I just, uh…"

"Did you come to help?" Riggs asks, and Logan shakes his head.

"No, I gotta get back to work. Libby, I just wanted to tell you that you can leave the key in the mailbox," he says quickly before casting one more glance at Cobra McSnugglebuns and returning to his car.

I slowly turn my head and lift my eyebrows at the grinning man beside me. "You seem quite pleased with yourself, Mr.

McSnugglebuns."

"Most fun I've had in a while," he says, "and we're friends, Libby. You can call me Mr. Cobra."

I follow Riggs in my Kia, and we make the drive to Port Saint Joe in a little over an hour.

"This is cute," he says, after we carry my couch into the cozy living room and set it down.

My shoulders hunch up with excitement at the prospects. I adore this darling one-and-a-half-story bungalow and was shocked that I'd gotten such a good deal on the rent.

"My lease says I can paint the walls and hang stuff as long as I don't make huge holes."

With his hands on his hips, he surveys the living area. "What are you thinking as far as art? Like photos or paintings or what?"

"I want it to be a true beach house with local photos of the water and sunsets, stuff like that. I guess paintings would be okay too, but I really love photos."

His eyes shift from side to side. "I think that would look great, but don't buy any. I think I can hook you up."

Despite me telling Riggs he can just leave the boxes on my wide front porch, he insists on carrying them inside and even takes each labeled box to its designated room. *Chalking up bonus points for chivalry.*

When we're done, we collapse onto the steps leading down to the sidewalk. "Thank you so much for everything, Riggs. Will you let me treat you to an ice cream?"

He leans back on his hands, and I have to force myself not to look at the veins in his forearms. "I never turn down ice cream," he says, "but I'll buy."

"Nope, not gonna happen," I insist, standing and clapping him on the shoulder. "Let's go, McSnugglebuns."

"So what's the plan for the BBB lessons?" Riggs asks around a mouthful of the salted caramel ice cream as we sit at a small, round table.

"Oh, you better shape up, mister. Coach Libby is a taskmaster."

He laughs. "I'll do my best, Coach. When do we get started?"

"I can meet with you on Saturday to go over my spreadsheets."

Riggs pauses with his cone an inch from his lips. "You have spreadsheets?"

I swipe my tongue around the top scoop of my ice cream and don't miss how Riggs's eyes follow the move. "I have spreadsheets and graphs as part of my rating system. I'm very… organized."

"Will I be your first client?"

"Actually, I'm meeting my first client tomorrow. I'm going to work with you and her concurrently. But on different days of course."

"Her?" he asks in confusion.

"Yes, she's in a same sex relationship, and she messaged me personally and asked if I would be willing to take her on as a client. After messaging back and forth, I told her I'd be happy to. She sounds like she honestly just wants to be a better partner for her girlfriend."

"That's kinda cool. I assumed it would only be men."

"I did too, but after thinking about it, don't we all want the same things? It doesn't matter if you're a man or a woman. You want someone to be attentive, someone who treats you like you're important to them."

He chews on the inside of his cheek. "That does make sense."

"I mean, I know our business is called the Book *Boyfriend* Builders, but I think it's just as important for us to be good book *girlfriends*. Relationships are a two-way street, and men—no matter how strong they are—want to feel treasured too."

His grin stretches across his entire face. "You're pretty damn smart, Liberty Hill."

I laugh and pat my hair. "Thank you, sir. Why don't you tell me a little about you and your girlfriend. Lucinda, right?"

"That's right. She's thirty, and our families are in business together. She's Salvatore's granddaughter."

"Oh, your grandfather's best friend?" I ask, remembering his family's story.

He nods and takes another lick of his ice cream. "Yes. We've known each other all our lives, but she asked me to go with her to a charity event a year ago, and we started dating after that. It made our families very happy."

"What does Lucinda like to do?"

"Her favorite things are shopping and traveling," he says with a chuckle.

"Where does she work?"

"She doesn't really. Her mother owns a high-end boutique, and she helps out there sometimes." Riggs rubs a hand through the scruff on his jaw. "What about you? What do you like to do?"

"I like being outdoors. I love spending time at the beach. The water soothes my soul."

His face softens at that. "The water is my favorite place to be. If I could spend every day deep-sea fishing, I'd be the happiest guy in the world."

"Oooh, I've been wanting to go on a deep-sea fishing trip, but I just haven't gotten around to it."

Riggs takes a bite of his waffle cone and leans back in his chair, his gaze contemplative. "I have a friend with a fishing charter business. We could have our first meeting on the boat on Saturday if you want. That is, if you don't have other plans."

"Seriously?" I squeal, wiggling in my chair. "That would be amazing."

He laughs and shakes his head. "I've never seen a woman so excited about fishing."

"My dad took me once when we were on a family trip to Galveston, and I've always wanted to go back. I think I was twelve." A thought strikes me. "Wait, how much does it cost?"

"No charge. Joe lets me use one of the boats when I want to take business clients out."

"For real?"

"Yep. Just a warning, the owner is a little… eccentric." Riggs lifts one dark brow at me, as if expecting me to back out.

I don't know what that means, but I bite my bottom lip in excitement and nod. "Consider me warned."

CHAPTER 6

After leaving the ice cream shop and dropping Libby off at her house, I dial Lucinda. I didn't get to see her when I arrived back in Florida last night because she goes to bed early.

"Hey, Lu," I say when she answers.

"Riggs, hi."

"Did you miss me?" I ask in a teasing tone.

"Sure." A less than warm response, but I'm used to it.

"I thought I'd swing by since I haven't seen you since last Wednesday."

"Okay, will you bring me a coffee, pretty please?"

"Of course."

"Do you remember my order?"

"Venti iced skinny hazelnut macchiato with sugar-free syrup, light ice, and no whip," I recite.

"Make sure the syrup is sugar-free," she reminds me.

A small ache throbs in my left temple, and I massage it with my thumb as I head to the local Starbucks.

Lucinda opens the door to her condo, and I lean in for her lips, but she turns her face slightly, offering her cheek, so I press a soft kiss there.

She takes her coffee, and I follow her into the living room. As always, I'm struck with a burst of minimalistic white. The lush rugs, the walls, the furniture. Everything is white, and my eyeballs beg for a splash of color.

As soon as she sets her drink down on the coffee table, I wrap my arms around her waist and lift her off her feet.

"Riggs! What are you doing?" she asks, and I kiss her along her jawline.

"I'm kissing my girlfriend." My nose nuzzles at her neck. She smells flowery and expensive, as always.

"Well stop. I'm mad at you for going to that stupid convention," she retorts, and my mood plummets.

Lucinda is surprisingly supportive of my side career as a book cover model. I think she likes bragging to her friends about it because they think it's cool. She still acts annoyed when I travel, even though I only go to a few book conventions a year.

"I only signed up for this one because you had that trip planned with your friends. And you know you're always welcome to go with me, Lucinda. I invite you every time."

She shoves against my shoulders in annoyance, and I set her on her feet. "Hanging out with book nerds isn't really my thing," she announces before easing gracefully onto her pristine white couch and picking up her coffee.

I sit beside her and push her dark-brown hair back over one shoulder, trying to preserve the day. Lucinda really is a beautiful woman. She's petite and has pretty brown eyes, but the scowl on her face mars her beauty.

"Let's not argue about that again, babe. Maybe we can talk

about more pleasant things." My lips drop to the side of her neck at the same time my hand slides up her toned thigh and beneath her white tennis skirt.

But her hand grips my wrist and halts my progress. "Riggs, stop it. I feel like all you want me for is sex."

Huffing out a harsh breath, I flop against the back of the couch and stare at the ceiling, calculating how long it's been since Lucinda and I slept together. It was… let's see… August?

"That doesn't even make sense, Lucinda. I could see it if we actually had sex at any point in the past two months, but you keep saying you're not in the mood."

"My choice," she retorts, leaving me with absolutely no response to that. Nothing I could say out loud anyway. I'm sure she doesn't want to hear about me jerking off in the shower morning after morning after a long string of lonely nights.

But I suck up all my frustration and force my head around to look at Lucinda. She's scrolling through her phone, obviously unworried about my irritating predicament.

"Would you like to go out somewhere Saturday? We can go to that seafood place you like."

"No, I'm going to Chicago to see Elizabeth this weekend." She glances up and shoots me a sly smile. "Liz is the one who told me about that thing I signed you up for."

I scruff my hand through my hair, mussing it up as I ask the question that's been burning through me since she sent me that text. "What exactly are you looking for with this book-boyfriend service, Lucinda? What am I doing wrong?"

She shrugs and turns back to her phone. "Liz said it's supposed to make your boyfriend swoonier. She's totally jelly that I could sign you up, but she can't do the same for Ethan because they don't offer that service in Illinois."

Ah, now I see. This whole thing has less to do with me and more to do with one-upping her friend. Or maybe *frenemies* is the better term to describe Lucinda and Elizabeth. They've been like this for as long as I can remember.

"Maybe you'll find this swoony," I say, going for a teasing tone that falls a little flat. I pull out the small box from my pants pocket and hand it over. It's wrapped in Lucinda's favorite color, white, with a silver bow.

She tears off the paper and opens the box to reveal a pair of elegant diamond earrings. Each has a huge central stone with smaller diamonds encircling it.

Lucinda's eyes light up. "These are beautiful, Riggs." She quickly takes the jewelry from the box and puts them in her earlobes before using her phone as a mirror to admire them.

"They were made by a Colorado jeweler," I explain. "I found his shop when I was walking around downtown, and I thought you'd like these."

"I love them."

To my surprise, she presses her lips to mine, and I lift my hand to cup her cheek. *Hmmm, maybe she's changed her mind about...* Before I can deepen the kiss, I hear a click and realize Lucinda has taken a picture of us. She pulls away and looks at the pic.

"Hmm, your hand is covering my earring. Let's try again."

Dutifully, I move my hand down to the side of her neck when she kisses me again. Chastely. "There. That's better," she says after taking another photo. "I'm posting this and tagging Elizabeth. She's going to be so jealous."

"Glad I could be of service," I say dryly.

"All done." Lucinda turns the screen toward me, and I read the caption: *My boo bought me new earrings. He loves me so much.*

Though we've dated for a year now, Lucinda and I have yet to say we loved each other, but she's always posting about our "love" on her social media accounts. That irritates me. I don't want to say those words until I mean them, and I'm fully aware I'm not in love with Lucinda. I want to be, but I just don't feel it yet.

She looks up at me and tilts her head, a smile playing across her lips. "Thank you, Riggs." Sliding across my lap, she seats her ass right on my dick, and the lonely fucker perks up and takes notice. Lucinda leans forward, and I think she's about to kiss me for real when the doorbell rings.

Lucinda pulls away and stands, leaving me with a rock-hard dick. "That's Mother. We're going to play tennis at the club."

Fuck.

As she goes to answer the door, I adjust myself in my pants to try and camouflage the obvious erection pulsing in my shorts. I stand as Bianca Farina sweeps into the room, looking not much older than her daughter, thanks to the talents of her plastic surgeon.

"Riggs," she purrs, "I didn't know you would be here, darling." She kisses me on both cheeks like we're European royalty and then pats my face.

"Mother, look at the earrings Riggs brought me from Colorado." Lucinda swivels her head from side to side, and the light glistens off the several carats adorning her ears.

"Ohhh, they're beautiful. Such a thoughtful young man." Bianca beams at me. "What are your plans for today, Riggs?"

I thought maybe I was going to get laid, Bianca. Alas, it's not to be.

"I'm going to pick up Ace from my sister's house and then go visit with Joe for a while."

Mother and daughter share a disapproving look, whether from the mention of my big, goofy black lab or of Joe, I'm not sure. Probably both.

"Isn't that nice," Bianca says with a fake-ass smile that tells me she doesn't think it's nice at all. "We'll let you get to it. My daughter and I have some tennis balls to smash."

"Okay, you ladies have fun." I kiss Bianca's cheek, and then take Lucinda's hand and lead her to the door. Her mother wanders to the kitchen, presumably to give us some privacy.

"Thanks again for the earrings," Lucinda says, and I cup both her cheeks, brushing my lips across hers.

"You're welcome. Do you want to come over tonight, sweetheart?" I ask, but I instantly know the answer when she scrunches her nose.

"Your dog will be there?"

"Not in my bedroom," I say suggestively. "You know he has his own bed." Actually my spoiled mutt has his own room.

"Oh, well, I'm going out with Eleanor and Stella. Girls' night, you know?"

"You could come over after," I say, trying to keep the edge of begging from my tone.

Her nose wrinkles again. "No, we planned to stay at El's house."

A voice comes from the kitchen. "Lucinda, we're going to miss our court time!"

"Gotta go," Lucinda says, pressing a chaste kiss to my cheek and herding me out the door.

Out in the hallway, part of the throb that was in my left temple migrates to the right, so now both sides of my head ache, though the previous throbbing in my groin is noticeably absent now.

"Hey, sis! How was Ace this weekend?" I greet Silvia when she opens the door.

Hearing his name, my boy abandons his chew toy and literally hops across the wood floor toward me. I squat and receive all the doggy loving he sees fit to bestow upon me, including lots of licks and nuzzles.

"Hi, buddy," I say, rubbing my hands up and down the sides of his neck, which is his favorite thing in the world. "Were you a good boy for Aunt Silvia?"

He does a full-body wiggle, followed by an affirming bark.

"He didn't eat any of my shoes," my sister reports, kissing my cheek when I stand.

"I've been working with him on that. Having lots of chew toys available seems to help."

Closing the door behind me, I step into Silvia's living room, which manages to be extremely bright and modern without losing that homey feel. Ace trots back to my sister's red-and-yellow throw rug and continues gnawing on his toy.

"I see you bought Instagram Barbie some new jewelry," Silvia says, rolling her eyes and shaking her phone at me.

I suppress a laugh. My sister is not a fan of my girlfriend.

"I always bring her a souvenir when I travel."

"A souvenir," she states flatly.

"Lucinda isn't exactly a T-shirt and shot glass kind of girl. My sister, on the other hand…" I pull a small bag from behind my back, and Silvia's eyes zoom in on it.

"Oooh, gimme gimme." She holds her hand out, and I let out a laugh as I pass it over. Silvia collects shot glasses, and I always try to find the most outrageous ones to bring to her.

My sister tears open the bubble wrap and immediately starts giggling at the shot glass with a cartoon hippo on it.

"Hippo-twat-amus? Where the hell do you find these?" Then her blue eyes widen when she looks inside. "Riggsy! What did you do?"

"Couldn't leave my best girl out," I say when she tips the earrings into her palm. These are different from Lucinda's but no less beautiful, with a large emerald in the center because it's Silvia's favorite stone.

She crashes into me and squeezes me hard enough to break my ribs. "I can't believe you did this, you big idiot."

I kiss the top of her head, and Ace hops up and trots over, nosing between us so he doesn't miss any excitement. "I hope you like them."

"I do though I'd have been happy with just the shot glass."

And that, folks, is why I love my sister so much. Though our family has money, she's the least pretentious person I know.

Unlike my girlfriend.

"Why are you frowning?" Silvia's voice breaks through my thoughts, and I realize my eyebrows are lowered over my eyes.

"Just a bit of a headache," I say honestly.

Silvia pats me on the chest and retreats to the kitchen, returning a minute later with a bottle of water and two ibuprofens. "Do you realize you always have a headache when you leave Instagram Barbie's place?"

I down the painkillers with a long swallow of water. She's not wrong, so I don't even bother to argue.

"When are you going to do something about this whole situation?"

Throwing a hand up, I let it fall in frustration. "What exactly do you expect me to do? Disappoint everyone in the family, including Nana?"

"So you'd rather disappoint yourself? When are you going to put yourself first?"

I pretend to think about it, though she already knows the answer. "Probably a week from never." Ruffling her dark hair, I fake a smile. "Don't worry about me. I'm fine."

Silvia encloses me in her arms and rests her head on my chest. "You deserve better than fine, Riggsy. You deserve laughter and fun and super-hot sex every day."

"Well, now you just made it weird," I reply, and my sister laughs before turning serious again.

"You're the best man I know, Riggs Romero. I just want you to find a woman who will appreciate you like you damn well deserve."

I pull her closer and kiss the top of her head.

If only, little sister.

CHAPTER 7

Riggs

"**A**fternoon, Joe!" I call, and the old man turns his head slightly, his dark-brown eyes finding mine before returning to his binoculars.

"Come aboard, Romero."

I let Ace go first and then climb onto the light-blue fishing boat. "What are you looking for? Are there storms coming?"

He shakes his head as one hand drops to pet my dog's head. "No, pterodactyls."

"Ah. That was my second guess."

Joe is undeterred by my sarcasm. "Everyone thinks those dinosaur movies are fiction, but every bit of fiction is based in fact. I saw on the internet where two of them had escaped."

My eyes follow the horizon, though I know with reasonable certainty I won't be seeing any prehistoric creatures flying around. I simply love looking out where the vast sea meets the even more vast sky. It's humbling and reminds me just how small I am in the grand scheme of things. How small my problems are.

"Any luck yet?"

He lowers the binoculars and lets out a sigh. "Naw. What can I do you for today?" Turning toward me, he smiles with teeth that are surprisingly white compared with the rest of his grizzled appearance. A full, gray-and-black beard lines the bottom of a face that's weathered from age and the sun.

"I need to borrow a vessel tomorrow."

"You takin' clients out?"

"No. She's not a client."

He lifts an overly furry eyebrow. "Lady friend?"

"She's a lady, and she's a friend, so yes."

Joe smiles again. "Course you can. You're part owner of this place, after all."

"I'm not part owner, Joe. I just loaned you some money."

"Whatever. You want to go out for a bit? I got some new cigars and a cooler full of beer."

I reach down and rub Ace's head. "Hey, boy. You want to go on a boat ride?"

His happy yip is all the answer I need.

"Hey! Am I late?" Libby asks as soon as she's out of her vehicle on Saturday morning.

"Two minutes early, actually," I let her know. *Not that I was excited to see you or anything.*

"Okay, good. I've gotten everything unpacked except the box with my sunglasses. I had to dig for them."

"You're unpacked already? You only moved in a couple days ago."

"I'm a very organized person," she says, hitching a soft leather briefcase thing with a long strap over one shoulder and a yellow-and-white striped beach bag over the other.

"I think you mentioned that before."

The sun hasn't risen yet, but Libby is lit by the pole lights in the small parking lot beside Joe's Marina. She's wearing a white sleeveless tee with a bright graphic beach design on the front, yellow flip-flops, and short denim cutoffs. Very short. *Not that I'm looking.*

"Are you sure I don't need to bring snacks?" she asks, her long, blonde ponytail bouncing as she walks across the parking lot toward me.

"Nope. Everything is provided." Just as I'm about to ask her if she minds Ace going with us, the crazy mutt bounds from the small office. "Ace, no!" I call sharply, but it's too late. He's on Libby, but to my surprise, she doesn't seem to mind.

Dropping her bags, she squats and opens her arm to receive all sorts of doggy loving. "Well, hellooooo, big boy? What's your name?" she croons, and the dog goes nuts, wagging his tail and wriggling his body in excitement at finding a new human.

"His name is Ace, and he's a tad overexuberant," I say dryly, striding the few feet to try and extricate my buddy from poor Libby. I reach for his collar, but he ducks me and licks the woman from her neck to her cheek. "Ace, cut it out you big oaf."

"Hims not an oaf is hims?" she asks in a baby voice, finding Ace's sweet spot with ease and rubbing up and down the sides of his furry neck. "No, hims a sweet fluffernugget."

I laugh and stop trying to pull my dopey pooch away. Libby seems to be a dog person. "Did you just call my dog a fluffernugget?"

"Of course," she says, sparing me a glance before turning her attention back to Ace. "He's fluffy, and he's just a big nugget of sweetness. Please tell me he's coming with us."

A grin rips across my face. "I was going to ask you if that was okay. If not, he can go out with Joe this morning."

Libby kisses the top of Ace's head. "I'd love for him to go with us." The *fluffernugget* takes that opportunity to stick his nose directly in Libby's crotch.

Goddammit.

I open my mouth to apologize, but Libby giggles and stands,

casting a look in my direction. "You didn't tell me your dog was a player, Romero."

"I'm sorry. You've only been here a few minutes, and you've already been licked and molested."

"Sounds like a good morning to me," she says with a cute wink. "Most action I've had in a while."

Fuck me.

My flag rises right up the old flagpole at the thought. Luckily, Libby doesn't notice because Joe walks out of the office and calls out a greeting as I spread my legs to make room. She smiles at the grizzled old man.

"Well, Romero, you didn't tell me your friend was such a looker. I'd have worn my good bibs," he says, slowing his pace as he hooks his thumbs in the straps over his shoulders. "Name's Joe O'Connell, pretty lady. What's yours?"

"Her name is *stop flirting, old man*," I interrupt, though there's no heat behind my words.

Libby laughs and holds out a hand. "I'm Liberty Hill, but you can call me Libby."

"Well, people call me Joe or Crusty Joe, but you can call me sweetheart, if the fancy hits ya." Instead of shaking her hand, Joe kisses the back of it.

Good grief… this guy…

"I'll call you Joe and reserve the right to call you sweetheart until after our second date," she says, flirting right back at the old codger.

He cackles before releasing her hand and turning to me. "Romero, I'm thinking of taking down that pine tree in my backyard. Think you could come over and give me a hand tomorrow?"

I frown. "Is there some kind of damage to it or something?"

Joe darts his eyes between me and Libby, leans close, and lowers his voice. "I heard they're putting listening devices in the pinecones."

"Who?" Libby whispers, and Joe widens his eyes.

"You know, *them*."

"Ah," Libby says, not missing a beat. "If you think it's just the pinecones on the ground, why don't you toss them in the ocean? Nothing to hear down there. Then you don't have to chop down your tree."

Joe's eyebrows crunch together, which makes him appear as though he has two caterpillars wrestling on his forehead. "That's not a bad idea. Hey, have you heard about the pterodactyl situation?"

And off he goes, telling Libby all about the dinosaur population *they* are keeping on a remote island in an undisclosed location. She nods along politely, and when he's done, she says, "You know what the smart thing to do would be? They should keep the dinosaurs on something like a space station. That way no one could accidentally discover them."

Joe's eyes widen like it's the best idea he's ever heard. "That's not half bad. I'll pass that along to my contacts." And with that, he wanders back toward his office.

"You handled that well," I tell her, picking up her satchel and looping it over my shoulder as we walk toward the docks with Ace trotting merrily beside us. "It was very kind of you to indulge him."

"You mentioned he was eccentric, and most eccentric people are that way for a reason."

"Very astute, and you're not wrong." As we approach, I gesture to the first two pale-blue boats, named *Stella* and *Hannah*. The crews are working to prepare the vessels for the day, and several wave in greeting. "Stella was Joe's wife, and Hannah was his daughter. They died in a car crash when Hannah was ten."

"Oh no," Libby whispers.

"I was a teenager when it happened, and I felt so bad for him, so I'd drop by to check on him. We'd go out on the boat because that was the only place he found any peace." I glance down at the woman beside me to find her with her hand over her heart and tears in her eyes. "Sometimes he talked about them, and sometimes we just cruised in silence. But he'd always let me have one cigar as long as I promised not to tell my parents."

She lays a hand on my forearm, and my skin heats from her soft touch. "That was nice of you to visit with him. Even when he didn't talk, I know it was a comfort to have you there."

"Joe floundered for the longest time, and then he discovered the internet. That's when he started…" I wave a hand back in the direction of the office, "you know, doing the whole conspiracy thing. It seemed to give him some kind of purpose or something. I'm not sure how to explain it, but it brought him back to life a bit. People call him crazy, but Joe isn't crazy. His mind is sharp, and he's just doing the best he can."

Libby's hands ball into fists. "You let me hear someone say that about him. I'll break their nose."

I resist the urge to put my arm around her and pull her into my side. She's just so fucking sweet. "I've threatened a few people with that a time or two myself."

We continue walking along the dock, and Libby says, "I really like Joe, and he's such a gentleman. He kissed the back of my hand. Do you know how rarely that happens these days?"

We stop beside the third blue boat, *The Dreamboat*, and I say, "Liberty Hill, I'm pretty sure you're the kind of woman who deserves to have her hand kissed every single day."

As Darryl, *The Dreamboat*'s captain for the day, cruises through the open waters of the Gulf of Mexico, Libby sits beside me and begins pulling folders from her satchel. The sun has yet to make its daily appearance, but Libby's movements are lit by a light on the side of the center console of the boat. Ace is up front, his paws on the bow as his ears blow back in the wind. The pooch is in his happy place.

"I thought we could go ahead and look over the paperwork so we can fish later," Libby says.

"Sounds good to me. That's, um, a lot of folders. I didn't know I was that terrible."

She laughs. "I'm sure you're not. This is just my system. Ah, here's the one." Around twenty folders in a rainbow of colors rest on her thighs, but she opens a navy-blue one. "This one contains your paperwork to fill out."

My eyes practically cross at all the boxes on the first page. The spreadsheet is titled "Book Boyfriend Ratings" and features a series of headings down the left side and numbers from one to ten across the top.

"Now, on the sheets behind this one, I have a detailed list of things every book boyfriend needs to know. Not every single one will be relevant to every couple, so don't worry if it's not something that pertains to you and Lucinda. You won't be rated on those."

"Um, okay."

"You can read through those when you get home. Next time we meet, we can go over them in more detail, or you can text me if you have questions about any of them."

"Sure," I say, a little speechless at the thickness of the folder. My eyeballs hang on the last row of the spreadsheet. "Dirty talk-ing?" I tap a finger on the words.

"Oh yes. Don't let that one intimidate you. Dirty talk is a key component of being a book boyfriend, but I'm not going to make you say anything uncomfortable out loud to me. On page forty-two, there's a form for you to fill out. Next time you and Lucinda are intimate, take note of the things you say. Then, when you have time, fill in the form with what you said and her responses to it."

"I, uhhh, I think I'm good in that department." *What the fuck? Am I blushing?*

She smiles indulgently. "I'm sure you're excellent, but how can I rate you on it if you don't fill out the form?"

"I… don't know."

"You don't have to feel embarrassed with me, Riggs. You've read my books. I'm obviously a huge fan of dirty talking. And you don't have to be ashamed of any kinks you enjoy. In fact, the kinkier, the better. I'm all in for whatever."

She pats my knee, and if she moves her hand up a few inches, she will feel exactly what this conversation is doing to me. And why the nickname Rocket Romero wouldn't have been off base at all.

She's all in for whatever? *Christ.* I try to push away the carousel of thoughts that evokes. Long legs wrapped around my head. Blonde hair fisted in my hand. Slender hands cuffed to my bed. I can practically hear the headboard smashing into the wall inside my head.

To be honest, it's been a while since I've heard that sound. Years, in fact. Lucinda is… I think the term we're looking for here is *vanilla.*

"I'll fill it out," I croak. My throat is completely dry because all the liquid in my body has migrated south. Shifting a little, I cover the evidence with the folder, but Libby doesn't seem to notice. In fact, she's flipping through pages and tapping on various things I can no longer comprehend because *she's fucking tapping on my dick!*

After god knows how long, I'm aware that she's stopped talking, and I worry that she asked me some question I didn't hear. But her face is turned to the side, giving me a glimpse of a profile with high cheekbones and a pert nose.

"Wow," she breathes, and I follow her gaze to the eastern horizon. *Wow, indeed.*

I motion to Darryl, and he cuts the exterior lights on the boat's console, bathing us in darkness.

In the distance, the sky is melting upward, away from the water, a thin line of dark purple that fades oh so slowly as we watch in silence. The purple turns into blue, which morphs into a dusky pink, and then finally a soft yellow.

The sunrise over the Gulf is one of my favorite things in the world to watch, but my eyes seem to gravitate from that awe-inspiring sight to another that's just as beautiful. Libby's face is radiant, her lips slightly parted as if she wants to say something but is simply too overwhelmed.

She enjoys this as much as I do.

"I feel so small right now," she finally says, her voice a mere whisper.

"No matter how many times I watch this, I always have the same thought."

Her face turns to me, and our eyes lock, my blue ones to her hazel ones, only inches apart. Flecks of green sparkle like emeralds in her irises as the sun continues to ascend without our noticing.

"I've watched sunrises before but never from this perspective. It's the most beautiful thing I've ever seen."

"I agree," I say, my voice low and dark, and I know in my heart I'm not talking about what's happening in the sky.

The moment is interrupted by Darryl poking his head out the door of the cabin, and we jerk apart.

He has dark skin and keeps his hair shorn high and tight, reminiscent of his days in the U.S. Marine Corps. Darryl is always steady and calm, excellent traits for a boat captain.

"This looks like a good place, Riggs. Gonna drop the anchor."

I'm kinda annoyed at the man right now, while at the same time, I'm grateful for his intrusion. I think I was heading into dangerous territory there for a minute.

"Thanks, Dare," I manage to say. I'm about to ask Libby if there's more we need to talk about, but she's already stuffing the folders and papers back into the satchel, her excitement for the day evident in her quick movements.

"What are we fishing for?" she asks, her tone vibrating as I place her satchel inside so it doesn't get ruined.

"Flounder and snapper should be good around here," Darryl answers before calling Ace into the cabin with him. The big doofus dog likes to bark at the fish when they're flopping around on the deck.

I start gathering the appropriate rods and bait and glance up at Libby. "I'll bait your hooks for you so you don't get dirty."

"Screw that," she says with a grin, waggling her fingers at me. "A little fish guts never hurt a girl."

Wow. I'm kinda blown away right now.

If I wasn't stuck in my current situation, I think I could really fall for this woman. But I am… so I can't.

CHAPTER 8

Libby

"Do you know how to cast?" Riggs asks, and my mouth twists to the side.

"It's been a really long time. I could probably use a refresher."

His lips crook up on one side, and I wonder if he's aware of how sexy that is. "No problem." He holds up a rod that's taller than he is and hands it over before turning me to face the water. "Now, hold it like this."

Riggs steps up behind me, and though he's not touching my body with his, I'm all too aware of his heat. He adjusts my hands and takes a couple minutes to instruct me on how to cast.

"Okay, here goes." I pull the rod over my shoulder, grip the handle tightly, and sling forward. Or at least I try to. It doesn't move. I give it another good yank, and Riggs lets out a yelp.

"Whoa, hold on, Libby. You got me."

"What do you mean, I…" Realization strikes me, and my mouth falls open in horror. Dropping the rod, I duck under Riggs's arm and circle around him as he leans over to grab the handle of the rod before it can splash into the water.

With him bent over the edge of the boat, I can clearly see the hook embedded in his backside. "Oh my god! Oh my god! I hooked your ass!"

I tug gently on the hook, and luckily, it appears as though I only hooked his shorts.

What happens next will forever be imprinted on the annals of my mind. For some reason, in my panic, I determine that it would be a fabulous idea to pull his pants down to check for damage.

I grip the waistband of his royal-blue swim trunks and tug downward until it's resting below his buns—and if I may interject, they are a stellar set of buns—and look for any wounds.

In retrospect, when I found no injuries, I should have pulled his pants back up, but oh nooooo. Not me. I proceed to run my hands over both ass cheeks—quite thoroughly, I might add—to assure myself there are no imaginary fishhooks embedded in his buttocks.

And that's when Darryl walks out onto the deck. "Hey, what's all the yell—Oh." He freezes and takes in the scene. Riggs bent over the boat. His bare ass exposed. My hands roaming all over said ass. Darryl studiously avoids my gaze and jerks a thumb back toward the cabin. "I'm just… yeah…" Then he sprints inside like a scalded dog.

"Um, Libby? Do you mind?"

I realize my fingers are digging into the fleshy man-meat of Riggs's behind, and I slowly loosen my grip, trying to think of something—*anything*—to alleviate this awkwardness. So I begin babbling nonsensically. Because that's *always* an outstanding idea.

"Welp, everything looks good back here. Your ass is fine. And I don't mean it's fine as in *you have a fine ass*, though you do. It's a very fine ass. Probably the finest I've ever seen. Very tan. You must sunbathe naked. Not that I'm thinking about you naked. And there's hardly any hair. Do you wax? Anyway, looking good in the buttocks region."

As if that isn't bad enough, I smack his right cheek twice before yanking his pants back up.

Mortified doesn't even begin to cover what I'm feeling right now. Riggs leans the fishing rod against the boat and turns slowly, lifting one dark, stern eyebrow. But do I shut up? No, no, I most certainly do not.

"Look, I know that got awkward for a minute."

His other eyebrow raises to the level of the first one.

"But the good news is that you don't have to go to the hospital to get a fishhook out of your booty." I do enthusiastic jazz hands and put on my brightest smile. "Yay for silver linings!"

The edges of Riggs's lips curl up slowly until he has a full-fledged grin on his handsome face as he crosses his arms over his chest. "Liberty Hill, when you said earlier that you like kinky shit, is this what you were talking about?"

My eyes turn into dinner plates, and I slap a hand over my mouth, but I'm unable to contain the giggle that erupts from my lips. And in the next moment, we're both laughing. Like, hysterical, hands-on-knees, barely breathing laughter.

"I can't… believe… you spanked my ass," Riggs gasps.

"Stop it," I giggle. "I was trying to think of a way to wrap up the entire situation without making it weirder."

"Oh, then that was definitely the way to go," he commends sarcastically, still chuckling. He picks up the fishing rod and nods toward the cabin. "I'm gonna get Darryl to cut this hook out of my swim trunks. And try to explain what happened."

"Poor man is probably traumatized."

"Or he's impressed with my *very fine ass*," he offers, sending my words back to me with a mischievous grin.

"Oh shut up," I chastise, lightly shoving his shoulder.

We spend the next few hours fishing without further butt-groping incidents. Riggs caught more fish than me, but I caught the biggest, a red snapper he estimated to weigh over thirty pounds.

As we wipe the fish and squid guts from our hands, I decide it's time to get back to work. "What kind of coffee does Lucinda drink?" I ask casually.

Riggs throws his wipe away and looks at me with confusion. "Venti iced skinny hazelnut macchiato with sugar-free syrup, light ice, and no whip," he recites with ease.

"Wow, and I thought my coffee order was complicated."

"What's yours?"

"Macchiato with one cream and two-and-a-half sugars."

He nods as he retrieves a basket and begins pulling out sandwiches and chips. "Why did you ask me that?"

"The other girls and I were talking about how a lot of men don't pay attention to the little things like their women's coffee order or favorite color. You're already a step ahead."

"Huh. Just seems like a normal thing to know. And her favorite color is white, in case you were going to ask that next."

I grin. "I was." Walking to the cooler that holds our drinks for the day, I open the lid. "Is it too early for beer?"

"Is it ever?"

Pulling out two Coors Lights, I take a seat on the deck in front of the spread. "This looks good. I'm starving."

"Fishing is hard work," Riggs comments, selecting a sandwich from the tray as I do the same.

Attempting to not stare at the way his strong jaw moves when he eats, I get back to business.

"You said Lucinda likes shopping. Do you go with her?"

He shakes his head. "No, she prefers to shop with her friends, so I got the bank to issue her a card from my bank account. She gets the best of both worlds, shopping with her friends while I pay from a distance." He flashes me a chagrined smile. *Wow, that's… something.*

"What about her favorite foods?"

"A mixed greens salad with two tablespoons of light Italian dressing," he says without pause. "Always."

"Oh. Okay."

Riggs pauses with a chip halfway to his mouth. "What's that look?"

"What look?"

"That uncomfortable look on your face."

Damn, he really is perceptive. "I just feel a bit over the top right about now," I say with a laugh. "Mine changes with my mood, and salad is no part of it. My comfort food is probably Oreos, but I love McDonald's french fries with extra salt too. And shrimp. Any kind of shrimp."

He tilts his bottle toward me. "I bet I can change your favorite food with one meal." I lift my eyebrows at him. "I make the best red snapper you've ever eaten."

"You cook?"

Nodding, he takes a long drink. "Yep, my Nana Viv taught me. If you want, I can cook that big boy you caught for our next meeting."

He's going to cook for me? "That sounds wonderful."

I'm so impressed with this man, and I keep waiting for the other shoe to drop. Why did Lucinda sign him up for Book Boyfriend Builders? I read the application she filled out, and it was very vague, only stating that she wants her boyfriend to be "swoonier."

Maybe he's nice on the surface but acts like an ass to his girl in private.

"What's the last gift you bought for Lucinda?"

Riggs swallows his food and says, "Diamond earrings I bought while I was in Colorado. I always bring her something back when I travel, but she's not really into what she calls *cheesy souvenirs*. She says they're cheap and stupid and she prefers jewelry, so that's what I get her."

I'm beginning to get the first inkling that maybe I don't like this Lucinda chick very much. But it's not my job to judge. It's my job to make this swoony man somehow swoonier.

"That's good, Riggs. It's important to know your woman's preferences."

He smiles, but it seems forced. "Yeah, I try. I also brought my sister some earrings and a funny shot glass. She collects them."

I lick my finger and make a tick mark in the air. "Bonus point for being sweet to your sister." He laughs, and I say, "I collect magnets. When my dad would go away for work, he'd always bring me one from whatever state or city he went to. I still have all of them on my refrigerator."

"It's nice that you have those. What did your dad do?"

"Insurance sales. He only had to travel to conferences once or twice a year."

Riggs's smile is soft and kind. "Will you tell me about your parents? If it's not too hard to talk about?"

We spend the rest of our meal talking about my family. We even discuss how my birth mother was a troubled young woman and ran away from home when she was eighteen, losing all contact with her family.

I know we're supposed to be discussing him and Lucinda, but he just seems so interested, which is a nice change. I'm not sure Logan even knows my parents' names.

Darryl pops his head outside, his eyes moving tentatively between us. Poor man's probably afraid of walking out on a scene like the ass rubbing incident. "I'm going to move us to another location, if that's all right with you, Riggs. We had some good luck there yesterday."

"Sounds good, man. Thanks." Riggs stands as the captain returns to his cabin. "Fuck it's hot," he says, reaching for the hem of his T-shirt. "Okay if I take this off?"

I barely hold back from screaming *fuck yes, take it all off, big boy* and manage to nod placidly. "Of course. I think I'll take mine off too, if you don't mind."

His grin is positively wicked. "Don't mind a bit, Liberty."

Is he flirting with me? Surely not.

I pull off my shirt, which is now stained with squid ink from the cut bait, and stow it in my beach bag. Then I turn and catch my first look at Riggs in all his shirtless glory.

Dear god! The man should be illegal. Or at least come with some kind of advisory label.

Warning: Staring directly at a half-naked Riggs Romero could produce spontaneous orgasms, rebellious nipples, and embarrassing wet spots. Proceed with caution.

His chest and shoulders are broad and taper down to a trim waist. Thank god I have my sunglasses on because I'm openly staring at his abs. I caught glimpses of them on the plane and when he was helping me move, but the full picture in the sun is nothing short of glorious. I would drop to my knees and lick sweat from those abs, trace my tongue between each hard muscle, worship them like they deserved to be worshiped.

And don't even get me started on his tattoos. His chest is bare of any ink, but both arms are covered with maritime tats. Waves, winding ropes, a gorgeous sunrise, the North Star.

As the boat begins to move, the azure backdrop of water and sky contrast beautifully with his darkly tanned skin, and I know behind his dark lenses, his eyes would perfectly match the lighter blue from overhead. I lift my pervy gaze to his face and find his tongue sliding along his bottom lip.

"I," he clears his throat, "I really like your swimsuit, Libby."

Maybe it's wishful thinking, but I believe he's looking at my boobs.

"I like yours too," I reply. He's wearing royal-blue swim trunks with a white anchor print, while I'm in a sunshine-yellow bikini top and ancient denim shorts.

"Is yellow your favorite color?"

"H-how did you know that?"

"You've worn yellow every time I've seen you so far."

And let's add acutely observant to the list of his attributes.

"I like it because it's a happy color," I reply. "I feel like we've been talking about me a lot. Tell me about you and your family."

"Hmm, I grew up here, as you know. I had good parents, and I love them, but I'm really closer to Nana Viv."

"Nana Viv is your father's mother?"

He nods, and by the way his face melts, I can tell he adores her. "She was always my confidant growing up. We'd spend hours in her kitchen or her rose garden just talking. I'd do anything in the world for her."

"I love that. What about your sister?"

"With her being six years younger than me, we didn't get really tight until we were both adults. Now she's my best friend. She's the one who got me into cover modeling. Some guy she used to date wrote a thriller novel and needed someone for the cover. Silvia volunteered me." He flashes a self-deprecating smile. "After that, I got approached by several photographers who wanted to work with me. They thought I had the look for romance covers."

"I agree." The boat slows, and we begin readying our tackle for the afternoon round of fishing. "What about your job?"

Riggs's smile fades a little. "It's a job. Just work, you know?"

"Are you happy there?"

"I'm… fine. It's the family business, so it's what I'm expected to do."

I read something unspoken between his words. "What would you do if you didn't have family obligations? If you could choose any career."

"This," he says, gazing out over the deep blue of the Gulf. "I'd be out on the water every day instead of stuck behind a desk."

His answer makes me sad. "I think that sounds like a dream. I would love to be out on a boat with my computer and simply write my books."

Riggs pushes his sunglasses to the top of his head and fixes me with his blue gaze. "Words and water?"

I bob my head up and down and confirm, "Words and water."

CHAPTER 9

Libby

The next Wednesday afternoon, I sit on a towel on the beach that's within walking distance of my little cottage. My computer is open on my lap, but the page is blank except for the chapter number at the top. I can't quite wrap my head around what I want to write next.

I just wrote an emotional scene, and the male character is now hanging out with his friends, so maybe it's time for something funny. A vague idea hits me, and I shoot off a text to my BBB friends and wait for an answer.

> Libby: I have a male character that's going to tell an off-color cum joke, but I'm struggling. Give me ideas.

It doesn't take long before I receive a barrage of replies.

> Gemma: A man asks his wife if he can come in her ear, but she says no because she's afraid it will make her go deaf. He replies, "Funny, I always come in your mouth, and you never shut the fuck up."

> JoJo: They say pineapple juice makes your jizz taste better. But for me, it just ruins the pineapple juice.

> Ava: From now on, I'm calling my cum "children alfredo."

I'm laughing uncontrollably when I reply.

> Libby: These are all awesome, but children alfredo for the win. I knew I could count on you bitches. Thanks!

I quickly type the joke into my document, and the words flow like a raging river after that. The male character has a hilarious group of friends, and I'm loving their banter.

My phone rings, and I pick it up and see that my friend, Sonya, is calling. She's an office manager for an optometrist in Port Saint Joe, and we instantly hit it off when she hired me to design a new website for the office. She's one of the reasons I chose to move to this particular town.

"Hey, lady," I answer, setting my computer aside and reclining back on my towel.

"Hi, Libby. What are you up to today?"

"Being a beach bum," I reply happily. "Well, I guess I'm working too because I'm writing on the beach."

"Do you have plans for tonight?"

"Nope, whatcha got?"

"Drinks at that little pub downtown at seven. Erica is coming too."

Erica is the optician at the office, and she has the most impressive collection of glasses I've ever seen.

"Sounds good. See you there."

"I've got so much to tell you."

I smile as I hang up. Those two are always good for some book fodder, competing to see whose crazy dating stories will end up in one of my books.

"I seriously don't know what's wrong with men today. They all seem to have mommy issues," Sonya says, her black curls bouncing with every shake of her head. Sonya is gorgeous, with dark skin, a huge smile, and curves I would die for.

"You went out with that Nathan guy that's been asking you out for a month?" I ask, and she nods.

"Yes. First *and last* date."

"What happened?" Erica asks, leaning forward on her forearms. She's a pretty brunette with soulful brown eyes framed by purple glittery glasses.

"This fool," Sonya starts, taking a sip of her Manhattan. "He shows up to the restaurant with his three-year-old daughter *and his mother.*"

"No fucking way," I breathe. "On a first date?"

"Yes, ma'am. And it was not a kid-friendly restaurant. The little girl screamed through the appetizer course, and neither of them did a thing about it. Everyone in the restaurant looked like they wanted to stab us. I finally pulled the kid out of her highchair and held her in my lap until she calmed down."

"Poor baby. It's not her fault her dad is an idiot," Erica says, her lips turning down.

"Why did he bring them with him instead of leaving his mom at home to babysit?"

Sonya rolls her eyes. "I asked him, and he said he wanted his three favorite ladies to meet."

I scrunch my nose. "Well, that just took a left turn into creepy town."

"Afterward, Nathan took his daughter, waved her hand at me, and said, 'Say bye-bye to Mommy.' I almost broke my ankles getting out of there."

Erica and I crack up laughing. "Did he at least pay for dinner?" I ask, and Sonya levels me with a flat glare.

"His mother paid."

Erica calms her laughter and holds up one hand. "I might be able to top that one. You remember that guy I had a one-night stand with a couple months ago?"

"Tyson?" Sonya asks. "The one with the big…"

"That's the one," Erica confirms. "Best sex of my life, so I was excited when he called me last week. This time we actually went out on a real date, and everything was going great. Good conversation and everything. He's really smart, some kind of engineer."

"Uh-oh," I say. "Sounds too good to be true. Did you sleep together again?"

"We did, and it was just as good the second time around. I'm talking *multiple* orgasms. The man can find my G-spot like he printed out the location on Mapquest."

"Is Mapquest still a thing?" Sonya interrupts. "I thought everyone used GPS now."

Erica waves her hand. "Whatever. You know what I mean. So afterward, we're laying in bed, and he turns the lamp on and tells me he wants to show me something."

"Oh shit, did he have a dick boil or something?" Sonya blurts, her brown eyes wide.

I laugh. "What the hell is a dick boil?"

"I have no idea. My cousin's boyfriend told her he couldn't have sex with her for about a month because he had a dick boil."

My nose scrunches. "She needs to get checked. He's probably got herpes." I turn back to Erica. "So what did Tyson have to show you?"

She lowers her voice. "He got my name tattooed on his dick."

I blink rapidly, my mouth falling open. "That's insane. Did you run for the hills?"

Erica averts her eyes and scratches the back of her neck as her words all come out in a rush. "No, I, uh, sucked his big Erica dick and then we fucked again. Three times."

"Good lord. Only you," Sonya moans. "And then you ran?"

"Not exactly." Erica gnaws on her bottom lip. "I told him I'd see him again."

"What? He literally got your name tatted on his penis after a one-night stand. He's probably a crazy stalker dude."

"I knowww, but the sex!" she whines. "It's, like, crazy good. Plus, him getting the tattoo shows he's not one of those guys with commitment issues."

Sonya and I almost fall out of our chairs laughing as Erica rolls her eyes and takes a sip of wine. "At least if he kidnaps me, I won't be horny."

"You are so ridiculous. If you end up dead in a ditch, I'm putting *But at least she wasn't horny* on your headstone," Sonya informs her before turning to me. "What about you, Lib? You dating anyone since the loser?"

"Nope, and absolutely no prospects."

"What about that book-boyfriend business you're doing? Maybe you can train up a man just like you want him."

"It's not a dating service," I argue. "And the man I'm working with now is taken. His girlfriend signed him up for the service."

"Must be a real loser if his girlfriend signed him up."

"He is not," I say defensively, feeling my cheeks heat. "He's a really great guy."

Sonya's eyes narrow. "Why are you getting so snippy about it?"

I huff out a long breath. "I'm not. He's just really nice."

My friends share a look and both smile. "Oooh, Libby has a crush on her client," Erica sings. "I smell a love triangle."

"There's no triangle or any other geometric shapes. He's just... different from what I expected. I was picturing someone clueless with women, but he's totally not, at least, from what I can tell so far."

"I'm sure the red flags will appear soon, and you can take care of it," Erica says. "There's no such thing as a perfect man."

"True," I say, signaling the waitress for another round.

But Riggs Romero is pretty damn close.

CHAPTER 10
Riggs

I approach the booth and find Mills and Salazar already waiting. "Sorry I'm late, guys. What did I miss?"

"We were talking about whether or not Salazar should shave his 'stache," Mills informs me.

I survey the bush on top of my friend's lip. "You look like a porn star."

"From the seventies or eighties?"

Assessing him once again, I proclaim, "Definitely the eighties."

"Cool. That's what I was going for."

Sliding in beside Mills, I motion the waitress to bring me my usual. "Then keep it. Some women love a good mustache ride."

"Speaking of that, did you see Salazar's shirt?"

My other friend leans back in his seat and straightens his Barbie-pink T-shirt with a bold black font that reads, *Real men don't just wear pink… they eat it.*

A chuckle rumbles up from my chest. "Fuck almighty, man. You really shouldn't be allowed to mingle with the normal people."

"We could chain him to his bed," Mills suggests. "Come by and feed him a couple times a day."

"As long as one of those times is a nice juicy—"

I interrupt. "Yeah, yeah. We get the idea."

"You and Lady Lucifer—I mean, Lucinda—still in a slump?" Mills asks, taking a sip of his beer, and I grind my teeth together. I got a little drunk and frustrated a couple weeks ago and spilled the secret of our *dry spell*.

"I don't want to talk about it," I grump, and my friends share a knowing smile.

"That means yes," Salazar says.

After the server drops off my McKenna on the rocks, I divert the conversation. "Mills, what's going on with you?"

He leans forward and lowers his voice. "I saw that chick again. The hot one, and it was even more spectacular than the first time. This girl blows my fucking mind in bed."

"And?"

"Well, you know I fuck with the lights off."

"We're all aware why you do that," Salazar says with a smirk.

"Yeah, because I let my stupid ex talk me into having her name tattooed on my fucking cock." He sighs and runs a hand over his blond hair. "I really like this new woman. A lot. She's freaky as hell, but she's also fun to be with. It was the best first date I've ever had."

"So did you finally unveil your little surprise?"

"First of all, it's not *little*, and second, yes, I did. I turned on the lamp when we were done. After I'd softened her up with a few orgasms."

"What did she do?" Salazar asks, leaning forward like the fucking gossip he is.

"She was surprised, of course, and then… wait, let me back up. Did I tell you new girl's name?" We both shake our heads, and he announces with a flair of his hands, "Erica."

Salazar and I stare at him in shock for a long beat. "The same name as your ex? The same name that's tattooed on your damn dick?" I ask.

"Yep," Mills says, popping the P. "And she automatically thought I'd gotten the name tattooed on my penis *for her*."

"Oh my fucking god," Salazar breathes. "You told her the truth, right?"

"I was going to, but then she scooted down and started sucking me off. And let me tell you, the woman's mouth is fucking amazing. She could suck the chrome off a trailer hitch."

Salazar and I slowly turn to look at each other in incredulity. "Why does this shit never happen to me?" he asks.

"Because you dress like a prepubescent whoremonger."

Mills slaps the table to bring our attention back to him. "Like I was saying, I really like Erica—the new one—and now I don't know what to do."

I shake my head. "I have so many questions. Do you only date women named Erica? Like some kind of name fetish?"

"No, it was purely coincidental."

"You have to tell her," I insist.

At the same time, Salazar says, "Don't tell her."

We discuss this ridiculous subject for a few minutes, and Mills finally decides he wants to try and make things work with New Erica, so he's going to tell her the next time they get together.

I turn to signal the server for another drink, and something yellow catches my eye. My heart rate practically doubles, and my legs push me to a standing position without my permission.

"Libby," I say as the blonde bombshell walks past our table dressed in a cute yellow sundress with a cherry print. Her hair is in one long braid that hangs over her shoulder, and her lips match the fruits on her dress.

Her eyes widen for a second, and then her lips curve into a genuine smile. "Riggs, hi! What are you doing here?"

"I'm having drinks with some friends. What about you?"

"Same. They just left, and I was on my way out."

"Do you… um, do you want to sit down?"

"Oh, I wouldn't want to intrude," she says sweetly.

The skin over my chest tightens. "It wouldn't be an intrusion at all."

"Yeah, you can class up the table a bit," Salazar throws in as he stands and flashes a huge smile beneath that porny mustache of his. "We'd love to have you."

"Okay," she says cheerily. "If you're sure."

"Positive," the lothario says, holding out a hand. "I'm Penn Salazar."

"Nice to meet you, Penn. I'm Libby Hill." Then she giggles. "I like your shirt."

"What about the 'stache?" He rubs a finger and thumb over the stupid facial hair.

Libby tilts her head and squints one eye. "You look like Ron Jeremy, pre-pot belly and receding hairline."

"I take that as a compliment, milady," he says with a little bow. Salazar is in full flirt mode, and it aggravates the shit out of me.

"I'm Ty Mills," my other friend says, rising to shake her hand. "Have a seat."

The only open seat is beside Salazar-the-mustachioed, so she sits there while I reluctantly take my place beside Mills.

"Sooo," Salazar drawls, "how do you two know each other, and why haven't you introduced us before?" He does the wide eyes across the table at me.

Libby gives me a soft smile that tells me she's not going to spill the Book Boyfriend secret. "We know each other from the book community," she says instead.

"Are you a model too?" he asks, propping his chin in his hand and giving her the full Penn Salazar treatment. "Because a beauty like you certainly should be."

Oh for fuck's sake.

"Libby is a romance author," I offer.

"Do you write the spicy stuff?" he asks, waggling his eyebrows.

"Would you think less of me if I said yes?" she asks coyly, and Salazar laughs like that's the funniest thing he's ever heard.

"Certainly not." The asshole leans even closer, and all I want to do is put some kind of barrier in his face. Like my fist. "How do you get the inspiration for your spicy scenes? From personal experience?"

"More like wishful thinking," she says with a wry grin.

My flirty-ass friend continues. "I've got a great idea for a book. A romance author—let's call her Likky—meets a handsome, intelligent attorney who we'll call Peen. She instantly falls for his superb facial hair and the witty pink T-shirt he's wearing, so he offers her a mustache ride."

Laughter bursts from her lips, and she slaps his arm. "Likky and Peen? You're funny, Penn."

"Funny-looking," I mutter under my breath, earning me a quizzical look from Mills beside me.

"Just hear me out. What starts out as a bit of fun turns into the most sensual night of their lives." He drops his voice to a sultry tone. "The charming Peen can't get enough of the extremely gorgeous Likky, and he treats her like a fucking princess. They fall madly in love and ride off into the sunset in his red Ferrari. That would be fucking epic."

Libby raises an eyebrow at him. "What do you do for a living, Penn?"

"Moi? Why, I'm a criminal defense attorney."

"And what kind of car do you drive?"

"I have several, but my favorite is my vintage Ferrari."

"Let me guess… red?"

"The same color as those lovely lips of yours," he purrs. "And let me assure you, the resemblance to our masculine, well-endowed hero is purely coincidental."

I hear a growling noise and realize it's coming from my own throat. Mills elbows me.

"It's a nice story, but there's no conflict," Libby says. "I pride myself on writing spicy stories that also have a plot."

"Ooh, I've got a plot twist for you," Mills adds, his green eyes sparkling with mischief. "The idiot hero has a best friend named… Romeo, who harbors a secret crush on the heroine."

Now it's my turn to throw an elbow—hard—and Mills yelps. Libby looks at him in concern, and he pounds the end of his fist against his chest and feigns a cough. "Sorry. Swallowed wrong."

"Well, I think we're getting somewhere with this story now," she muses before leaning forward on her forearms. I try not to notice how that move pushes her cleavage up, but I am unsuccessful. "What if we make it really juicy, and Likky can't decide between the two men?"

"How will she decide?" Mills asks, getting into the story now.

Libby purses her lips and rolls her eyes up to the ceiling. "Umm, maybe… Ooh, I know. There can be a fuck-off to see who she's most compatible with."

Every male member of our party chokes on their own fucking tongues, and Libby sits back with a huge grin on her face as we try to recover.

When he's able to speak again, Salazar croaks out, "Oh, our hero, Peen, would definitely be the victor in that kind of contest."

"Or maybe Likky likes an antihero," she tosses out. "The one who treats her like a queen in the streets and a slut between the sheets."

I need another fucking drink. Now.

Mills and Salazar are openly gaping at her while I'm frantically waving my arm for the server. I've never met a woman who's so cool about sex talk with three guys. Maybe it's her profession that makes her so nonchalant.

I see the server nod and hold up one finger as Libby announces, "I'm running to the restroom."

"You want me to order you a drink?" I ask, and she smiles.

"I've had a few, so maybe I'll just get a coffee."

"Macchiato with one cream and two-and-a-half sugars?" I ask.

She looks surprised and… pleased, which makes me feel pretty fucking pleased myself. "Yes please."

As soon as she's out of earshot, Salazar practically launches himself across the table until he's only a few inches from my face. "Oh my fucking god, Romero. I think I'm in love."

I give him a playful shove that's more forceful than I intend. "Sit down, you fuckwit. You just met her."

Bouncing back in his seat, his eyes go dreamy. "They say when you know, you know. And I know she's going to be the first Mrs. Salazar."

"The first?" Mills snorts. "How many wives do you plan to have?"

"Well, my dad is on his fifth, but he probably has his eye on Miss Number Six as we speak."

The waitress drops by, and we order drinks and a bunch of appetizers before Ty starts in on Penn again.

"Are you blind, Salazar?"

He waves a hand in front of his face and frowns. "No, I think I'm good."

Mills reaches across the table and smacks him on the side of the head. "I'm talking about the obvious. Romero likes Libby."

"No I don't," I insist, as Penn's eyes snap to mine. Then a myriad of expressions crosses his face, from confusion to realization. "I don't like her," I drive home.

He wags a finger at me. "Yes you do. Why the hell didn't I notice?"

"Because you were too busy sticking your head up Libby's ass," I retort.

"Jealousy. Yep, he definitely likes her," Ty says with a chuckle before turning to face me. "Why don't you ask her out?"

"I have a girlfriend." Even I can hear the regretful tone in my voice.

"Dude, your nana would not want you to stay with someone you have no chance of ever falling in love with."

I avert my eyes. "You didn't see the look on her face the first time I told her I was dating Lucinda. Nana and Lucinda's grandmother were best friends, and she told me they had always dreamed that their grandchildren would one day get together. Plus, Lucinda's father runs my fucking company."

My two friends look at each other, and I can see the pity in their eyes. They're the only ones I can really be honest with about my relationship. I don't even tell Silvia everything.

"Riggs," Penn says, sounding uncharacteristically serious, "your nana and papa were the perfect love story. She would want nothing less for you. Just explain it to her."

"But she's so happy, and her health has improved drastically over the past year. I can't... I can't risk disappointing her and seeing her health decline."

I rub a hand over my heart to try and quell the ache that's formed there at the thought of losing Nana Viv, especially if I contribute to that by upsetting her.

"She's coming back," Penn mutters, glancing over my shoulder before letting out a very loud, very fake laugh. We all follow suit like we hadn't just been talking about some serious shit.

"What's so funny?" Libby asks, sitting down and grinning at us.

"We were just talking about Ty's penis tattoo," Penn blurts out. "Get this, about a year ago, he was crazy for this girl, and she wanted him to get her name tattooed on his dick to prove his love for her."

Libby frowns. "And did you?"

Ty rolls his eyes. "I did, and then she left me two weeks later."

She covers her cherry lips with one hand. "That's terrible. Can you get it removed?"

Ty lifts an eyebrow. "Do you have any idea how painful laser tattoo removal can be? Especially in such a… delicate area."

"His penis is very delicate. And tiny," Penn says, earning him a middle finger from our other friend. "Anyway, her name was Erica, and now Ty is dating *another* woman named Erica, and when she saw the tat, she thought he had it done for her."

Libby's mouth drops almost to the floor. "You've got to be kidding me. Wh-what does the new Erica look like?"

"Totally fucking hot," Ty replies, closing his eyes. "Dark hair, and these nerdy glasses that make her look like a sexy librarian."

"Oh my fuck," she whispers, blinking rapidly.

"I know," Ty laments. "And I really like her a lot. I want to see if this can go somewhere between us, but now I feel like I've started our relationship out on a lie. At the same time, I don't want to hurt her feelings. Maybe you could give me a woman's perspective on what to do."

Libby purses her lips and lifts her eyebrows before shocking the hell out of us all. "Seeing as how the Erica you're talking about is one of my friends and she was just telling me this story about an hour ago—"

"No fucking way!" Penn yells, and she nods.

"Yes fucking way. Ty, you really need to tell her. Erica likes you a lot but she's a little concerned that you're a stalky weirdo who got his peen tattooed after being together one time. I can assure you, if you tell her the truth, she'll understand."

Four sets of eyes dart between one another before the ridiculousness of the situation hits us at the same time, and all we burst into laughter.

"Um, I have your food and drinks," the server says, looking concerned at the crazy folks in her booth. "Is everything okay here?"

"Fine," Libby says, wiping tears of mirth from beneath her eyes before pointing at Ty. "We're just trying to help our friend with an unfortunate penis incident."

The waitress quickly slides her entire tray onto the table and sprints back to the kitchen as another bout of hilarity roars from our table.

Could this woman be any more perfect?

CHAPTER 11
Riggs

My friends may be idiots, but they were a hundred percent right when it came to Libby. I fucking like her.

And there's absolutely nothing I can do about it.

Knocking on the door, I force a bright smile when Lucinda answers, and I lean in for a kiss. She offers her cheek, not her lips, and I brush it lightly. "You ready to go?"

"Sure. Let me get my purse." Then she looks over her shoulder at me. "You didn't bring the truck, did you?" Lucinda hates my truck.

"No, I brought the Mercedes."

"Good."

The ride is made in silence while she scrolls on her phone, which gives me time to think. The first month after Lucinda and I got together a year ago was great. I took her to all her favorite places and doted on her.

The second month, I tried to introduce her to things I liked—fishing, the beach, parasailing—but she despised all of it. I thought it was okay though. Couples could enjoy different things, right? We could have our own interests that we could do with our friends when we weren't together.

In the third month, we became intimate. It was... fine. We had sex a couple times a week. Nothing mind blowing, but it fulfilled a need.

On paper, our relationship was perfect. Our families were bound by business and old friendships, so I hoped love would blossom, but by the half-year mark, it withered on the vine. The closer I tried to get, the more she pulled away. Since then, I'd tried to foster *more*, but it wasn't something you could force.

I treated Lucinda with the respect she deserved as my girlfriend, but the bone-deep feelings I'd always craved? Yeah, I couldn't quite get them to surface.

But it was okay. I would gladly give up a few years of my life if it made my grandmother happy. So, I'd bide my time and wish I could free myself of the noose I wore as my daily jewelry.

"We're here," I announce, pulling up the long, curving driveway, the white gravel crunching beneath my tires. Nana's home came into view when I topped the last hill. Her manor is enormous, but it is also warm and full of love.

I get out of the silver luxury car and round the front to open Lucinda's door. She's wearing a gauzy white shift dress with tiny rhinestones dotting the neckline. "You look really pretty today," I tell her, and she smiles.

"Thanks." I hand her the flowers I'd picked up on the way, and she loops her fingers with mine as we ascend the steps. The only time Lucinda initiates contact is when we're in front of our families. Maybe we're both pretending.

"About time," Nana says, swinging open the door. My heart performs a little tap dance in my chest. My grandmother appears small at first glance. She's barely above five feet tall, with an ample figure that's the result of a lifetime of pasta and garlic bread. But the woman's personality is larger than life.

"Nana, what are you doing answering the door?" I ask, leaning down to kiss her cheek. She smells like an Italian bakery.

"That's what you do when someone comes for a visit," she tells me in her no-nonsense tone. "Unless it's those folks trying to tell you about Jesus. Then you hide in a windowless room till they go away."

Lucinda gives her a simpering smile and hands over the flowers. "You look lovely today, Nana."

My grandma's eyes flicker down to our joined hands. "You do too, dear."

"Where is Nelda?" I ask, wondering why Nana's house-manager-slash-butler didn't answer the door.

"Probably banging the gardener," she says, winking mischievously at me. "I've been trying to set those two up for ages, and I think it's finally starting to take."

"You're something else, Nana," I tell her with a laugh. "Why don't we sit down?"

She loops her arm through my free one, using me for support as we walk to the back of the house. "I was totally kidding about Nelda, by the way. She ran to the store to get me those crackers I like. Let's go sit in the garden." I hear the low sigh from Lucinda. She hates being outdoors, but I know she won't complain in front of Nana.

My grandmother's gait is slow, but she seems pretty steady today. A nurse jogs down the curved staircase, a little breathless. "There you are, Ms. Viviana. I told you to wait for me so I could help you down the stairs."

"Psshhht, I'm fine," Nana scoffs. "You act like I'm an old lady with congestive heart failure." Then she cackles at her joke because that's exactly what she is.

Stopping, I link Nana's arm with Lucinda's and say, "You two beauties head on outside. I want to talk to Ophelia."

"They're going to talk about me behind my back," Nana tells Lucinda in a loud voice as they exit through the french doors that lead to the garden.

"How is she today?" I ask the nurse, a lanky Jamaican woman with a lovely accent I could listen to all day.

"Having a good day. The cardiologist came by this morning

and gave Ms. Viviana a good report. He said he will talk to you about it tomorrow."

"Thank you, Ophelia. I appreciate everything you do for my grandmother, and please call me if you need anything."

"I will. You're a good boy, Riggs."

"That's what they tell me," I say with a cheesy grin. "Thanks, Ophelia," I pat the woman on the shoulder before heading outside.

The visit with Nana goes well. Lucinda and I put on a good show, mimicking the kind of affection we shared when we first got together, which is pretty much absent now. My grandmother is glowing the entire time, her eyes not missing a single gesture, and I know I'm doing the right thing.

Even though, for the first time, pretending like Lucinda and I are still an adoring couple feels very, very wrong.

"Do you want to come over tonight?" I ask Lucinda on the way home.

"No," she says breezily as she stares down at her phone, "I have to pack since I'm leaving tomorrow."

"Okay."

From my peripheral vision, I can see her look up from her phone and at my face. "That's it?"

"What's it?"

"Just *okay*?" On the last word, she lowers her voice to copy my own.

"You said no, so yes, that's it."

"Fine," she huffs, returning to her regularly scheduled scrolling.

"Fine," I repeat, and for reasons I can't define, a tiny spark of relief shines inside my chest.

CHAPTER 12

Libby

I wiggle excitedly in my seat when, one by one, my author friends' faces pop onto my computer screen. Well, except for…

"Can you see me?" Ava's voice asks.

"No," we all chorus.

"Shit. Hold on." Five minutes later, she figures out how to turn on the camera, and all four of our faces appear in squares on the screen like the spicy author version of *The Brady Bunch*.

Another ten minutes is spent catching up on life events before we get down to business. "Who wants to go first?" Gemma asks, and I raise my hand like a sixth grader.

"I'll go. As you know from my texts, I'm actually working with two BBB clients right now. The first is Gina, the woman that's one half of a lesbian couple."

"I've been curious about that. How's it working out?" JoJo asks.

"Really well, actually. I think most people want the same basic things from a relationship, no matter their gender or sexual orientation. The lady is really sweet and very in love with Lauren, but Gina had a hard home life growing up. She didn't receive much affection as a kid, and now she's not sure how to show affection to her partner."

"That's sad," Ava says.

"It is, and Lauren's love language is physical touch. I'm trying to be cautious because I don't want Gina to do anything she's uncomfortable with, so I told her to take it slowly. I gave her a few assignments for the week, things she said were within her comfort level, and she was eager to try."

"Sounds like you're doing everything right," JoJo says. "What about your other client?"

Closing my eyes, I puff out a long breath. "I'm struggling with this one."

"Asshat?" Gemma asks.

I open my eyes and massage my forehead. "No. Actually, it's Riggs Romero."

Beat of silence.

And then my speakers erupt with a cacophony of yells.

"Riggs fucking Romero?"

"Holy shit!"

"Lib's totally going to bang her client."

"Lucky bitch."

"Yep, totally banging him like a screen door in a hurricane."

I wave my hands at them and laugh. "Stop it! I'm not going to bang him." Three sets of skeptical eyebrows raise. "Seriously, I'm not. His *girlfriend* signed him up. Plus, it would be totally unprofessional."

"She's right," Gemma says with a firm nod. "Libby wouldn't sleep with a taken man."

"She'd think about it," JoJo says, and they all grin knowingly.

"Well, I'm not dead. I think every woman who's seen him has thought about getting Riggs between their sheets." *And in their showers. And against their walls. And...* "Anyway, my struggle is that I can't seem to figure out anything for him to improve on."

Ava twists a lock of dark-brown hair around one finger. "What did the girlfriend say in the application?"

"It was vague. She just wants him to be 'swoonier,' but she didn't give specifics. I've questioned him a lot, and he knows all her preferences, seems attentive, and get this… for a souvenir from Colorado Springs, he bought her diamond earrings."

"Wow, I was lucky to get a ball cap from Aiden when he went somewhere," Gemma quips dryly.

A titter of amusement goes through the rest of the group. None of us has ever seen Gemma wear a ball cap. "See, that's what I mean. A hat is a thoughtless gift for you, but Riggs bought Lucinda jewelry because he knows that's what she likes."

"Why don't you contact this Lucinda and get more info from her," Ava suggests.

Gemma nods. "That's a good idea. People always try to put their best foot forward, but you never know what they're like privately."

"Okay, I'll do that. Riggs just seems like a very thoughtful guy. Like, I mentioned that I wanted to go deep-sea fishing, so he took me for our first meeting. His friend has a charter business."

"Did you see him shirtless?" Ava asks breathlessly.

"And bottomless," I say, rolling my eyes, and everyone gasps. "Not like that. There was an… unfortunate incident."

Gemma leans forward and widens her eyes. "Do tell."

I recount the entire story about hooking Riggs and the ensuing chaos, including the impromptu spanking I delivered. By the end, the other girls are howling with laughter, and Ava actually disappears from the screen because she slides onto the floor like a limp noodle as the ridiculousness gets the better of her.

"That's fucking hysterical, Libs," Gemma wheezes. "Can I use that in my next boo—"

"No," I cut off with a good-natured roll of my hazel eyes. "I'm totally using it. My humiliation, my story."

"Fair enough," she grumbles. "At least tell me you wore the red bikini while you were spanking him. The one that practically shows your areolas?"

I giggle. "No, you ass. I wore the yellow one. Perfectly respectable."

I remember the blue gaze that heated my skin more than the sun when Riggs looked at me that day, and I change the subject to distract from my blushing.

"Ava, how is your first client?"

Ava peeps up until her eyes are visible, and she lets out a tired sigh before sitting in her chair again. "I'm actually doing more of a classroom setting. I have three men, and two of them are so sweet and genuinely want my help. The third…"

Her eyes roll to the top of her head, and JoJo asks, "What's wrong with the third guy?"

"He's like Zach 2.0. He doesn't seem to take the BBB or anything else seriously."

"Just cut him loose and tell him maybe this program isn't for him," Gemma suggests.

"I did, but then he came back. And now it's like a battle of wills. I'm not backing down until he does. Maverick McKinney has met his match as far as stubbornness goes." Her green eyes blaze with determination as she jabs a finger against her desk, and I feel a little sorry for this Maverick dude.

"What about you, JoJo?" Gemma asks.

"I met with Jacob last week. It was a quick coffee to discuss what he was looking for and how or if we could help. About an hour after the meeting, he confirmed he did want my help. I'm meeting with him again this afternoon. We will cover some do's and don'ts when attempting to court a woman. I'm hosting a Friendsgiving at the farm and inviting the girl he's had his eye on for a while now, so fingers crossed he doesn't get trigger shy."

"What about Colton, the guy you got snowed in with?" I ask.

JoJo's lip curls in derision. "Oh, you mean Boston's most eligible bachelor?"

"Yes, isn't he your brother's best friend?" Gemma asks. "Sounds like a romance book waiting to happen."

We all laugh, except for JoJo. "I'm *not* taking him on as a client," she insists, "but, admittedly, he is different. He's a walking red flag, and while that happens to be exactly my type, his brand of asshole wouldn't be good for business."

"What about you, Gemma? Your client is the funny plumber, right?" Ava asks.

"Yes." Gemma's face crunches into a grimace. "He's the hottest... plumber I've ever seen, but I know he's hiding something."

Worry threads through my veins. "In what way? Do you feel unsafe? If so, take one of the guys with you when you see him. And only meet in public places like—"

"I know, *Mom*," she says with a teasing grin. "And it's nothing like that. I'm just waiting for him to trust me enough to fully open up."

"A lot of men have trouble opening up and making themselves vulnerable," JoJo says wisely.

We discuss that for a while and then hang up and promise to talk again in a week or two. Pulling up Riggs's application, I find Lucinda's number and give her a call.

On Saturday morning, I dress in denim shorts, a melon-colored T-shirt, and matching flip-flops. I'm heading to Riggs's home for our next meeting because he offered to cook the snapper for us. He said I could come early if I wanted to hang out on the beach for a while.

I've gotten a ton of writing done the past couple days, so a beach day is exactly what I need.

The drive to the town of Mexico Beach is only about fifteen minutes, and as I turn down a quiet lane, I wonder if my GPS is broken. Then I make a curve, and my mouth drops open.

This is where he lives?

It's the most stunning house I've ever seen, managing to be huge and humble at the same time. At first I think the siding is white, but as I creep closer, I note that it's actually the palest of blues, like the sky hidden behind a wisp of clouds.

The home is two stories, covered with Hardie-plank and a gray wood shake roof. Four white columns flank the wide front porch that's dotted with comfy-looking padded chairs in a charcoal that pops against the pastels.

But the best part of the house is the view that spreads out behind it. Every imaginable color of blue is reflected back at me, from the deepness of the Gulf waters to the brightness of the sky.

I park in the oyster-shell driveway, and the door opens as I'm gathering my bag. Riggs steps out onto that gorgeous porch, one hand stuffed into the pocket of ivory linen shorts, and the other lifting for a wave. He's almost knocked on his ass when a blur of black fur bursts out the door and directly toward me.

"Hey, big boy," I coo at Ace as he skids to a stop a second before he's about to barrel into me. Squatting, I rub the spot he seems to love on his neck, and the pooch goes into a full-body wiggle as he nuzzles my shoulder. "I brought you a present. You wanna see?"

He backs up a step and turns in a circle before sitting attentively with his tongue hanging out one side of his mouth. I pull a huge chew bone from my bag and toss it out into the grassy yard. Ace takes off after it, ears flying behind him as I laugh at his pure doggy joy.

"You've made a friend for life," Riggs says as I climb the white painted staircase up to where he's standing. "That was really thoughtful of you."

"I didn't leave the dog dad out," I say, pulling a bottle of red wine from my bag. "Thank you for inviting me over."

He grins as he takes the bottle and reads the label. "Thanks, Libby. Shiraz is my favorite."

"I hope that one's okay. I remember you mentioned you like

Shiraz on one of the flights." I had passed over the very expensive ones in the liquor store, opting for a moderately priced one.

"It's perfect. Come on inside."

Ace trots up the steps with his treasure, and Riggs opens the door for him. "Go to your room, Ace." The dog dutifully prances down the hallway.

"Your dog has his own room?"

Riggs gives me a smile that's slightly shy yet completely unabashed. "Yeah, he's a spoiled brat. But that keeps him out of my room. I love the big goof, but I get no sleep if he gets in my bed. It's like sleeping with a damn furnace."

We walk into a spacious living room. The floors are covered with textured tiles in an alternating square and rectangle pattern. The honey color lends a rustic air to the room, despite the obviously expensive furnishings. The brown cushy couch is upholstered in some kind of suede material that I run my fingers over.

Riggs toes off his loafers, and words erupt from my mouth before I can stop them. "No fair. Even your feet are pretty." *Ohmygod, stupid, stupid, stupid.*

He stares down at the long, perfectly tanned things holding him up before lifting an eyebrow at me. "But are they prettier than my *very fine ass*?"

I groan. "A true gentleman would never bring that up again."

"Never promised I was a gentleman all the time," he says with a wink.

"When aren't you?" my lips ask, and I really need to get a grip on those blabby bitches.

His blue eyes darken a shade, as does his voice. "When a woman doesn't want me to be."

Hoo boy.

"That was a very book-boyfriend thing to say," I tell him, putting a playful tone in my voice as I wonder why he said *a woman* and not *Lucinda.*

Riggs rolls his eyes with a grin on his face. "Anyway, this is obviously the living room."

"I love the walls," I say. "What color is that?"

"I had the paint specially mixed to match this," he says, walking toward a panoramic photo that stretches the length of the mantel over the stone fireplace. Riggs traces a finger over the sunrise and shows me the thin line of peachy yellow where the sun is just about to make its appearance. "There's so much to love about sunrises, but this strip where the sun is just cresting is my favorite. Like a moment of hope that widens as the day begins."

"That's really beautiful," I say. "The photo and the thought." My eyes drift around the room, taking in all the photos on his sunrise-colored walls. A vista of an empty beach. A raging storm over the water. A crusty anchor on the deck of a boat. A silhouette of a palm tree and a dog looking out over the Gulf.

Doing a double take at the last one, I crane my neck closer and squint. "Is that Ace?"

Riggs stands beside me with his hands in his pockets, and his voice goes mushy. "Yeah, that's my buddy. I can't believe he sat still long enough to let me take it."

It hits me then and my eyes skate over the photos again. "Wait. Did you take all these pictures?"

"Yeah," he says so bashfully it makes me want to hug him. "It's just a hobby, but I enjoy it."

"They're great, Riggs. Like, really beautiful. You capture so much."

"Thanks," he says, and I can see the passion for his hobby in his light-blue eyes. "Do you want to see more?"

"I'd love to." I take off my flip-flops and place them next to his beside the door.

Riggs gives me a brief tour as we walk into another section of the first floor and arrive at a closed door, which he opens. "This is kind of a mess because I build frames too, but I like the light in this room better than working in my garage."

"I can see why," I tell him, a little breathless at the view of the beach through the floor-to-ceiling windows. The other three walls are covered with so many stunning photos, framed in what is obviously driftwood.

"I told you I could hook you up with pictures for your house. Just choose whichever ones you want." He shrugs, seeming embarrassed. "I mean, if you like any of them."

"I like them all!" I assure him, walking around and inspecting each one. "I wouldn't feel right about taking them without paying you though."

"No way, Libby. You provided dinner with that big snapper you caught, so consider this a repayment."

My house is significantly smaller than Riggs's, so I decide four would be a good number. I select two beach and water scenes from different angles, and then I come across a replica of the one Riggs has in his living room… the one with the dog and palm tree.

"Would it be weird if I wanted the one with Ace? I love the dark silhouettes against the colors."

"Nope, not weird at all," he assures me, taking it off the wall and adding it to my stack. "What's your last selection?"

"I don't know," I whine. "They're all so pretty, and they each tell a different story."

"What about this?" He takes down a small panorama print of a sunset. There's no frame because it's on one of those one-inch-thick canvas things. "See all the reds and purples? That would look great over your couch."

Picturing it in my mind, I smile. "Sold."

"Cool. I'll wrap them up and put them in your car for you. Why don't you use the spare room down here to change into your swimsuit and then meet me on the back deck? We can talk there."

"Bring your paperwork," I say as I pick up my bag and head for the bathroom.

CHAPTER 13

I step barefoot onto the wooden deck behind Riggs's home. I've changed into a blue-and-white-striped bikini with a sheer white cover-up. The salty air hits my nose, and I'm not sure I've ever smelled anything more appealing.

Pulling my folders from my bag, I arrange them neatly on the wrought-iron patio table and take a seat in a padded chair. Riggs appears a few minutes later.

"All loaded in your car."

"Thank you again for the photos. I wish you'd let me pay—"

"You're insulting me, Liberty," he says with a stern voice, and I give him a chagrined smile.

"Okay, I'll shut up. Do you have your paperwork?"

He hands over the navy-blue folder, and I page through it. "This looks good, but can we talk about the self-assessment?"

A slight flush rises up and spreads across his cheeks. "M'kay."

"You pretty much gave yourself fives across the board, except in honesty. You gave yourself a ten there."

His shoulders lift and fall. "That's the only one I feel confident that I'm a ten in. I don't lie. Ever."

"What about attentiveness? Do you not pay enough attention to Lucinda?"

"I try to," he demurs.

"And?"

"She's not always receptive to it, so maybe I'm doing something wrong. Same with all the rest of the categories."

My eyes stop on each category down the left side. "And do you give her compliments?"

"I do. I know women take time with their appearance, and I always try to mention it so she knows her efforts haven't been wasted."

"Then why did you give yourself a five?"

Riggs drops his head and runs a hand over the top of his hair. "I don't know. I'm just not sure why Lucinda signed me up for BBB. I must be doing something wrong."

"Maybe…" I don't finish the thought because it doesn't seem professional. *Maybe you're not the problem.* I hate seeing him blame himself when he honestly seems to be putting in the effort. "I contacted her for more information, and we're meeting for lunch week after next."

"Really?"

I smile. "Yes. She's the one who signed you up, so I'm going to try and get more specifics from her."

"Oh, okay." His nonchalant response tells me it doesn't bother him that we're meeting, which makes me happy. If he's secretly an asshat that treats his girl like crap, he would have protested, right?

"You did give yourself a seven in the dirty-talking category."

"Yeah, I told you I think I've got a pretty good handle on that."

I shuffle through the papers. "I don't see page forty-two. The one where I asked you to document some examples?" I let that hang in the air like a question.

"We, uh, haven't had the chance to… Lucinda's been busy."

Now it's my turn to blush. "Okay, no problem," I say a little too brightly. "You can give it to me next week."

His almost-admission confuses me. They haven't been intimate in the past week? Or maybe he's simply not into dirty talk, though he looks like he would be. Hell, the man looks like he could growl out the filthiest shit imaginable while pummeling a woman's cervix into submission.

Stop thinking things like that, Libby, I scold myself, moving on to discuss romance. I read over page thirty-one, which is the list of romantic things he's done for Lucinda since they've been together, and I have to be honest. All these things are sweeter than anything I could have come up with. Maybe he needs to be the coach here.

"This all looks great, Riggs." I rap a knuckle against the paper. "Especially the private, candlelit dinner on the beach. That sounds super romantic. Did she enjoy it?"

His face looks pained. "Not really. She got sand in her new shoes, so she wasn't exactly happy with me."

"Oh." I move on to the next one. "And the trip to Switzerland for your one-year anniversary? That sounds awesome, and very… sandless."

Riggs chuffs out a laugh. "The sandless-ness is why I chose Switzerland, but we, uh…" He pulls at the back of his neck. "We didn't end up going. I was trying to be spontaneous and surprise her, but she already had plans I didn't know about."

Jesus, who is this woman? If a man who looks like Riggs Romero wanted to whisk me away to Europe—or hell, pretty much anywhere—I'd have my bag packed in about four-point-five seconds.

I pat the back of his hand and try to reassure him. "Riggs, I think you're doing your best, so much more than a bunch of fives. But all relationships take two people to work."

I stop short of saying, *It doesn't sound like a YOU problem; it sounds like a HER problem.* His reluctant smile tells me that maybe he's getting what I'm putting down.

"I think that's enough for now," I declare, letting my gaze roll toward the beach and the soft waves bubbling at the shore.

"You want to hit the beach?" he asks, perking up, and I nod happily.

We spend the rest of the day on the beach. Sitting lazily on blankets and soaking up the vitamin D. Throwing a ball for Ace and laughing when he bounds after it and trots goofily back to us, pride in his big brown eyes when he drops the ball at our feet. It's too cold to swim, but we walk through the front edge of the surf and let the gentle water wash the sand from our toes.

I've had a crush on Riggs Romero since the first time I saw him on a book cover, but the real-life version of the man—the one behind the face and the killer body—is even better. He's so fun to be around, and I find his attentiveness almost disarming. Throughout the day, he constantly checked to see if I was hungry or thirsty or if I was tired of playing with his energetic dog.

Not to mention, the man can cook like a five-star chef. The snapper was delectable and flaky, with a buttery sauce that held a hint of lemon. Paired with braised brussels sprouts, it was one of the best meals I've ever had.

After our meal, I check my bag to make sure I've put away all my folders and papers, and I catch Riggs staring at me, an amused smile on his face. "What?" I ask.

"Have you always been this organized? With the spreadsheets and charts and stuff?"

I shrug. "Since I was four." His eyebrows shoot up in surprise, and I clarify, "Of course not with all the computer stuff, but I started organizing my closets and drawers by color. I tried to make everything as neat and tidy as possible."

He's quiet for a long moment. "Did something happen when you were four?"

Damn, he's astute.

"It did. Nothing all that bad in the grand scheme of things. A lot of kids had it worse than I did."

"Will you tell me?" His voice is low and his eyes seem to be piercing directly into my soul, making it almost impossible to say no.

"Why do you want to know?"

His pink lips crook up on one side. "I feel like we're becoming friends, Libby, and I'd like to know more about you. The sun is about to set, and the view is beautiful from the beach behind my house. We can sit back there and talk."

"Will there be wine?"

He chuckles. "I can open the bottle of Shiraz you brought."

"So I get wine and a sunset, and you get a sad story. Seems fair."

We make our way down the short, sandy path to the beach. Riggs is wearing the green swim trunks he swam in today, and his white linen shirt is open and unbuttoned, leaving a small strip of yumminess visible.

He spreads a blanket, and we sit side by side but not touching. We're silent as he pours deep-red wine into two plastic wine glasses. Sipping slowly, we watch the greatest show on Earth.

"It's like the sun and moon are on opposite sides of a seesaw," he says, "and as one lowers, the other rises."

"It is," I say, loving his analogy. "And it's like they trade their lights, the bright yellow one being replaced with the muted blue."

Quiet falls between us, the gentle lapping of the waves the only sound as the seesaw raises the moon and lowers the sun into the water. "You don't have to tell me anything you don't want to," Riggs says softly. "I feel like I pressured you."

I turn to look at his profile, which is so perfect it makes my teeth hurt. "Not at all. I don't tell many people because it's really not that interesting."

Riggs pivots his head slowly to face me. "Everything about you is interesting, Liberty."

"Wow, that's a lot of pressure," I laugh out, and we both turn back to the water. "I told you I was in the foster care system after my mom died."

"Yes, I remember."

"Well, I'd been with this family for a couple years, the Coopers. As I look back now, I realize they probably didn't have very much money. That's something you don't really notice as a child… the lack of money. I remember the house being a little shabby, but they were nice, and I liked being there."

"Did… did someone hurt you?"

"No, nothing like that. They were a very kind couple, and they asked me if I wanted them to adopt me. I didn't know what adoption was, but they explained it, and I said yes. It was the only home I'd ever known. Or that I could remember anyway."

I take a sip of my wine, and the soft richness soothes my throat. "Then they did a vision screening at my preschool, and the school nurse sent a note home saying that I needed to see an eye doctor."

From the corner of my eye, I see Riggs nodding along, so I continue. "I had something called strabismus, which is basically when the eyes aren't aligned."

"Like crossed eyes?" Riggs asks, breaking his silence.

"Pretty much. Crossed eyes is when one eye turns in, but strabismus can refer to any kind of misalignment." I take another sip of my wine. "When I got out of bed to go to the bathroom late that night after my appointment, I overheard the Coopers talking."

Riggs inches a little closer. We're still not touching, but I can feel the warmth of his body seeping through the tiny space between us.

"I remember a bunch of words like insurance and surgery.

Again, I was four, so I had no idea what any of that meant, but one thing the wife said was very clear in my little mind."

"What did she say?" Riggs's voice is barely audible.

"She said, 'We can't keep her, Craig. She's too… messy.'"

"Fuck," he spits out, glugging back the rest of his Shiraz. "And you thought she meant you weren't tidy."

"Right," I say as he refills our glasses. "I immediately turned into a tiny, organizing beast. When I was placed with another family, all I could think was that I had to be perfect. I had to be… *not messy*."

Though I kept my gaze straight forward, I could feel Riggs looking at me. "Libby, I'm sorry."

"Nothing for you to be sorry for," I assure him. "I became a very difficult child after that, crying if a single thing in my room was out of place. Like full-on tantrums if a blue shirt got hung up in the middle of the red ones."

"That's a lot for a child to deal with," Riggs says, and I nod in agreement.

"So, Libby the brat was passed from home to home until…" My voice breaks, and *goddammit*, tears form in my eyes. I haven't cried about this in years, but something about this night with this sweet man seems to turn on the waterworks.

Before I know what's happening, a warm, strong arm encircles my back, and I'm being tugged hard against Riggs until my face is pressed against his shoulder. I let the tears loose like someone has turned on a faucet. Not sobbing, heaving cries, but a slow, gentle release of emotions that feels so fucking good to get out.

The big, warm man holds me in silence, not uttering that it's okay or any other inane thing. He simply lets me soak his shirt with my pain.

After a long while, I clear my throat and attempt to pull away, but a large hand holds my head in place. And I don't hate it. At all. Riggs Romero is comfort personified, like the softest blanket in the world wrapping around me and making me feel safe.

"Anyway," I continue, speaking into the damp linen of his shirt, "I got placed with the Hills when I was eight. My mom noticed my eye turn right away and took me to the optometrist."

"Your eyes look straight now, so they must have gotten you the surgery you needed."

"They did. My parents weren't rich, but they had good insurance."

"And everything's okay now?"

"Pretty much, though we received a crash course in visual plasticity. That's a neurological concept where a human is only able to develop normal vision up until the age of seven or eight. After that, there isn't much plasticity."

"What does that mean?"

"It means after that critical period, vision is unable to develop, so I'm legally blind in my left eye."

Riggs pulls back and looks down at me, his eyes seeming even bluer in the moonlight as they dart between mine. "Blind? You don't… never mind. I was about to say something dumb."

"I know. I don't look blind," I tell him with a small smile. "The muscle alignment was corrected, so they look perfectly normal. But since that eye had been out of alignment for so long, it didn't receive the visual stimulation it needed to function like a normal eye. It's called amblyopia, though most people call it a lazy eye."

His eyes are still flicking slowly between mine, as if looking for a discernible difference. "When you say legally blind, what does that mean?"

"That distinction usually means a person can't be corrected to better than 20/200. The big E on most eye charts is 20/400, if that gives you some idea."

"And yours is worse than that?" he asks incredulously.

"I'm 20/1000, so I have to stand at twenty feet to see what most people can see from a thousand feet away. Pretty much everything looks like blurry, barely discernible shapes in that eye."

"No fucking way."

"Yes fucking way. If they were giving out bad vision awards, I'd definitely get a trophy."

Riggs barks out a laugh and then clamps his lips shut, eyes widening in horror. "I'm sorry. I didn't mean..."

I nudge him with my shoulder. "Don't worry about it. I can joke about it."

"Of course you can," he says, with the tiniest of smirks.

To prove my point, I ask him, "What do you call a blind gynecologist?"

Warily, he replies, "What?"

"A pain in the ass," I sing, and after a beat, we both fall back onto the blanket and laugh like maniacs at the dark sky. The stars seem to twinkle in time with each giggle that passes our lips.

"You're something else, Liberty Hill."

"That's what my dad always said."

I'm still staring at the glow of the moon against the depths of midnight-blue, but I can sense that Riggs has tilted his head in my direction. "How did you end up staying with the Hills, if you were such a brat? Which I don't believe, by the way. You're entirely too sweet."

If it wasn't so dark, I'm sure he would notice the blush shining on my cheeks.

"Oh, I can assure you I was, but instead of expecting me to adapt to them, my parents adapted to me. *Around* me. Mom always told me she and Dad fell in love with me the moment I entered their house and that love trumps all."

"I like that. They sound like wonderful people."

"They were. It didn't hurt that Mom was a librarian, so she was very orderly herself."

"Ahh, the good old Dewey Decimal System. Who knew something so confusing could change a child's life?"

I smile up at the heavens. *Such a beautiful and apt analysis.* "I know, right? I was lucky to have them."

Riggs rolls on his side and props his head on his hand. "How could you think that story isn't interesting?"

Angling my head toward him, I allow my lips to squeeze into a wan smile. "I guess if you're into fit-pitching children with vision conditions, you would think so."

"That's not how I read it. I think it's more a story about love and acceptance on your parents' part and perseverance and grit on yours."

"Or just brattiness," I say, and he presses one long finger against my lips. I stifle the urge to kiss it. But I really, really want to, which is confusing. I've never been a finger-kissing freak before.

"Don't you dare call yourself a brat again, Liberty Hill, or you'll have me to deal with. You were a scared child who was coping by trying to control the only things you could in your small world."

"I guess."

"Turn and look at me."

My body recognizes the demand in his voice and moves me onto my left side without any conscious input from my brain. My left arm tucks beneath my head, and Riggs lowers into a mirroring position.

We're so close our elbows are pressed together, and though it isn't exactly an intimate part of our bodies, someone forgot to inform my vagina of that fact. Because she's all fucking in with the whole elbow cuddling thing we've got going on. Oh yes, my needy little downstairs neighbor is slick with need, like Riggs has his face between my legs instead of some innocuous elbow touching.

And now I'm thinking of his face between my legs. How his broad shoulders would spread my thighs impossibly wide so he could get all up in there. How those full, pink lips would feel kissing every inch of me. How he would lose control and use his teeth because he was so fucking hungry for me.

"Say, *yes, Riggs*," his deep voice commands.

"Yes, Riggs." I don't mean for it to, but that totally comes out in a sort of Marilyn Monroe voice, all breathy and wanton. *And what was the question again?*

"So no more brat talk," he confirms, and I nod, remembering what we were talking about before the elbow-inspired porn that took off in my brain.

"Yes, sir," I agree, and his nostrils flare a little bit as his eyes drop to my mouth.

After a very long moment, they rise slowly to meet mine, and I see regret there. "I wish..." he starts, and I wait for him to finish, but he closes his lips.

"You wish what?"

"A lot of things."

We're so close, I can smell the sweetness of the wine on his breath, and while most of his face is in shadow, those blue eyes shine like beacons. If I was writing a book about this moment, I would say those beacons were guiding my soul home, but this is reality, not fiction. There's absolutely no eyeball soul guiding here, and I'd be obtuse to think otherwise.

I mean, the man is madly in love with his girlfriend. He puts so much effort into trying to make her happy that he's going along with the whole boyfriend building thing, even though I know he thought it was silly at first. Hell, maybe he still does, and he's just doing it to please Lucinda.

But when Riggs Romero looks at me, covered by the depths of the sky, it seems like the big world has shrunk until we're the only two people in existence. We lie like that in the dark for what could have been ten minutes or ten hours.

"What's the one thing you wish for most?" I finally whisper.

"For my life to be my own," he whispers back. The anguish on his face forces the next words from my mouth.

"Then do it."

His answer is immediate. "I can't disappoint anyone."

"What about yourself?"

Riggs searches my face with those azure eyes. "That's not what's important."

"As a self-imposed people pleaser, I think I can say with certainty that never pleasing yourself will lead you down a slippery slope that's difficult to reclimb."

A smirk crosses his lips, and he says, "I never said I don't please myself."

I giggle and shove at his shoulder until he falls onto his back. "Ugh, you're such a guy."

Riggs shifts his eyes toward me, and he's so fucking beautiful it gives me a full-body shiver, earning me a frown. He obviously mistakes my tremble for something weather related.

"Shit, I'm sorry, Libby. It's getting cold out here." Pushing gracefully to his feet in one swift movement, he reaches out a hand to pull me up.

"Sorry our conversation got heavy," I say as he shakes out the blanket and folds it over one arm. "It was such a great day, and I hope I didn't spoil it."

"Not at all," he assures me. "I'm glad you felt comfortable enough to tell me."

Without another word, I pick up the empty bottles and glasses, and we head up the path to the house. I don't trust myself to talk because I'm afraid I might blurt out exactly how comfortable Riggs Romero makes me.

"Thanks for coming over today," he tells me once we're inside. "I'm actually enjoying my lessons with Coach Libby."

"I'm going for Coach of the Year," I joke, and he grins.

"You have my vote. You definitely give me lots to think about." Looping my bag over his shoulder, he says, "I'll walk you out."

I know better than to argue that I can carry my own bag. I'm learning that Riggs is very chivalrous, but he does it without being condescending.

"Um, my shoes are missing," I say when we reach the door, and Riggs curses.

"Dammit, Ace!"

The dog pokes his head out from under the coffee table, takes one look at his owner, and takes off down the hall. Riggs stomps over and digs beneath the table before coming up with two completely mauled melon-colored flip-flops.

"Shit, Libby, I'm sorry. I'll replace them."

"No, it's okay," I assure him. "They're just the cheap ones from the dollar store."

He checks the bottom, probably looking for the size. "No, I insist. I have the goofy mutt trained pretty well. He goes to his room when I tell him to, and he never gets on the couch. His only toxic trait is that he seems to have a hunger for shoes."

"I have a couple pairs, so it's fine."

He's still shaking his head when he leads me outside. As Riggs walks in front of me, I gingerly make my way over the crushed oyster shells that make up his driveway. Then he turns and notices, and his eyes widen.

"Hold on. Don't move," he directs, jogging back and turning around. "Hop on my back."

"I can't… I mean… you don't… no, it's…" I've lost complete control of my verbal abilities at this point.

"Now, Libby. Don't make me tell you again."

Oh sweet balls of fire! That tone of voice that leaves no room for debate is my weakness, and I hop up onto his broad back when he dips his knees slightly.

Riggs surprises me by taking off at a gallop, and I squeal. "Riggs, you're going to hurt yourself!"

"Whatever. You're light as a feather, Libby-girl."

"I'm totally not. My long legs make me much heavier than a feather, or even the whole damn bird."

"Bet you're lighter than an emu," he says, and I giggle.

When he reaches my car, he opens the door, turns, and squats so I can slide directly into the driver's seat. "There you go. Safe and sound. You didn't cut your feet, did you?" Riggs bends and picks up both my feet, and I have to brace my arms on the seat to keep from falling over backward.

"Riggs Romero, do not look at my feet! They're all dirty from walking barefoot on the beach."

He completely ignores me, inspecting each one while I squirm, before releasing them. "I don't see anything. I'm sorry again about your shoes." His chagrined smile is so goddamn adorable, and I'm in real fucking trouble here.

"I told you, it's no biggie. They're super cheap." I swing my feet into the floorboard, and Riggs stands in the open door.

"Text me when you get home so I know you made it okay."

"I'm grown and perfectly capable of driving for twelve miles," I protest, and his lips kick up on one side.

"I don't mean to insult your capabilities, Libby, but anyone can have an accident or a flat tire. I always have my sister call me, and she only lives five miles from here." Then he pauses and cocks his head to one side. "Please. It would make me feel better."

"For Christ's sake, stop doing the puppy dog eyes. I'll call you," I grump, and he grins broadly.

As I drive away, I glance into my rearview mirror and find him standing in the driveway with his hands in his pockets. And I wonder...

How the hell am I supposed to make this man swoonier than he already is?

CHAPTER 14

Libby

I leave my coffee date with Lucinda Farina in a tailspin. I'm confused… and angry as hell. Somehow, I managed to hold my temper and not tell her where to stick her pretentious coffee. Barely. And only because it would be unprofessional.

After texting my BBB cofounders that I'd like a meeting, I drive home and quickly change into lounge clothes before logging onto my computer. One by one, my friends pop onto the screen.

"My client is a complete jackass," I snap without preamble, earning me shocked looks from the other three.

"Riggs?" JoJo asks. "Because that's surprising. He seemed so—"

"Not Riggs. He's…" *Sweet? Kindhearted? Perfect?* "Riggs isn't the problem. It's his girlfriend and her vague and unrealistic expectations."

Ava's eyes widen. "Ruh-roh. What happened?"

I begin a rambling account of my meeting with Lucinda. "First of all, I arrived right on time, and she was on the phone with her mother. She glanced at me and waved an imperious hand at the other chair like she was the queen granting a peon an audience. Then she stayed on the phone for *fifteen minutes.* And they weren't even talking about anything important. Just stuff like which clothes they're bringing on their Italy trip next year and gossip about some woman that goes to the same country club as them."

"Fucking rude," Gemma comments, a sneer lifting one corner of her perfectly painted lips.

"Yes!" I practically shout, jabbing my finger toward her on the screen. "So fucking rude. Anyway, when she finally decides to grace me with her attention, I get down to business and ask her why she enrolled Riggs in Book Boyfriend Builders."

"What did she say?" JoJo asks, leaning her chin onto one palm.

"She gave me the whole *I want him to be swoonier* bullshit, and I told her I was going to need something more specific. So then… THEN! She proceeds to call someone named Liz to get her opinion, and they low-key bash on Riggs for about ten minutes. They finally decide that he should buy her more expensive stuff and take her on more trips."

My voice begins to rise as I really get fired up. "Oh, and she wants him to get rid of his dog, which is completely ridiculous because he's the sweetest. Okay, Ace does like to chew on shoes, but other than that, he's very well-behaved."

"Wow," Gemma says.

"Yeah, that's about all I've got too," Ava chimes in. "She really said she wants him to get rid of his pet?"

I nod, and JoJo's jaw tightens. "That's ridiculous, and materialistic shit is not what being a good boyfriend is all about. As far as gifts go, it's more about the thoughtfulness, not the monetary value."

"Speaking of that, she showed off the diamond earrings he bought her, and holy fuck, y'all! They were huge and had to be worth thousands."

"The ones he brought her as a souvenir?" Ava asks, scrunching up her nose.

"Yup. Oh, and after she got off the phone with that Liz person, she got all smug and told me Liz was totally *jelly* of her because Liz wanted to sign her boyfriend up for the BBB, but couldn't because we don't have anyone in Chicago."

All my friends look disgusted as I continue. "I honestly think she just signed up Riggs to stick it to her… friend or whatever." I roll my eyes so hard they hurt. "So meanwhile, I'm still trying to do my job, and I ask her about the anniversary trip. You know, since she said she wanted to travel more."

"What anniversary trip?" Ava asks.

"Oh, he booked a surprise trip to goddamn Switzerland for their first anniversary, but he told me she couldn't go because she already had plans. So I ask her about it, and do you want to know what those very important plans were?"

My friends nod in eager agreement, and I announce with much hand-flailing fanfare, "She was going clubbing with her friends."

They all stare back at me in stunned silence.

"Anyway, I wanted to talk to y'all about it, but I really think we need to drop this client. What Lucinda Farina wants is the exact opposite of what the BBB is about." It makes me sad to say that because it means I won't get to see Riggs anymore.

"I agree," Gemma says, nodding thoughtfully. "I don't think we should offer a refund on what's already been paid because you've put in the time working on this account. But we should definitely stop the billing going forward."

The others agree, and we decide I'll draft a message that our business dealings are now concluded.

"How is the move going?" Ava asks as we're wrapping up.

"Great. I got the walls in the living room painted this week." I move my head out of the way so they can see the fresh sky blue on my walls.

"That picture is beautiful," JoJo remarks, pointing at the chair behind me, and I smile.

"Riggs gave it to me, along with some others he took."

Rising, I gather the pictures and hold them up one by one for the girls to admire. "I was going to hang them up later today."

"Those are phenomenal," Gemma breathes. "He could sell them."

"I agree," I call over my shoulder as I prop the pics against the chair again. My attention is drawn by a knock on the door. "Hold on a sec. That's probably my Amazon order."

Walking swiftly to the door, I swing it open and do *not* find a brown-clad delivery driver. No, I find a suit-clad Riggs Romero. And dear, sweet baby Jesus, the man can wear the fucking hell out of a suit.

I haven't seen him in person in over a week, though we text almost every day. Nothing serious, just funny memes and jokes to make the other laugh, and he occasionally calls to ask a book-boyfriend question that I'm pretty sure he already knows the answer to.

Christ, I've missed his face. And that's not good. Not good at all.

"R-riggs, hi," I practically gush as I rein in my urge to grab him by his red tie and yank him into my house. "Come in."

He blesses my soul with one of those radiant smiles. "I can just stay for a second because I'm on lunch break. I wanted to bring you this."

Closing the door behind him, I take the proffered bag and look inside. Flip-flops… the exact same color as the ones Ace had gnawed to shreds.

"I told you not to worry about it," I protest.

"I know, but I felt bad." His teeth sink into his bottom lip, giving him a shy appearance. "There's something else in the bag too."

I dig around until my fingers wrap around something small and cool, and I pull it out. A magnet sparkles from my palm, a glittery sunset with *Port Saint Joe* beneath it.

"I didn't know if you'd gotten one since you arrived." His cheeks pinken in the most adorable flush. "They had several, but this one had lots of yellow, and I know that's your favorite."

"I love it." I run my finger over the sparkly plastic. There is indeed a lot of yellow. *Why the hell are my eyes feeling extremely watery right now?* "This is the most thoughtful gift I've gotten in a long time, Riggs. Thank you."

His grin is wide and happy. "Good, I'm glad you like it." He squeezes my shoulder, and that big hand of his gives me thoughts I most definitely shouldn't be having. "When are we meeting again?"

Fuck. My mind scrambles for a way to tell him that he can't be my client anymore. Faking a smile, I put on my chirpiest voice. "I have great news for you, Mr. Romero."

"What's that, Ms. Hill?"

Why does he have to sound so decadent when saying my name?

"You've, um, graduated from Book Boyfriend University. With honors!" God that sounds so fakely cheerful. To add to my awkwardness, I shake both fists in the air in a *YAY* gesture.

A frown creases his brow. "What does that mean?"

"It means I've assessed everything we've done and determined we're all done with the book-boyfriend training."

Cupping a hand around the back of his neck and massaging, he appears to be upset. "So you're saying I'm hopeless."

"Not at all," I say quickly. "I'm saying you are officially a book boyfriend and don't need my help anymore." *You're perfect...*

"So we don't get to... we can't..." The lines between his eyebrows turn into deep ditches as he pulls his eyes to the side and spots the pictures, hammer, and nails on the chair. "I can come help you hang the pictures later," he says suddenly.

"Oh." I blink rapidly, unsure what to say.

"I have one of those laser levels that will make sure everything is hung properly."

Against my better judgment, I acquiesce. "Okay, that would be great."

Riggs visibly relaxes. "Okay, good. I'll call you. Maybe this weekend after Thanksgiving?"

"Sure." The thought of seeing him one last time is bittersweet.

"Do you have plans for Thanksgiving? I know you're new in town."

"Yeah, my friend Sonya invited me to her family's celebration."

"That's good. I'm glad you have someone." His right hand twitches and then balls into a fist at his side, like he's trying to keep from touching me. "Do you think we can still be friends, Libby?"

I'm touched but also a bit apprehensive. This does not seem like a good idea, given my crush on this man who's in a relationship with someone else. "I'd like that," I say anyway, and he smiles down at me, mischief draping over his gorgeous lips.

"Good, maybe we can go fishing again. I'll call you next time I feel the need to be spanked."

I prop one hand on my hip and point to the door with the other, my face a mock scowl. "Out. I'm not having this conversation with you, Romero."

He laughs, a long and deep sound that rumbles directly into my bones. "I won't bring it up again." Then he shocks the crap out of me by pulling me into a hug. "Thanks for everything you've done for me, Liberty."

He smells like the ocean, even in his tailored suit, and I inhale as I return his hug. "You're welcome." My voice is thick with emotion as he releases me and heads for the door.

Once he's gone, I stare at the spot where he disappeared until I hear a throat clear behind me. *Shit, my friends are still on my computer screen.*

I paste on my most innocent smile and sit back down at my small table. Three sets of wide eyes stare back at me.

"Was *that* your Amazon order?" Gemma asks, her eyebrows

almost disappearing into her hairline. "Because those bastards never show me anything like that in the suggestions."

Letting loose with my loud, goofy laugh, I shake my head. "No, his dog chewed my flip-flops, so he insisted on replacing them."

JoJo leans forward until all we can see is her face. "Gemma, Ava, did you see what I just saw?"

"See it?" Ava asks, fanning herself with one hand. "I could practically smell the pheromones through the computer."

"You know how we always write about electricity snapping in the air between our couples?" Gemma points at me through the screen. "*That* just happened in real life."

"Y'all are crazy," I scoff, staring at the corner of the screen so I don't have to look them in the eyes. Because I feel that electric sensation every time I'm with Riggs Romero.

CHAPTER 15

As I drive away from Libby's house, I try to decipher all the feelings that have been swirling in my head since she said our business is concluded. I'm not sure I've ever felt more… discontent.

While I haven't been excited by my relationship with Lucinda for a long time, a dissatisfied feeling now hangs over my head. Like a storm cloud waiting to douse me with gloom.

Have I been in denial about my happiness for months? In all honesty, yes, but I've been pushing it all down and ignoring it. Like a disease you know you have, but if you avoid going to the doctor and getting the diagnosis, you can deny its existence.

But the thought of not seeing Libby again brings that disease to the surface and makes it impossible to ignore. The ache to get to know her better is palpable, a visceral thing that's crawled inside me and refuses to leave.

I can't deny I'm attracted to Liberty Hill. And I'm fully aware you can't help finding another person attractive. What you can control is how you react to it. I'm not some cheating asshole, I've never been unfaithful to a woman, and I never would be.

That doesn't assuage the guilt I feel though, the thought that I'm being mentally unfaithful. I find myself thinking about Libby all the time, wondering what she's doing, wanting to send her a funny meme or joke I found. I've tried my best to stop it, but she just pops into my head at random times.

So I know what I have to do.

I need to break things off with Lucinda. We're obviously not suited, and it's not fair to either of us to carry on like this. Hell, we barely see each other anymore except when we go for our weekly visits to Nana's.

Nana. My only weak spot in this decision. The Romeros and the Farinas always spend Thanksgiving together, and I don't want to make things awkward, so I think I'll try to get through tomorrow and then cautiously bring it up to her.

And then… so many maybes. Maybe Nana will understand if I explain that I'm unhappy. Maybe Libby will want to explore this thing between us. Maybe she's feeling the same intense chemistry I've been trying so hard to suppress.

Even if I'm reading the signals wrong and Libby isn't interested in me, I still don't want to continue this charade with Lucinda. We don't love each other, and I can't fathom a pathway to those kinds of feelings with her.

And that's why I have to at least try to broach the subject with Nana Viv. Even taking Libby out of the equation completely, I still have no desire to stay in this farce of a relationship. Liberty Hill was merely the catalyst that made me realize how much I'm having to force myself to be with Lucinda.

Silvia is right. Nana wouldn't want this for me.

A honk snaps me out of my reverie, and I realize the traffic light has turned green. Pressing my foot on the accelerator, I drive through the intersection and head back to the office for my afternoon meeting.

"Mister Romero, Ms. Farina is here to see you."

"Send her in, Mackenzie."

Lucinda enters my office and closes the door behind her. She's wearing a white dress, as usual, but today the neckline plunges much deeper than the conservative dresses she normally wears.

"Hi, honey," she purrs, strolling in and perching on the edge of my desk.

"Hey, Lucinda. I was just about to go into a meeting, so I don't have much time."

"It's ok," she says amiably, leaning forward to give me a look at her boosted-up cleavage. I avert my eyes. "I wanted to invite you to come stay at my house tonight." Her eyelashes flutter suggestively as she drags a long pink nail down the sleeve of my suit.

Is she fucking kidding me right now?

"I can't," I say, attempting to keep the coolness from my tone but failing as I pull my arm away from her touch. "I have to get the manicotti ready for Thanksgiving tomorrow."

"Oh." Her lips puff into a pout. "But I want to see you."

You should have thought about that before you iced me out for the past three months.

"Mister Romero, you told me to remind you when the meeting is ten minutes out." I smile and rise from my desk as Mackenzie unknowingly saves me through the intercom.

"Thanks, Mac," I reply before walking to my door and opening it, a not-so-subtle invitation for Lucinda to vacate the premises. "I'll pick you up tomorrow to go to Nana's."

Lucinda drags a hand across my chest as she sways by. "Okay, come over tonight if you change your mind. I got new panties."

The thought of that doesn't even earn a spark of desire from what lies beneath my zipper, and I know I've made the right decision. If everything goes well with Nana, I'm going to have a talk with Lucinda and end things. I feel lighter than I have in months as I walk down the corridor of our corporate office and toward the conference room.

Carrots. So. Many. Fucking. Carrots.

We've been discussing the vegetable for over an hour, and I legitimately hate my job right now.

Carrot sticks, baby carrots, organics, rainbow-colors, and what seems like a million different varieties that we're considering for our stores. The previous hour was spent on goddamn potatoes, and I am fucking done with root vegetables today.

Silvia sits beside me, listening with a raptness that I don't understand. My sister is the Chief Financial Officer for the corporation—a complete whiz with numbers—and I wish, not for the first time, that she was the firstborn. Taking over Mercato Industries would be right up her alley.

I, on the other hand, feel like I'm stuck in a rut here. My eyes wander to the window, to the Gulf waters beyond, and I long to be out there, smelling the salty air and feeling the gentle spray of droplets against my face.

"In conclusion…" *Thank fuck,* I think as Mildred, one of our produce experts, wraps up. "I think we should add Parano carrots to our stores because they are excellent for juicing, and that's very popular these days."

Leo Farina, Lucinda's father, nods and makes a note in his leather-bound notebook. "Excellent. Thank you, Mildred." He taps his fancy pen twice on the table and nods to me. "Riggs, what have you come up with for expansion options?"

I stand and walk to the other end of the table where a large screen has been lowered from the ceiling. Pulling up my Power-Point presentation, I begin. When I get to the fifth slide, I can't hold back my smile. It's a spreadsheet, and it makes me think of Libby.

Once I reach the end, I summarize the facts and figures I've just laid out. "Since the Savannah store we opened two years ago is doing so well, I think it's safe to say that expanding farther north into Georgia is a good bet. I recommend Atlanta."

Nods from around the table boost me for my next recommendation, the one I feel most strongly about.

"For our second new location, I think we would do well between Mexico Beach and Port Saint Joe. Since we don't have a store within two hours, our employees from here at our headquarters can't even shop at Mercato. They have to shop with our competitors."

More enthusiastic nods from everyone… except the president. Leo Farina frowns, but I press on. "From the figures I ran with Silvia, and after talking to the heads of marketing and construction, we think a smaller, market-style store would fit with the laid-back vibe and would pull customers from both towns."

Leo flips through the paperwork in the folder I compiled and tilts his head back and forth. "I'm inclined to agree with Atlanta, but it's a no on a local store. The population wouldn't support it."

"The numbers say otherwise," I argue, and Silvia gives me a grin and a subtle thumbs up. "If you'll look more closely, you can see that a small store would be very profitable—"

"We don't want small," Leo insists. "We want to grow bigger."

"Our flagship store in Tallahassee thrived when the families started it, and that was the starting point for this entire business," I shoot back. "And it's still the most profitable, despite being the smallest. People love shopping at an intimate family-owned business."

Leo's spine goes ramrod straight, and he narrows his eyes. "My answer is the same as when you brought up this idea a year ago, Romero. No." Then he shuts his laptop with finality before glancing around the room. "Everyone have a good Thanksgiving, and I'll see you on Monday."

And he leaves the room. *Goddammit.*

The other ten people rise, and each of them acknowledges me with a nod or a pat on the shoulder as they pass.

"I like the idea, son," Carlos Garcia, our head of marketing, says, firmly squeezing my bicep. "Going back to the basics. Every store we've built recently has gotten bigger and bigger, and I don't like it. We seem to be getting away from what the founders wanted."

"Thanks, Carlos," I tell him, and he gives me a small smile before exiting, leaving me alone with my sister.

"Fuck Leo," Silvia says loyally. "Once he retires and you take over, we'll build that store."

She wraps me in a solid hug, and I kiss the top of her head.

Lucinda is wearing a baby-pink dress that drapes dramatically off one shoulder when I pick her up on Thanksgiving morning. "You look nice," I tell her out of habit.

"You too. Very handsome," she says, stroking one hand down the lapel of my charcoal-gray suit jacket. I'm wearing matching pants, a white shirt, and no tie.

We make the short drive to Nana's in silence. After pulling into the driveway, I grab the food from the backseat, open Lucinda's door for her, and we walk side by side up the steps.

Normally, I would hold her hand, but I just can't bring myself to touch her today, not knowing I'm hopefully going to break up with her this weekend. I honestly don't think she'll be too upset. Her interest in me has dwindled for almost half a year, except for yesterday. I still don't know what the hell that was about.

Since my hands are full, she rings the doorbell before reaching into her Gucci bag and pulling something out. Then she stuffs it into my front pants pocket.

"Do it during dessert," she hisses a second before the front door opens. "Vera, Happy Thanksgiving!" Lucinda greets my mother with enthusiasm.

Vera Romero looks beautiful in a beige Chanel dress that hits just below her knees. She's tall and dark-haired, with only a few streaks of gray near her temples.

"Happy Thanksgiving, dear," she says, before turning to me and beaming. "And how's my handsome son?"

"I'm good, Mom." I give her an affectionate kiss on the cheek. "I brought your favorite."

My mother gives me a giddy smile. "Ohh, I do love your manicotti. Let me take that into the kitchen for you. Go say hi to everyone." She removes the glass pan from my hands, and we make our way into the living room.

My father, Sergio, greets us and steps behind the black, leather-topped bar. He fancies himself as the designated bartender and pours us both a drink. Leo and I exchange cool nods, and Uncle Roberto, my dad's younger brother, gives me a merry wave.

"Where's Frank?" I ask him, referring to his only child.

"He'll be along. I'm sure he's running late because he has the little one by himself today."

"Theresa's working?" My cousin's wife is an emergency room nurse, and she often has to work holidays.

"Yep. He was trying to get Allegra's shoes on her feet when I talked to him about fifteen minutes ago."

We chuckle. Frank and Theresa's three-year-old is full of sass and energy. Sticking my hand in my pocket, I frown when I remember Lucinda putting something in there on the porch. It seems to be a small square wrapped with paper.

"I need to run to the bathroom," I say as Dad fires up the

blender. I exit to the hallway and walk quickly to the powder room two doors down.

"What is this?" I whisper, pulling the object from my pocket. A sheet of computer paper is folded around… *what the fuck?*

Setting my drink and the paper on the vanity, I open the velvet box to find the biggest diamond ring I've ever seen. An engagement ring, to be exact.

"She's got to be fucking kidding me," I mutter as my mind tries to process. I slug back the rest of my bourbon before picking up the paper and reading the typed words.

> HOLIDAY PROPOSAL
>
> As soon as dessert is served, get down on one knee with our families surrounding us. Say the following:
>
> My dearest Lucinda, from the very first time I saw you, I knew you were the one for me. Your beauty is indescribable, but your warm heart is what captured my own. The love I have for you burns from within my soul, and I can't wait to spend my life with you. I'll strive every day to make you the happiest—

My eyes dart from side to side, and I stop reading about halfway down the page, and a boulder of alarm sits heavy in my gut.

Lucinda expects me to propose to her.

Today.

And she wrote me a fucking script.

CHAPTER 16

I force myself to read the rest of the script Lucinda expects me to recite, and I almost gag. It's full of flowery language I would never use, not to mention it's a load of crap, expounding on Lucinda's "sweetness and goodness."

Stuffing everything back in my pocket, a thought hits me. *How did she pay for this ring?* I think I know, and when I pull up my banking app, my suspicion is confirmed. I see a charge for almost forty-thousand dollars from a jeweler in Miami. *Goddammit.*

I march from the room in search of my *not-fiancée* with fire in my every step. The audacity of her, thinking she can dictate when and how I... god, I can't even think the word. We are nowhere near that point in our relationship. I'm ready to end things, and she's thinking about marriage? No.

Before I can find Lucinda, I'm waylaid by a ball of pure energy. "Riggsy!" Allegra shrieks, hurtling toward me and jumping. I grab the toddler in mid-air and pull her to my chest, twirling us around. Then I gobble at her face, making her laugh until she's holding her stomach and informing me her *giggler* hurts.

My angry demeanor softens immediately. Besides being on

the water, nothing is more soothing to my soul than a child or a dog. "How are you, kiddo?"

"Good. I go to preschool, and Timmy Noles is a poot-head."

I laugh and prop the little girl on my hip, listening to her happy chatter. With her dark, wavy hair and big brown eyes, Allegra Romero is simply precious. When she informs me she has to go potty, I drop her off with her dad and resume my search for Lucinda.

I find her in the kitchen with Nana, Silvia, our mothers, and two of Nana's household staff. After greeting everyone, I'm about to ask Lucinda to step outside with me, when my mother interrupts.

"Riggs, can you carry the turkey to the table?"

"Of course, Mom," I say, trying to keep the frustration from my voice.

Everyone begins piling into the formal dining room and taking their seats, and I grit my teeth, wanting to set Lucinda straight as soon as possible. *How the hell can she think this is okay?*

She sits on my right side, and my sister plops down on my left as Dad begins carving the turkey. Our families celebrate Thanksgiving with a mixture of traditional holiday fare and Italian food, including my manicotti.

The mood is jovial, and as it always seems to do, the conversation shifts to the business. My father sits on Mercato's board of directors, and at one point, he asks Leo when he plans to retire.

"Soon," he says cryptically, "and then Riggs and Lucinda can take over."

The table falls silent until Nana speaks up. "You know that's not how it works, Leo. With each generation, the head of the company switches between the families. My Luca was Mercato's president until I took over when he died. Then you became president. This generation, it switches back to the Romeros."

Leo's sly glance at me grates on my nerves. "But if Lucinda is also a Romero, they can run it together." His lips curl into a Grinch-like grin, and my stomach curdles at the realization.

This is why she wants to marry me.

"Oh, I didn't realize you two were thinking about that," Nana says, shifting her eyes between me and Lucinda as the staff removes our dinner dishes and replaces them with dessert plates. Then her face creases into a tight smile. "I'll not say no to more great-grandchildren. Allegra is such a blessing to us all."

Great. Now Nana has her hopes up about marriage and babies. How am I going to break this news to her?

"I'm not having children," Lucinda announces, and my mother's mouth drops open. "It makes your body all… blehhhh."

Nana looks like someone just clipped their toenails at the table, and to break up the uncomfortable silence falling around us, my mother begins dishing up the desserts the staff has brought in. As Mom slides a piece of pecan pie onto my plate, Lucinda nudges me with her knee beneath the table, lifting an eyebrow like she's waiting on me to get the whole proposal thing started.

Her teeth sink into her bottom lip and she smiles in anticipation as I push back from the table and stand. The ring feels like an anchor in my pocket, threatening to pull me under and drown me. "Excuse me, I need some air," I say, striding from the room and heading for Nana's study.

I push open the french doors and inhale, the cool November air stinging my lungs as I step onto the stone patio. My mind is a jumble of thoughts, but I can't even get my head around this day before my solitude is broken.

"What the hell, Riggs? You're supposed to be proposing to me right now. You're fucking it all up."

Turning to face her, I walk back into the room and narrow my eyes. "I'm not proposing to you, Lucinda. You can't stuff a ring and a goddamn proposal instruction manual into my pocket and demand I ask you to marry me."

She crosses her arms over her chest and rolls her eyes. "Fine. I wanted to do it at Thanksgiving so we could have a Christmas-themed engagement party, but I guess you can do it on Christmas Eve."

My blood reaches lava levels, but I temper my tone. "We don't even love each other."

Lucinda scoffs. "That doesn't matter. We make sense. Our families are friends and have the business together."

"That is *not* a reason to get married. We don't even want the same things. I don't want to marry you, Lucinda," I tell her, softening my voice. "I'm not going to propose to you."

Her teeth grind audibly as she tosses her ebony hair over one shoulder. "Fine, then I'm breaking up with you."

I nod solemnly. "I think that would be best."

Shock paints her cheeks red, and she sets her hands on her hips. "You don't mean that."

"I'm sorry, but I do. I tried to make things work, but I'm tired of forcing it. We have nothing in common, and we hardly spend time together. That's not the type of relationship I want, and honestly, you shouldn't want that either."

Lucinda runs her tongue over her top teeth. "Okay, if that's the way you want it, but when you come to your senses and beg me to take you back, don't get your hopes up. I'll probably have moved on by then."

I nod. "Then I'll wish you all the happiness."

With anger clouding her brown eyes, she spins on her high heel and storms from the room, calling out, "Fuck you, Riggs," on her retreat.

It doesn't surprise me when my sister walks into the office approximately thirty seconds later. Her nosy ass was probably listening to the entire exchange from around the corner.

"You okay?" she asks, and I nod.

"I'm more than okay. Would I sound like a giant asshole if I said I feel about thirty pounds lighter?"

Silvia's lips flatten into a sarcastic line. "Not at all. It's probably because you got rid of Lucinda's giant head." I chuckle, and she whispers, "Warning, Nana is on her way to talk to you."

We hear the unmistakable sound of Nana's footsteps punctuated by the clomp of her cane, and she appears in the doorway a minute later.

"Hi, Nana. I apologize if I ruined Thanksgiving."

"Are you kidding?" she asks, walking straight to her desk and settling into her chair like it's her own personal throne. Silvia and I sit across from her. "That was the most holiday excitement we've had since Theresa's water broke at Christmas."

I laugh. "That was memorable. Poor Frank fainted, and I had to carry him to the car."

My grandmother levels a look at me. "Please tell me you've finally broken up with that shrew."

Silvia and I exchange a shocked look. My sister jerks a thumb in my direction. "This moron has stayed with her so long because he thought that's what you wanted."

Nana literally clutches at her pearl necklace. "Oh, heavens no. Whatever gave you that idea?"

I shake my head to clear the cobwebs. "You… you seemed so excited when we started dating."

"I was at first. Mary and I always dreamed that our grandchildren would marry, but it was just that. A dream. Lucinda was a sweet little girl, but she's grown up to be exactly like Bianca. I can't stand that heifer." Silvia snickers as our grandma continues. "As time went on, I knew Lucinda wasn't the one for my Riggs. I was just waiting for you to figure it out for yourself."

"Oh, um…"

"Took you long enough," she mutters. "And why the hell do you think I have any say in who you date?"

To say I'm flabbergasted would be an understatement. "Your health has been so good this past year, and I didn't want to rock the boat."

Nana Viv waves a hand at me. "The doctor put me on some new medicine about a year ago. It's helped." Then her shrewd caramel eyes shift between me and Silvia. "Did I ever tell you why we moved to this country?"

"You said it was to have a better life," Silvia says.

"It was, but I think I need to tell you the specifics." She leans back in her chair and stares at the ceiling. "My parents owned a grocery store back in Italy. They arranged for me to marry the son of a local dairy farmer for business reasons."

Silvia and I share a wide-eyed look.

"But I wasn't in love with this farmer. I had my eye set on Luca Romero, the most handsome boy in our town." Her lips curve into a secretive smile. "We had quite the torrid affair."

I mask my chuckle with my hand.

"So you left Italy to get out of an arranged marriage?" Silvia asks.

"I did. Also, my best friend, Mary, was in love with the dairy farmer's son." Nana's eyes came back to me. "His name was Salvatore Farina."

My mouth drops open. "So you're telling me you were supposed to marry Sal? Lucinda's grandfather?"

The old lady smiles and nods. "Yes, so we all four snuck out in the dead of night and caught a boat to America. It caused quite the scandal in our little village from what I've heard." Her mouth turns down into a frown. "Our parents disowned us."

"Do you regret it?" I ask softly, and Nana's face warms.

"Not for a second. I never could have been with anyone but your grandfather. I should have told you this story a long time ago, and maybe you would have realized that I'd never want you to marry someone because of the business or any other stupid reason." She punctuated her next words by slapping the surface of her desk with her wrinkled hand. "You. Marry. For. Love. That's it. Period. End of story."

"Yes, ma'am," I say, standing and rounding the desk. Dropping to my knees, I allow my grandmother to pull me against her. Despite her heart failure, her hugs never fail to be strong and sure.

"I love you, my boy. I want you to find the kind of love your grandfather and I had." Tears sting my eyes as she kisses the top of my head. "You have such a pure heart, Riggs, and I never want you to give that heart to someone that doesn't deserve it."

"Thanks, Nana," I tell her, resting my face against her shoulder and smelling her sweet pastry scent.

"Anything else you want to talk about?" I lean back and look into her watery eyes, and she reads my apprehension. "Be honest with me, mio nipote." *My grandson.* I always know she means business when she speaks Italian.

"I don't want to take over the presidency of Mercato." Damn, that feels good to say out loud. "I'm so proud of our company, but I'm miserable sitting through endless meetings about carrots and shit. Being behind a desk every day."

For about the millionth time today, I'm surprised when Nana Viv smiles and pats my face. "My boy has always liked the outdoors."

"I don't want to shirk my duties. I still want to be involved." I flick my eyes to my sister. "But I think Silvia would make an excellent president."

Silvia's mouth drops open, and she blinks rapidly a few times. "A-are you sure? You're the oldest Romero."

"But it doesn't make me happy, and I'm sick of doing crap that doesn't make me happy. I don't enjoy the corporate world like you do, Sil. You thrive there."

Nana looks so pleased and holds out a hand for her grand-daughter, who rises and takes it. "Is that what you want, sweet-heart? To become Madam President of Mercato Industries?"

Silvia's cheeks bloom with pride and joy, and she nods. "I would love to if you think I'm capable."

"You're more than capable, nipotina, and I would be proud to recommend you to the board." Then Nana turns to me. "You can have a place on the board of directors like your father, if you still want to be involved."

"I'd like that," I say in relief.

"What would you like to do instead, Riggs?"

Taking a deep breath, I say, "I'd like to help Joe run the

marina. A few years ago, he was struggling. Business was booming, but his boat kept breaking down, so I bought him two more. Now he thinks he owes me, but I won't accept any money from him. He says he's leaving the marina to me when he retires or dies."

Nana smiles her approval. "I think it's a fine idea. My grandson and my granddog can spend every day with their tails in the wind out on the water."

As the matriarch of our family pulls my sister and I into a hug, my heart feels like it's about to burst with happiness.

As soon as I get home, I stick the ring and note in my underwear drawer. I'll deal with it later. The ring is probably custom, so I'm sure the jeweler won't take it back, but maybe I can sell it.

My legs take me back and forth across the wooden floor of my bedroom. Things are finally starting to look up for me, but I'm restless, so Ace and I go for a run on the beach.

I wake several times during the night, inundated with thoughts of Libby. All I want to do is talk to her, tell her about yesterday, see if there's any way she wants to explore a relationship with me.

After trying to distract myself by spending all of Friday outside with my camera, I can't take it anymore. Yesterday started out shitty but ended better than I could have imagined.

As I grab my keys and head out the door, I hope my luck will hold out.

CHAPTER 17
Libby

Friday evening, I pull out the to-go containers and warm up some dinner. Yesterday was the first time I'd met Sonya's family, but by the time I left, I felt like I was part of it. They were funny, loud, and the most genuine people I'd ever met.

And holy cow! The food was delicious. I'm sure I put on at least five pounds during the Thanksgiving lunch.

I'm rinsing my plate when I hear a knock at the door. I swear, if that's Sonya trying to give me that damn sweet potato pie again…

I swing open the door and almost drop my teeth. It's definitely not Sonya with a pie.

"Riggs, uh, hi. Happy belated Thanksgiving."

He's dressed in a baby-blue sweater, faded jeans, and a brown bomber jacket. He looks damn fine, though his hair is disheveled, like he's been running his hands through it. It only adds to his deliciousness.

"Happy Thanksgiving, Libby. You look… wow… you look beautiful."

My blood warms as he runs his gaze up and down my fitted orange tee and yellow sweatpants.

"Uh, thanks. You look pretty dashing yourself."

He shifts from foot to foot and finally asks, "Do you mind if I come in?"

"Oh, crap. Sure. I'm sorry. I was just surprised to see you."

Riggs strides in and crosses the room before staring at the wall for a few long seconds as I close the door. Then he begins to pace restlessly back and forth, one hand sliding through the top of his hair. He appears quite agitated.

"Riggs, are you okay?"

"Lucinda and I broke up yesterday," he blurts.

My heart does an odd little flip-flop in my chest. "I'm so sorry. I know how much you love her."

He stops walking and stares at me. "What makes you say that?"

Shit, why is he frowning? "It was obvious. You worked so hard to make her happy."

His eyes clench closed, and he shakes his head. "No, I don't love Lucinda. I never loved her. It was about my Nana Viv."

I'm trying to decipher what the hell he's talking about. "You're in love with your grandmother?" My voice sounds kinda squeaky.

Riggs's mouth drops open for a second, and then he bursts into laughter. "Liberty Hill, you always know how to make me smile. But no, I definitely don't love my grandmother. Well, I do, but not like *that*."

"I'm confused. Maybe you can explain."

And he does. He tells me the whole crazy story where he was only staying with Lucinda because his grandmother is sick and he thought it would make her happy. Meanwhile, Nana knew almost the entire time that Lucinda wasn't right for her grandson. She was just waiting for him to realize it.

"Your nana is right about Lucinda not being right for you," I say without thinking and then wince. "Sorry, that's not my place to say."

Riggs shakes his head. "No, I want to hear what you think."

"It's just, um, Lucinda doesn't seem very down-to-earth, and you're the sweetest, most normal guy I've ever met, despite being a bazillionaire."

His lips twitch. "Actually, I'm only a millionaire."

"Well, bless your heart," I tell him in my best Texas drawl.

He chuckles, and then his face turns solemn as his blue eyes hold me captive. "Do you feel it, Liberty?"

A bolt of lightning shoots down my spine. The way he's looking at me is just so… intense. "F-feel what?"

Riggs takes a step toward me, his gaze never leaving mine. "This. This thing between us."

I watch his finger move back and forth between us like I can actually see the *thing* he's talking about. "I don't… I don't know."

His feet, clad in Gucci loafers, bring him another two steps closer, and I take an involuntary step back until my back is plastered against the door. He's so close, I can smell his seductive aftershave.

"Do you think about me when we're not together, Libby?"

"I do," I admit immediately, like the man is sucking the truth from my mouth with that deep voice. "I know I shouldn't, but —" I can't finish that sentence because I have no good excuse.

"I think about you too," he murmurs, and I resist the urge to look around for a hidden prank camera. "All the time."

Riggs places his forearms on either side of my head, caging me against the door. He's not touching me, but I can feel his heat radiating against my body like he's the sun.

"What kind of thoughts?" I ask breathlessly, and he leans forward until I can feel his breath whisper against my ear.

"I think of watching sunrises with you. I think of playing on the beach and laying in the sun and swimming in the water. I think of eating meals with you, taking you for a drive, and dancing in the moonlight."

"I like those thoughts." My voice sounds like I'm talking through a bowl of Jell-O, thick and quivery.

"And then I think of putting my hands on you. My mouth." He hesitates, and my eyes close as he seduces me into a trance with the rough rasp of his voice against my ear. "All over you, Libby."

Sweet baby Jesus in a rocking chair! This man sorely underrated himself in the dirty talk category. He hasn't uttered a single *cock*, *pussy*, or *fuck*, but he paints a provocative picture with his words and the gravel in his voice.

"Ohhh." It's a breathy moan, a single drawn-out syllable, but I think it gets the point across because he finally touches me. His forehead rests against mine, and we share the same breaths for a long moment.

"So, I ask you again. Liberty Hill, do you feel this thing between us?"

In answer, I lift one leg and hook it over his hip as my chin tilts forward a scant inch until our lips are touching. "I feel it," I whisper, and in the next second, Riggs Romero is kissing me.

No, that's not quite accurate. He's fucking *consuming* me. His lips pull mine with perfect suction, over and over as he drops one hand to cup my face.

"I've been wanting to do this since the first time I saw you on that plane," he says. "Since I caught you staring at my dick."

"It was market research," I argue, and he chuckles as his nose nuzzles mine.

"Did you get all the data you needed?"

Infused with an unexplained boldness, I purr against his lips, "Not yet."

"Fuck," he curses a second before covering my mouth with his own. His warm tongue parts my lips, and he takes a half step forward, closing the distance between us.

Heat infuses me as soon as our tongues make contact, circling tentatively at first, before engaging in an all-out battle for supremacy. He wins, hands down, taking control of the kiss. Of me.

I'm a limp noodle, held up only by the door at my back and

Riggs's big, hard body at my front. And he is hard ev-er-y-where. My hips jerk involuntarily, and we let out mutual groans as the firm ridge of him nestles exactly where we both need it.

His hips roll, and he's far from tentative now. No, he's dominant and powerful, sliding one hand to my knee that's still wrapped over his hip and yanking my leg farther around him. I almost orgasm on the spot.

Riggs pulls his mouth away, his breaths ragged against my wet lips and his eyes showing the haze of lust. "I'm sorry, Libby. This isn't what I came over here for. I just wanted to talk to you."

"We talked," I point out, nipping his bottom lip, and he groans. "Now, do you have more to discuss, or can we get to the good stuff?" I ask impatiently, digging the back of my bare foot against his butt and locking him to me.

His grin is slow and goddamn sexy as he circles his thick erection against my pussy. "I vote for the good stuff."

"It's unanimous then."

Riggs trails his lips across my cheeks and to my ear. "You want me to fuck you, Libby-girl?" His hips thrust gently against my needy sex, and I nod.

That's apparently not satisfactory because he fists my long hair and jerks my head back until I can see his eyes. They blaze like the hot, blue fire at the center of a flame.

"Say. The. Words," he growls. "I want to hear it from those full red lips." His thumb swipes over my bottom lip, and I open my mouth and take the tip inside. Riggs's nostrils flare when I take it deeper, sucking hard and cupping my tongue around the pad.

Then I release it and drop a hand between us to grip his hard length. And it is quite… lengthy. And girthy. *Holy shit, he's going to break me with that thing.*

My voice is raspy and sweet. "Please fuck me with this big, hard cock, Riggs."

His chest rumbles in satisfaction, and he drops my leg, taking a couple steps back as he shrugs off his jacket. "Undress, baby."

I've never gotten into it when a man calls me baby, but I'm fucking into it now. Riggs Romero could recite a list of cleaning products with that deep voice, and I'd bow at his feet and beg for more.

I can't help but stare when he tugs off his sweater. The veins of his forearms are barely covered by the perfect smattering of dark hair, and I want to trace each one with my tongue.

Riggs looks up at me and lifts an eyebrow, like he's waiting for something. I have the feeling I'm supposed to be doing something, but this damn sexual brain fog has my head in the clouds. Oh. Wait. He told me to get undressed.

"Sorry," I say sheepishly. "You distracted me with your forearm porn show."

His mouth quirks up on one side, and I'll be damned; smug looks good on Riggs Romero. Damn good.

"After reading your books, I've always wondered if you had a forearm fetish," he tells me, stepping forward with mischief in his eyes.

I lower my eyebrows. "It's really more of an appreciation than a fetish. But they have to be good forearms, muscled, veiny." He props one hand against the wall beside my head, and I'm momentarily distracted by the muscled, veiny arm *right fucking there.*

Continuing, I say, "They have to have the perfect amount of hair, just a dusting." *Like yours.* "Not Chewbacca-level. And some…" I pause when he places his other hand on the wall, and now there are two orgasm-inducing forearms bracketing my face. "Some well-placed tats are always good," I squeak a second before I turn my head and bite his left arm, circling my tongue against the warm skin between my teeth.

We both groan when I release him and trace one bulging vein with the tip of my tongue. "God. Damn," he grunts as I move to the sensitive underside and lap at another vessel.

Then his arms are gone, and his fingers rip my T-shirt over my head.

"You seem a little impatient, Riggs. You're not a premature ejaculator, are you?" I ask in a teasing voice as he makes quick work of my pants.

They fall to the floor, and his eyes rove my body, clad only in a nude bra and panty set. "I've never had that problem before," he assures me as his gaze roams. "But I'm not making any promises with you, Libby. I'm ready to blow right now. You are fucking stunning."

I can feel the flush from desire and his praise rising up my neck, and he traces the pink flow with gentle fingers.

Then he drops to his knees, and *dear lord!* My panties are drenched.

"I've been dreaming of how your pussy would taste when it melts on my tongue," Riggs says, sliding my underwear down my legs.

"I… oh!" I yelp when he hauls my left leg over his shoulder. "That, um, sounds like something you should investigate."

"Oh, I plan to, Libby-girl. Thoroughly." He licks the arousal from the inside of my thigh, and my standing leg almost buckles. "I just need to get close enough to the target."

Holy fucking hell. I hope he's not all talk and knows how to actually locate *the target.*

That hope is fulfilled when he drags his tongue through the lips of my sex and immediately zeros in on my clit.

"Oh. Wow. You… you found it," I pant, grinning goofily as my head falls back against the door. "Congratulations, you're now in the top tenth percentile of men in the world."

He closes his eyes and savors me with another long lick. "Mmmm, baby, I'm going to eat you so good and make you come so hard, I'll skyrocket into the top one percent before your legs stop shaking."

Mother of fuck! That was a damn good line, and I kinda want to pull a Gemma and write it down to use in a book. But all thoughts of writing are dispelled as Riggs really starts to go to town on my sex.

He shoves his entire face between my legs and licks me like a man possessed. His frequent hums of pure pleasure make my clit throb in time with my racing heartbeat. He's enjoying himself as much as I am.

With one hand, I grip the top of the door frame to steady myself, and with the other, I thread my fingers through his hair. It's thick and soft, just like I knew it would be on those nights I fantasized about this.

"Mmmmm, this is the best pussy I've ever tasted," Riggs moans against me. "I want to eat it until I get fucking lockjaw."

"Holy shit, that feels good," I breathe as he slides one finger inside me. It searches against my inner walls until he finds a spot that makes my hips jerk, and he smiles smugly into my crotch.

"There it is." He adds another finger, and the tips of both give my G-spot the attention she so desperately needs. He finger-fucks me slowly and adds some kind of fucking swirl thing with every thrust. Out… in… swirl. Out… in… swirl.

Meanwhile his lips latch onto my clit, and he sucks as his free hand drops to his cock. Tilting my head to the side, I can see the impressive bulge in his pants.

"Dear god, Riggs. Let me see it." I don't have to specify. He knows what I want.

One handed, he unfastens his pants while his mouth and fingers never stop their sweet torture. When he pulls his cock out, I gasp. That fucking thing looks brutal, the enormous purple head crowning a thick, rigid shaft.

"I want to watch you stroke it while I come on your face."

"Fuck, baby." The vibration of his moan sets me directly on the edge of an orgasm. And when he begins fucking his tight fist, the edge crumbles away, and I fall into the blissful depths of my climax.

"Riggs!" I call out as I see kaleidoscope colors around the edges of my vision. His cheeks hollow with the strength of his suction, his fingers pump me, and his hand jerks that big ole cock.

Finally, his movements slow as he brings me out of the stratosphere, and I loosen my hold on his hair.

"I need to add a few more rows to your spreadsheet," I pant as he gives me one last lick and grins up at me.

Then he stands and holds my face with both hands. "You are breathtaking when you come for me, Libby-girl."

I seriously feel like I'm in one of my books right now. Glancing down at the cock standing at attention, I say, "That's a very book-boyfriend-worthy penis you have there, Mr. Romero."

He laughs. "Is this where you're supposed to get all concerned about it fitting inside you?"

Pressing my tits against his chest, I drag my tongue along his bottom lip and purr my response. "We'll make it fit, baby."

With his mouth hovering over mine, he murmurs, "I think that's my line."

"What can I say? Orgasms make me sassy."

He chuckles. "Then prepare to be sassy for the rest of the night, Libby, because I'm nowhere close to being done with you."

CHAPTER 18

Cupping Libby's chin, I lift her face to mine and search her pretty hazel eyes. "Are you sure this is what you want? I know this all happened so fast."

This isn't what I had planned at all when I decided to come over here. I wanted to do a gentle probe into her feelings and see if she was interested in pursuing a relationship with me. And now I want to do a not-so-gentle probe into something else.

"It's not that fast," she argues. "We've been circling around this for a month. I felt our connection on the plane."

"When you were staring at my crotch?" I tease, and she smacks my chest.

"Would you stop bringing that up?"

I laugh and shake my head. "No, I don't think I will."

Her look turns sly, and she reaches down to grip my cock, which is still hanging out of my jeans. *Holy fucking hell.*

"Seeing as how you just gave me an epic orgasm, I guess I can let it slide." She mimicked that last word with the slide of her hand up and down my length. I could have coated her flat, bare stomach with my release from that single stroke.

Her hand feels so right around me. Soft skin. Tight grip but not too tight. Just fucking perfect.

"I want to make sure you're good with it, Libby. I don't want you to have any regrets."

"I'm a big girl, and you're a big boy." She looks down as her fist tightens, and she gives me another of those delicious strokes. "A very big boy."

Christ, this woman is seduction in a ponytail.

Libby continues. "We're both adults who are obviously attracted to each other, so why shouldn't we?" Her full lips press together for a second, and she looks almost shy. "Unless *you* don't want to."

I kiss her lips softly. "I want you more than I've ever wanted anything. I'd give my left nut to be inside you right now."

"That seems a little dramatic and completely unnecessary," she says with a cute giggle before sinking her teeth into her bottom lip, giving me more of her vulnerability. "It's been a while for me."

"How long, baby?"

"Months."

"Your ex is a fucking moron." I lay a kiss between her eyebrows and reassure her. "I'll be gentle with you."

"Let's not be too hasty about that. Because if you're as good with this as you are with your mouth…" She lifts an eyebrow in challenge as her hand moves up and down my dick a few times, using my pre-ejaculate to lubricate the glide. Libby leans forward until her lips rest against mine, and she whispers, "I like it rough, Riggs."

I slap a hand against the door for support because *those words*… not to mention she's still doing very magical hand shit to my cock.

"I need this bra off so I can suck your pretty tits while I fuck you against this door."

Seconds later, we're both naked, and I'm rolling on a condom. The fit is tight because my dick has never been so engorged with need. Libby is fucking gorgeous, her breasts high, pert, and a perfect handful. I run my thumbs over each rosy nipple while my erection throbs painfully between my legs. Then I trail my hands down her sides, loving the goosebumps I bring to life on her skin, before grasping the backs of her thighs and lifting.

"Libby…" I start, and she wraps her legs around me and kisses my nose.

"Riggs, if you ask me one more time if I'm sure, I'm going to punch your lights out and use your body for my pleasure while you're unconscious."

I've never been so amused and turned on at the same time. I didn't think it was possible. "That wasn't what I was going to say," I tell her dryly. "I wanted to tell you if I break your door, I'll buy you a new one."

A cheeky grin spreads across her face. "Good to know. I think there's a clause about that in my lease agree— Ohhhh."

That sound is elicited when I nestle the head of my dick just inside her entrance. "Hold on tight, sweetheart," I tell her, my voice barely recognizable because, despite only being an inch inside her, I can already tell I'm going to be addicted.

Then I take her in one hard thrust, burying my hardness deep inside her. We both let out guttural noises as our mouths find each other. I rotate my hips to loosen her up because, *fuck me*, she's tight, smothering my cock with her wetness.

We kiss frantically as I pull my dick halfway out and slam back in. Her pussy clenches me, the muscles rippling as I begin fucking up into her at an almost unimaginable pace. And she takes every bit of me, her sexy hips churning in time with my own.

Libby's long legs wrap tightly around my waist, her heels digging into my ass to urge me on. She's driving me fucking wild, and I take her harder than I'd ever taken any woman. When I hit one particular spot inside her, she moans loudly into my mouth and scores the back of my neck with her fingernails.

I fist my hand in the back of her hair and yank her head back, giving me access to that long, beautiful neck. Her eyes close as I drop my mouth to her neck and lick a long stripe up the side and to her ear.

"You were made for me, sweetheart," I growl, nipping her earlobe with my teeth. "Your cunt is the most perfect thing I've ever felt in my life."

Her hands dive into my hair and twist, and I love that she's as uninhibited as me. "Riggs, no one has ever fucked me like this."

"That's a shame, baby, because this is exactly how your tight little pussy deserves to be fucked. Deep and rough." I kiss down her neck and chest until I arrive at those sweet tits of hers. Taking one nipple in my mouth, I suck with long, firm pulls as I continue to pound into her.

The uncontrolled writhing of her body tells me she's getting close, and thank fuck for that because I'm about to blow so hard inside this woman.

I switch to her other breast, but this time, I bite and suck at the silky underside until she's marked with my love bites. And then I devote all my attention to her hard nipple. Libby goes absolutely feral, sliding that delicious little pussy up and down my shaft as we do our best impression of a scene from Animal Planet.

"That's... ohhhh... right there, Riggs. Your big, hard cock is making me come."

Sweat drips down my back and chest, and beads of perspiration dot my forehead. With a strength I didn't know I had, I maintain my pace, resisting the urge to speed up. Because the cardinal rule of giving a woman immeasurable pleasure is to not change one fucking thing when she says she's coming.

With her tit in my mouth, I allow my release to take over with a loud groan as Libby comes undone around me.

"Riggs... Riggs," she chants, and it's the most beautiful sound I've ever heard, my name dripping like honey from her lips as she climaxes, long and hard. My own orgasm is so intense, I have to fight to keep my legs underneath me.

Sex with Libby Hill is like a rollercoaster, the climb, the thrill of reaching the top and falling over it, and finally, the slowing of the ride as we pull into the proverbial station together.

And that's where we are now, our slick bodies grinding together in an unhurried dance of satiation. My gaze takes her in, the dreamy eyes, the blonde hair falling out of her ponytail, the upward curve of her lips and flush of her cheeks that can only come from being utterly satisfied.

Guilt begins to seep in around the edges of my psyche. I haven't even taken this woman on a date yet I show up at her house, eat her pussy, and then attempt to fuck her through the door.

She doesn't seem bothered in the least though. Libby clings to me and rests her damp cheek sweetly on my shoulder, a move so feminine, it makes me want to cuddle up and stroke her body for the rest of the night.

"Please tell me this wasn't a one-and-done," she mumbles against my neck.

Lifting her chin until we're face-to-face, I tell her, "I'm not a one-night-stand kind of guy, Libby. I know I didn't act like it tonight, but I really love being with you, and I don't mean sexually, though you did just blow my damn mind."

"I know, Riggs." She leans into my body, and I can feel the strong, fast beat of her heart. "I like spending time with you too. I'm so glad you came over."

That assuages a metric-ton of the apprehension I was holding on to, and I rub her back. "And to answer your question, hell yes, we're going to do that again."

Her grin is wide and infectious. "Good. I need to ice my vagina for about an hour, and then I'll be good to go again."

I laugh and hold her close as I carry her upstairs to her loft bedroom.

CHAPTER 19
Riggs

I awaken in the dark and immediately smile. I'm in my soft, cozy bed with a long, lean blonde wrapped in my arms. We'd come to my house last night because I had to take care of Ace, and I'd asked Libby to come with me. Thank god she'd agreed because I wanted to spend all the time in the world with her.

After checking the time on the bedside clock, I lean up on one elbow and kiss Libby's cheek. "Baby?" I whisper, not wanting to startle her. She stirs and presses her fine ass back against my crotch.

"Again?" She says it amenably, and not in a *good lord, you want to fuck again?* way. Which is how Lucinda used to say it when I wanted sex more than once.

But Libby—this beautiful, wild woman—has a sexual appetite that rivals my own. We went at each other all night, with long naps in between. Once I'd roused with a warm mouth around my cock, her soft suction gently waking me from a bone-deep sleep.

"No, baby. I mean, yes. Always yes with you, but first I thought you might like to watch the sunrise from my balcony."

She rolls over, and I can feel the curve of her smile against my neck. "Yes, please."

Turning on the bedside lamp, I get up and grab us some clothes, wrapping Libby in my fluffy lavender robe. Don't judge. My sister bought it for me as a joke, but I kinda love it. I slip on a sweatshirt and pajama pants and lead Libby out the glass doors to my flagstone balcony.

The first hint of the sun lightens the strip of sky just above the water as I settle onto a sling-back patio chair with the most gorgeous woman in the world curled in my lap.

As the yellow orb turns the sky into a rainbow of pastels, the scene before us is simply majestic. But the beauty of it pales in comparison to Liberty Hill. The emerging sunlight sets her hair aglow. Her locks hang loose and messy down her back, the ponytail having been disposed of during one of our romps.

I like her like this, and I can feel the earth shifting beneath us. Nuzzling my nose against her cheek, I say her name. "Liberty."

"Hmm?" She turns her pretty face toward me, and I can see a few freckles dusted across her nose.

"I meant what I said last night. I'm not into one-night stands. Do you think you'd…" I inhale a deep breath and expel it, letting the air take the nervous butterflies with it. "Do you think you'd like to be with me?"

She's silent for a long moment, her eyes searching mine. "Are you sure that's what you want? You had a girlfriend about five minutes ago."

My fingers tangle in the hair above her right ear, and I pull her toward me for a tender kiss. "That's been over for a while. I was just too dumb to realize it. But I think being with you is the smartest thing I've done in a long time."

"Genius, really," she comments, making me smile. "I'd love to give this thing between us a try."

Relief floods my every vein, and I pull her head to my shoulder. "That makes me happy."

Libby sighs as we resume our sky watching "It's so easy

being with you, Riggs, and the chemistry is off the charts. People who say physical stuff doesn't count are deluding themselves. You make me feel special when we're together." She cuddles closer, and I can hear the smile in her voice. "Even when you go all panther on me."

"Panther?" I ask with a laugh, and she gazes up at me.

"Oh, don't act like you don't know what I'm talking about. Every time you came back from the bathroom, you prowled at me like a big, dark cat."

Dragging my thumb across her bottom lip, I ask, "Were you afraid I was going to eat you up, little girl?"

"Terrified," she says, widening her eyes in mock-fear.

"Is that why you kept spreading your legs for me?"

She giggles. "I spread them because you, sir, are a master with your tongue."

"The better to lick you with, my dear."

"I think that's the big, bad wolf you're quoting."

I stand, holding Libby in my arms and carrying her back to my bed. She bounces when I toss her onto it, and then I crawl up over her, attempting to be as prowly as possible.

I untie my robe from her waist and part it, my eyes hungrily taking in the sight of her naked body.

"Brace yourself, little one. The panther-wolf is ready for his breakfast."

Libby and I took a nap after our morning activities. It's a little after noon, and I'm singing along to "Sittin' on the Dock of the Bay" as I make meatballs in my kitchen.

My head snaps around when I hear a commotion, and I find my sister bustling in with about fifty shopping bags.

"Come on in, Silvia. Don't bother knocking," I snark, internally freaking out. Libby is somewhere in my house, and I really wasn't planning on telling my family about her just yet. Hell, I just broke up with Lucinda two days ago, and today I have another woman in my house. It makes me look like a bit of a manwhore.

"Well, that's a fine way to greet your sister," she says, dropping a kiss on my shoulder before plopping her bags onto the counter. "I've been Christmas shopping. You should see the shoes I got for Mom."

"I-it's really not a good—"

"And I got Nana an Hermes scarf at a steal. It's purple. What are you making? It smells delish. God, my feet hurt. I'm turning the music down; I can barely hear you." Silvia is a bit of a babbler when she's excited.

As soon as she turns down the volume on my phone, her head swivels slowly toward the first-floor corridor. The unmistakable sound of a woman laughing filters into the kitchen, and Silvia's head whips back toward me like something out of *The Exorcist*.

"Swear to god, if you're back with Lucinda, I'm going to stab you in the face," she hisses.

I put myself between my sister and the knife block she's now eyeing. "It's not Lucinda," I sigh, turning to wash my hands. After drying them, I turn to find Silvia marching down the hallway.

Goddammit.

I chase her and almost slam into her back when she stops outside Ace's room. My silly dog is leaned down on his front paws, butt in the air as he raptly watches his favorite toy, a large cardboard box.

For the record, yes, I buy my dog nice toys. And no, he doesn't like them as much as a stupid empty box. He's like a fucking toddler.

All of a sudden, Libby pops up out of the box, her back to us, and yells, "Boo!"

Ace goes nuts, waggling his butt and grinning his doggy grin as he barks at his own personal jack-in-the-box. When Libby sinks back down into the box, Ace assumes the ready position once again.

The next time she jumps into view, she yells, "Fluffernugget!" before giggling and disappearing again. My excited pooch runs in circles around the box.

I'm pretty sure a grin is permanently etched on my face. Libby is playing the canine version of peek-a-boo with Ace.

My sister hooks a hand around my wrist and drags me to the spare room next door. "What the hell? Who is that?" she whisper-yells as soon as the door is closed.

I rub the back of my neck. "That's, um, her name is Libby."

Silvia's lips form a coy smile. "Oh. My. God. My big brother has got a rebound fuck in his house. Good for you, Riggsy."

"She's not a rebound fuck," I snap, and Silvia lifts her dark eyebrows. "She's… my new girlfriend."

My sister stares open-mouthed for a long moment before a snort fills the air. "Since when?"

"Last night," I admit.

And then she's laughing, hands on her stomach as she cackles at my expense. "What the actual fuck, bro?"

I riffle my fingers through the top of my hair. "Look, I've been interested in Libby for a while, but I haven't been in a position to ask her out because of, you know… my situation. So I went to her house to talk to her last night to see if she might want to pursue things with me."

"And, of course, she said yes," Silvia fills in. I nod. "Well, I already like her better than the wench you were with. At least she likes your ridiculous dog."

Thoughts of Libby flood my mind. Her hooking my pants on the boat, playing on the beach with Ace, the way her eyes sparkle when she laughs. Though a fair amount of my thoughts are of the tits bouncing while riding my cock variety. "I like her too," I finally say.

Silvia's grin is laden with mischief. "I can tell. You're letting her wear *the jersey*. You yelled at me last time I wore it."

"That was ten years ago, and you were dribbling chocolate ice cream all over a special-edition, signed Dan Marino jersey."

I'm not sure why I draped that particular garment over Libby's head after our shower this morning. I guess I just wanted to see it on her.

"Come on. Introduce me," my nosy-ass sister insists, grabbing my arm and dragging me toward the door.

"No," I hiss. "It's too soon to be meeting family members."

"But it's not too soon to be clapping cheeks?"

"No one says clapping cheeks, Sil."

"Would you prefer I say *making whoopie*?"

"Only if you're a contestant on Family Feud in 1986," I say dryly.

"Pleeeeease, Riggsy. Please let me meet your new friend."

I sigh and roll my eyes. "All right, but don't call me Riggsy or say anything else embarrassing for fuck's sake."

"Okey dokey," she says, giving me a quick hug. As we retrace our steps back to Ace's room, Silvia whispers, "One question though. What the hell is a fluffernugget?"

CHAPTER 20
Libby

I love Silvia Romero. During our lunch of spaghetti, meatballs, and garlic bread, we get to know each other while Riggs watches, amused, occasionally piping up with a comment.

Halfway through the meal, his phone rings, and he excuses himself to answer it. When he returns to the table, a frown mars his perfect face.

"What's wrong?" Silvia asks, and he forces a smile.

"I have a book event in New York next week, and my PA just called and said he broke his foot. It's fine though. I can deal with everything myself."

His sister's lips twist to the side. "I would say I could go with you, but then who would keep the wonder dog?"

"Ace can stay at my house," I offer.

Silvia is quiet for a few seconds and then she lifts an eyebrow at her brother. "Or I could watch the mutt, and you can take Libby with you to New York."

I'm about to protest, but Riggs's face lights up. He takes my hand, and his damn smile melts me. "Would you, Lib? I'll cover all your expenses if you'll be my assistant."

Is this crazy? Going away with a man I started dating last night?

Actually, we haven't even been on a real date. We banged like bunnies all night. That's it.

Despite that, I find myself saying, "Sure. I'd be happy to."

"I'm coming to New York," I announce into the phone as soon as my cousin, Gianna, answers.

"Oh my god, when?"

"Next weekend," I tell her, my body vibrating with excitement. "You know that cover model I've sent you pictures of? Riggs Romero?"

"How could I forget that hottie?"

"We're, uhhh, dating now."

I have to pull the phone away from my ear to keep from being deafened by Gianna's scream. "You have to tell me all about it when you get here."

"Same. I want to hear every detail of what you've been up to. I still can't believe you're engaged to Auburn Bouvier. I bet your wardrobe is killer now." Gianna's fiancé is the head of the Bouvier fashion house in New York City, and he recently proposed to her.

"Girl, if I even glance at something in a magazine, it magically appears on our doorstep a few days later. Last month, I mentioned to him that I love the new lipstick I'd bought, and he had his designer whip up two dresses and a pantsuit in the exact shade."

My heart is so full. My gorgeous cousin deserves all the pampering in the world. She's a little younger than me, but she's so damn strong and has the best heart.

"I'm happy for you Gia, and I can't wait to see you. Riggs has a book event at the Javits Center on Saturday until four, but we're free any other time."

"Do you need a place to stay?"

"No, he booked us at the Four Seasons."

"Oooh, there's a great steakhouse there. It's practically impossible to get in, but Auburn can get us reservations."

"I'll check with Riggs and let you know. I'm so excited to see you," I tell her, feeling emotional. Gianna is my only family, and I haven't seen her in over a year.

"Me too, babe."

I rub my forehead and glare at my computer screen, like that's going to scare it into spontaneously typing what I need it to.

"What's wrong, babe?" Riggs asks from the window seat beside me. We're in the first-class section of the plane on the way to New York.

"The words aren't wording right now," I tell him in frustration.

"Do you mind if I take a look?"

At my wit's end, I nod and hand him my laptop. "Here's the character analysis for them," I say, showing him my detailed notes.

Riggs reads them thoroughly before switching back to the scene I was working on. "Ah, you didn't warn me this was a spicy scene," he says after perusing it twice.

"It's not. They're arguing," I say.

His eyes meet mine. "Don't you feel the tension you're building here? I do, and there's some serious steam going on. They need to fuck it out."

I stare at the words I've already written and nod. "You're right." I take the laptop back and poise my fingers over the keys. "Who breaks first?"

The crooked smile Riggs gives me has my thighs clenching

together. "He does. He's had it with Sophia's shit and tells her to put that smart mouth to good use on his cock."

My eyes widen, and I bite my lip as I begin to type. "Yes, this is good. She's a bit of a loose cannon, so I think she would try to slap him."

"Oh, but Xavier would never put up with that. He'd grab her wrist and yank her to him." My fingers fly over the keys, and Riggs leans over to watch what I'm writing as his mouth whispers near my ear. "He's hard as stone, and she feels it against her hip."

I write out some snarky dialogue from Sophia, and Riggs commentates for the filthy-mouthed Xavier. "I think he would grab the back of her hair, and when he sees how turned on she is, he gets rougher. Tells her she has two choices. He's either going to fuck her mouth or her tight little ass."

"Ooh, I like," I tell him, rearranging the words in my head and allowing them to flow like a river through my keyboard. "She's an anal virgin, so of course she'll choose oral."

"Are you an anal virgin, Libby?" Riggs rasps in my ear.

My fingers fumble and type *Therrrr's no why I let you in my ash, Xaxier.* I fix my errors before shifting my eyes to the man beside me and letting my lips curl into a smirk. "No, but I've been told I'm as tight as one."

He swallows hard, his blue eyes blazing with desire. "Christ, that made me so fucking hard," he hisses, the muscles in his jaw quaking.

"Maybe I'll let you try it for yourself if you're a good boy," I tell him sweetly before going back to the blow job scene that's now appearing on the screen as I type. Riggs feeds me dirty dialogue in my ear, and *fuck me*, this scene is fire.

I'm done with the chapter way sooner than I expected and stow the laptop in my backpack. Leaning my head on Riggs's shoulder, I kiss his jaw. "Thank you, Riggs. You got my creative juices flowing."

"What about your other juices?" he asks quietly.

"Like a waterfall," I admit. "And yours?"

"Why do you think I took off my jacket and laid it on my lap? My dick is attempting to escape from Alcatraz, and I'm pretty sure I have a wet spot on the front of my pants."

My smile is coy and full of promises before I lean down, rummage through my backpack and pull something out, concealing it in my right hand. My left hand snakes beneath the black London Fog jacket draped over Riggs's lap.

"What the hell are you doing?" he murmurs, excitement lighting his eyes as I find the tent in his dark-gray athletic pants.

"Paying my coauthor for services rendered," I say in a low voice, reaching beneath the waistband of his pants and boxer briefs.

Riggs adjusts the jacket to make sure he's covered as I wrap my hand around his cock. He's hard and hot in my hand, and his eyes dart around the cabin. The couple across the aisle is asleep, and the flight attendants are nowhere to be seen.

"Libby, you can't," he whispers, but he lets out a low groan at the end of the sentence because I circle my thumb over the wet tip of his penis. He was right earlier; he's positively dripping.

"Is that a challenge, handsome? Because I'm pretty sure I can."

His lips twitch as I began a slow up-and-down motion with my hand. "Oh, I don't doubt your ability, sweetheart. I meant that I can't come in my fucking pants."

"Shh, you're interrupting my rhythm," I say, stuffing the item in my other hand into his mouth. His eyes widen before he quickly pulls it out, staring down at the red satin panties I'd taken from my backpack.

"My mother always taught me to carry an extra set of clothes on a plane with me, though I'm pretty sure this isn't the reason she had in mind," I tell him, allowing my hand to stroke him faster.

"You want me to... come... on your panties?" he pants quietly. Oh, he's close already, his big cock throbbing in my palm. Pre-ejaculate drips over his crown and lubricates the glide.

I lean over and place my lips against his ear. "Would that turn you on, big boy? Blowing a fat load into my silky panties?"

"Fuck, fuck, fuck," he chants as I really let him have it. "Lib, I'm…"

"You better get ready. I can tell this big cock is ready to explode." His hand slips beneath the jacket, and I can feel the satin against my finger and thumb as he covers the head of his dick.

His free hand grips my thigh with white-knuckle force as his hips lift from the seat, fucking my hand.

"Be still, Romero, or I'll stop. Let me handle this. All you have to do is come for me. I know you wish it was my hot mouth you were coming in," I purr. "Don't you?"

Riggs's head presses back against the headrest, and he nods curtly. With his eyes closed, I know from his harsh exhale that he's finally losing it.

His body trembles through his release, and I kiss the spot right in front of his ear. "Such a good boy," I whisper, and he swivels his head to look at me.

I can read the satiation in his eyes as he warms me with a smile. "You, baby, are fucking diabolical."

Smooshing a kiss against his full lips, I take the panties from him and readjust his pants over his softening cock. After checking the aisle behind me and finding it clear, I bring the garment to my mouth and drag my tongue over a particularly wet spot.

Riggs's eyes drop to dreamy slits as he watches me. "I never knew I needed to watch you lick my cum from your panties until right now."

I toss him a flirty wink and reach for my phone. "Ooh, that's a good line. Can I use it in a book?"

As he laughs, I think, *God, I'm turning into Gemma.*

CHAPTER 21

I stare at the two bags on the floor of our hotel room. There should be three. "I need my suit bag," I tell the man on the phone, the third one I'd talked to today.

"I'm so sorry, Mr. Romero, but we're still trying to locate it."

"I have an event tomorrow. I can't show up without my suit," I complain. "Find it and get it to the Four Seasons before I go to bed tonight."

Libby walks into the room as I hang up and toss my phone on the bed. With a sexy sway of her hips, she walks right into my space and wraps her arms around my neck.

"Have I told you how hot it is when you get all bossy?"

As bad as my mood is, she pulls a smile from me.

"Is that so?"

"Mmhmm. So hot, I almost don't want to tell you my good news."

I lift a sardonic eyebrow. "You've magically procured me a suit?"

"Why, yes, Mr. Romero. I certainly have," she says with a southern belle drawl.

"This isn't the time to be fucking with me, Libby. I have to dress the part tomorrow, and most of my suits are custom-made because of my height."

"Have you forgotten who my cousin is dating?" she sings, and my eyebrows rocket up my forehead.

"Bouvier?" I murmur, and she nods.

"He's sending over a suit as we speak. Gianna and I compared notes, and we think you and Auburn are about the same size."

The relief that shoots down my spine is laced with adoration for this woman. While I've been fighting with the airline, she's been working on another solution.

"Babe…" I'm lost for words, so I kiss the hell out of her.

When we come up for air, she presses her lips against the corner of my mouth. "Gianna said something similar happened to her when she moved to New York, except the airline lost *all* her luggage. So she's very sympathetic to your situation."

Thirty minutes later, the concierge calls our room, saying we have a delivery, and I tell him to send the person to our suite. When he arrives, I'm surprised to find a well-dressed man in his fifties with dark-brown hair shot through with a healthy dose of gray.

"I am Devereaux," he says formally, "Bouvier's head designer. This is my assistant, Tora." He nods toward the thin man behind him with huge brown eyes.

I resist the urge to say *holy shit!* I'm not a fashion guru, but I'm well-versed enough to know that getting a personal visit from the head designer of a major fashion house is a big fucking deal.

"Devereaux, Tora, thank you so much for coming. Come in." I gesture for them to enter, and they do, Tora pushing a hanging rack ahead of him.

"I've brought a selection from Mr. Bouvier's personal collection," Devereaux says. "We're here to make sure whichever you pick fits properly."

Tora's voice is teasing as he winks, "We can't have ill-fitting

Bouvier suits floating around out in public. Dev would rather eat a carb than to see that happen."

"For your information, I ate a carb last week, Tora." He shudders. "It was delicious, but I did a two-day juice cleanse to counteract it."

Tora goes to work sliding the suit bags down the rack. "I ate four doughnuts for breakfast today. And I did a cheesecake cleanse at lunch."

"Not everyone is lucky enough to have the metabolism of a toddler, Tora," Dev retorts, circling a finger at the rack. "Give me the black one."

"Of course, Your Majesty," the thin man says, affecting a royal curtsy at his boss before pulling out a suit bag.

These two are hilarious.

Libby walks out of the bedroom, dressed in a dark-green wrap dress that sits just at the curve of her shoulders. I forget for a moment that we have visitors as I practically leave a puddle of drool on the floor.

"Oh, hi?" she says, eyeing the two men. Like me, she probably expected a delivery person to simply drop off a suit.

"Libby, this is Devereaux, Bouvier's head designer, and his assistant, Tora," I explain.

The latter lets out a squeal and dashes toward Libby, squeezing her in an overly enthusiastic hug. "Look at you, you gorgeous thing. You look so much like your cousin. The cheekbones, the adorable little nose." He boops Libby's nose, and she laughs.

"Thank you. That's quite a compliment."

Tora holds her at arm's length. "And your shoulders. Look, Dev! Libby has our Gianna's shoulders."

Devereaux gives her a deferential nod. "You are stunning, Libby. I've brought something for you as well." He snaps his fingers twice. "Tora! The dress!"

Tora hops to attention and pulls another bag off the rack.

"Gianna picked this out for you, Libby. It's to wear to your event tomorrow."

"No, I couldn't," Libby demurs, and Dev levels her with a glare.

"You'll have to take that up with your cousin, but I'm certainly not leaving here with that dress. What Gianna Moschella wants, Gianna Moschella gets. Mr. Bouvier would fire me on the spot if I displeased his bride-to-be."

"Oh, well. I wouldn't want to get you in trouble."

By the time the designers leave two hours later, I have a bespoke navy suit and shoes for tomorrow, as well as a more casual black suit for this evening's dinner with Gianna and Auburn. Dev and Tora hand-altered the cuffs of both suits for the perfect fit.

Libby is the proud new owner of a flirty red cocktail dress that looks amazing with her tan. She will wear it tomorrow to the book event.

"I can't wait to see Gianna," she says as we walk downstairs that evening. She's vibrating with excitement, and I place my hand on her lower back when we enter the restaurant. It's stunning, decked out in dark woods and red upholstered chairs.

"Hello, we are meeting Auburn Bouvier," I tell the maître d', and he practically bows at the waist.

"Right this way. You're in the private dining room."

While we walk behind him, Libby looks up at me and mouths, "Ooooh, fancy-pants!"

As soon as we're inside the large room, which is set with one intimate four-top table, Libby and her cousin squeal with delight, jumping and hugging each other.

I've seen pictures of Auburn Bouvier, and he's just as impressive up close, tall and imposing, though his face is complete mush as he watches his fiancée's happy reunion. He turns to me and holds out his hand. "Auburn Bouvier."

"Riggs Romero," I tell him, giving the man a firm shake.

"I figured these two would be loud as hell, so I got us a private dining room."

I laugh, liking this guy already. "Thank you so much for saving the day," I tell him, fingering the lapel of the jacket I'm wearing.

"No problem. My fiancée set it all up." He beams at the F-word, obviously thrilled to be marrying Gianna. And who could blame him?

Though Gianna has dark hair and green eyes and Libby is blonde with hazel eyes, the relation between them is unmistakable. With similar facial features and builds, they're both fucking knockouts.

The ladies finally make their way to us, and the rest of the introductions are made. "Gianna," I say, lightly kissing her cheek, "it's so nice to meet you. Thank you for handling the wardrobe issue. You have no idea how much I appreciate it. I'll get the suits cleaned and shipped back to you next week."

Auburn waves a hand at me. "Don't worry about it. Just keep them."

I shake my head. "I couldn't do that."

"You look great in a Bouvier suit. Very good advertisement for the brand." He winks. "Maybe you could wear it on a book cover."

"I'd love to, but are you sure?"

Gianna rolls her eyes. "Trust me, he won't even miss them. Right now Auburn has eleven navy suits, seven gray, two ivory, three light-blue, and fourteen black ones in his closet. And that's not even including the tuxes."

I can't help but laugh at the man's chagrined smile. "Well, that's very kind of you, Auburn. I'm going to take care of dinner tonight as a token of my appreciation."

"I couldn't let you do that," he says with a frown, but I shake my head.

"I insist."

We sit, and after some excellent appetizers, the chef brings out a selection of Wagyu beef dishes from America, Japan, and Australia. Each bite is more delicious than the last, but the company is even better.

I really like Auburn and Gianna. It's obvious the two are head-over-heels in love with each other, and I'm surprised to learn they've been dating for less than a year.

"How did you two meet?" I ask, and the couple exchange a bemused smile as Libby giggles. She's obviously heard this story before.

After they tell me about their meet-cute, I burst out laughing. "Damn, Bouvier. You actually said, 'she'll do?' You're lucky to have this lady on your arm. You were a bit of a dickhead."

"Huge dickhead," Gianna agrees, bumping Auburn's shoulder with affection. "But he's more than made up for it. Now, tell me about you two. How long have you been dating?"

Libby inches her eyebrows up and nods at me. Taking a deep breath, I announce. "A week."

"Wow, dude. You move fast," Bouvier says, and his woman narrows her eyes at him.

"Says the guy who had me in his bed on our first date."

Auburn cups Gianna's face with a tenderness I wouldn't have expected from the billionaire. "I was taking care of you, sweetheart."

"Is that what we're calling it these days?" I tease, and Auburn wraps an arm possessively around his bride-to-be with a grin.

"I actually *was* taking care of her. She got really sick. Nothing happened between us that night."

"Except for when you undressed me and put one of your T-shirts on me," Gia shoots back with a look of amusement on her face.

"So you'd be comfortable, baby girl. I didn't even look." His head tilts to the side. "Well, maybe a quick peek but purely for… medical purposes."

We all crack up at that, and Libby's crazy laugh makes me loop my arm around her chair to pull her closer. Something about this woman makes electricity hum through my body, especially when she's being so real.

Oh, who am I kidding? She's always real and her authentic self, and that's so goddamn attractive to me. I kiss her temple, and she lifts her eyes to mine. There are little laugh crinkles around the corners, and her lips are turned up into a happy smile.

"I'm crazy about you," I whisper before pressing my lips softly against hers.

"I'm crazy about you too," she says back, and suddenly, I'm anxious to get her back to the room.

CHAPTER 22

Riggs backs me into the room, our lips fused and his fingers already finding the snaps that hold my dress in place. The green fabric is in a pool on the floor in a matter of seconds.

"Fuck, you're sexy," he says. "I love your ponytails, but when your hair is down like this, I want to watch it spill down your back while I fuck you from behind."

I'd worn my blonde locks in loose curls tonight, curls that are currently being destroyed by Riggs's impatient hands as his mouth plunders mine.

He lifts me with strong arms, and I curl my legs around his waist, allowing him to carry me to the living room. My fingers work on the buttons of his dove-gray shirt while he settles onto the cream couch against the wall.

Something about this man and the way his tongue strokes against mine turns me into a wild woman. I've never craved anyone so deeply. One kiss from Riggs, and I have the overwhelming urge to rip his clothes from his body.

And the beautiful thing is, he's the same with me. The desire runs both ways, and within minutes, we're both bare. As I reach to remove my shoe, a large hand stops me.

"No, leave those on," he orders, and my lips tip up at the corners. *What is it about men loving to fuck a woman with her heels on?*

Riggs swivels and slams my back against the seat of the couch before settling between my thighs. "So hungry for you, baby," he growls into me.

His mouth manages to be precise and unrestrained at the same time as his tongue goes to work, lapping fiercely at my sex and barely grazing my clitoris.

"Riggs, please."

Spreading my pussy lips, he glances up at me with a wicked grin before dragging a long lick directly up my center. I cry out with pleasure.

"This what you need, sweetheart? You want me to lick this cunt until you paint my face with your creamy goodness?"

"Yes!" I pant, and my world flips as Riggs rolls onto his back and plants me on his face.

"Then take it, baby girl. Take what you need from me."

This is one of the things I love most about being with Riggs. He's dominant as fuck when things turn sexual, but he's also secure enough to cede control to me sometimes. His number one priority is my pleasure, and I can't say I've ever been with anyone like that before.

Riggs gently eases my thighs apart so that I sink farther onto his face. "That's it, Libby. Ride my mouth like a good girl."

My hips begin to move, and he hums his approval against my center, the vibrations ramping up my arousal tenfold. He always sounds like he's eating the most decadent dessert when he has his mouth on me.

"Mmm, so fucking good," he groans, tongue fucking me while his hands grip my hips. My clit glides across his rough, wet tongue, and I increase my pace, chasing the orgasm that's right on the horizon.

"Talk to me," I whimper, needing to hear his dirty words to push me over the edge.

"I think about eating this sweet, pink pussy all day at work. Mmmm, baby, yes. I feel you dripping into my mouth. Give it all to me."

Holy fuck, this man… My fingers dig into the cushy arm of the couch as I find a sensual rhythm. Riggs guides my hip motions into small circles, and his scruff abrades my pussy and the insides of my thighs.

All the sensations combine to get me to my release, and I come with a loud cry of nonsense words as my pussy jerks rapidly back and forth over Riggs's eager mouth. His constant hums of approval as he laps up every drop only serve to prolong my climax. Every time I think I'm done, another wave of bliss rolls through me until my spine goes loose.

"Mmm, so good, Libby-girl. You taste like delicious sin on my tongue," he groans into me as his mouth finally slows between my legs. When his big hands grip my hips and slide me down his body, I notch my sex over his impressive erection, wetting him with the evidence of what he does to me.

I kiss him, tasting myself in his mouth, and he strokes soothing fingers up and down my back. "I want to ride you," I tell him, and his thick cock twitches against me.

"Let me get a condom."

I move off him, and he quickly grabs a foil packet and a towel before returning to the couch. He lays the towel down and sits on it and then rolls on the condom. His dick is hard and red, resting against his stomach, and I've never wanted to sink onto a man so much in my life.

Riggs said earlier that he wanted me from behind, so I position myself in reverse cowgirl on his lap. "Fuuuuck," he groans, holding himself up so I can swirl my opening over his swollen head. "Take me slow, Libby-girl. I want you sore, but not so sore I can't have you again and again tonight."

Holy shit, this man is a sex god. And I want to be his goddess.

Arching my neck back so my hair drapes dramatically down

my back, I lower myself onto his length. It has the desired effect because Riggs's hands sink into my hair and tug.

"So fucking beautiful taking my cock inside that tight little pussy, baby."

I circle my hips and whimper, trying to deal with all of this man. He's so thick, and this position only amplifies it. Keeping one hand fisted at the base of my neck, he grasps my hip with the other. I love his touch, the gentle and the not-so-gentle.

"You fill me up so good, Riggs. You touch places I've only dreamed about," I moan as I begin to move.

"No one else will ever touch those places," he growls, tightening his grip on my hair. "Only me. Do you understand?"

Good lord have mercy! His possessiveness has me panting like a horny bitch in heat.

"Yesss," I hiss when the crown of his erection drags across a particularly sensitive spot inside me. I lean forward a little, placing my hands on his knees, and his balls ride full and firm against my clit.

"Do you have any idea how goddamn hot you look, Liberty? You're the culmination of every wet dream I've ever had. So beautiful. So perfect for me, baby girl."

My praise kink is in full effect as I ride him harder, take him deeper, fuck him faster. When Riggs grabs both my hips and starts pounding savagely up into me, my orgasm is on a fast track to becoming reality.

"Yes, just like that," I say breathlessly because the man is seriously knocking the wind from my lungs. "Be rough with me, Riggs. I need it."

A slap to my ass jolts me and turns me on even more as my release perches on the horizon. "You like that, baby? You like me spanking this naughty little ass? I think you want me to fuck it."

Oh, sweet heavens! This is some next-level shit.

"I'll let you," I tell him, and then I feel his thumb slide to where we're joined and gather some moisture.

"This okay, Libby-girl?" he asks, smearing my arousal around my back hole.

"Yes. Please," I beg, and his thumb slowly breaches the entrance. "God, I'm so full of you, Riggs."

He presses in deeper, and then his other thumb follows the path of the first one, lubing up and then sliding in beside its counterpart. The sex becomes untamed and frenetic, his fingers gripping my butt cheeks while his thumbs explore my ass.

"You're so tight back here, Libby. I'm going to wreck this tiny hole with my cock."

Riggs is behind me so I can't see him, but the sounds of our bodies slapping together and the thick smell of sex in the air surround me like a sensual cocoon of lust.

"Fuck, coming!" I cry out as a tidal wave slams over me.

"Me too," he grunts, never letting up as he jerks inside me and fills the condom with his release. His voice is low and ragged. "God. Damn. Libby. Never. Come. This. Hard."

I reach down and cup his balls, loving the taut feel of them as they pulse and contract in my hand.

Riggs pulls his thumbs out of my backside, and I collapse back onto his hard body, sweat drenching both of us.

"Hands down, that was the sexiest sex ever," I inform him, and he chuckles as he turns sweet and presses gentle kisses across my shoulder.

"I couldn't agree more, Libby-girl."

After a shower, Riggs and I are on the king-sized bed between sheets that are so soft, they must have been woven by literal angels.

Our legs tangle as we face each other, whispering and laughing in the dark. It's so damn intimate. I was afraid of this kind of connection at first. Sex is sex, but intimacy is something entirely different.

That's why, besides the first night we spent together, I insisted on going home to sleep in my own bed every night afterward. It wasn't Riggs; he's been an excellent boyfriend this past week. It was me. He texted me multiple times a day, just to say hi or that he was thinking of me. We had dinner together every night, sometimes at restaurants, and sometimes at his house. Then we had insane gorilla sex that left me wrecked and sore.

But now, lying with this beautiful man after sharing my body with him, I have no idea why I've been so apprehensive. Despite his astounding good looks, he's not a playboy. He's deep and kind and loyal.

"I have an idea," I tell him, nuzzling his neck.

"You're naked in bed with me. I have lots of ideas," he replies, mischief in his voice.

"Stop it, you maniac," I say, swatting his firm butt. "You know that children's home Gianna and Auburn were talking about tonight?"

"Yeah."

"What if we could help out?" I tell him my thoughts, and he listens intently without speaking.

"I love that, Libby-girl. Count me in." He kisses me slowly. "I love how big your heart is."

I blush in the darkness.

Riggs smoothes a strand of my mussed hair behind my ear. "Can I ask you a question? If it's too personal, you don't have to answer."

"You had your thumbs in my butthole less than an hour ago. I'm not sure we can get more personal than that."

He laughs, and the sound vibrates the mattress. "I wanted to know if you're on birth control."

"I am. I'm on the shot."

I can barely see his eyes in the dim light seeping in through a crack in the curtains, but they're serious now. He rubs a lazy hand up and down my arm. "I want to sleep with you without a condom."

"You do?"

"Yes. When and if you're ready. I don't sleep around, Libby, and I wouldn't ask this if I wasn't entirely serious about you. I know this has happened fast, but I've never been this drawn to a woman before. I think we're something special."

Unbidden tears sting the backs of my eyelids, and I run my fingertips down his cheek. "I think we are too. Have you ever done that before?"

He nods. "Only with one woman though."

"Lucinda?"

Riggs chuckles a little. "Definitely not. It was a woman I dated a few years ago."

"Did you love her?" I regret the words as soon as they leave my mouth because if he says yes…

"I did." *Fuck, why does that give me an irrational sense of jealousy?* "I met Anastasia at a photo shoot in Florida. We had good chemistry on camera, so I thought I'd ask her out. We dated for almost two years, and she's the only woman I've ever said those three little words to."

Great. A model.

"What happened?"

"She moved to Arizona to take care of her father, and the long-distance thing was too hard. She asked me to move out there with her, but I didn't want to leave my family." The high I've been riding is rapidly sinking, but Riggs kisses my forehead. "I'm glad I didn't though because then I probably wouldn't have met you."

"Okay, Romero. Are you trying to swoon me right out of my panties?"

"You're not wearing panties," he whispers conspiratorially, and I giggle.

"Have I told you what a good book boyfriend you are?"

"I'm still waiting on my gold stars," he complains.

"I'll see what I can do." Wrapping an arm around his waist, I kiss his chin. "And I would like it if we didn't have to use condoms."

He hardens instantly against my stomach. "Starting now?"

CHAPTER 23

Riggs rolls on top of me, and I cradle his hips with my thighs as he holds up his weight on his elbows. With gentle lips, he sucks at my mouth as the round head of his erection finds my center.

"I'm not even inside you yet, and I can already tell you're going to blow my mind," he whispers. Then he reaches over and flicks on the bedside lamp. "I want to watch your face the first time I take you raw."

My arousal, which had been perfectly satisfied only moments ago, rears its needy head.

"You are so beautiful," I tell him, cupping his face as he rotates his hips and grinds against my clit.

His smile takes my breath away. "There you go stealing my lines again, Libby-girl."

We both gasp when his tip breaches my entrance, and the muscles of his jaw clench into steel as he pushes in a little further. His cock is hot and smooth, stretching my swollen tissues as he bores into me with unhurried precision.

I close my eyes and wrap my arms around him until our bodies are flush. "Riggs, it's… god, so good. Better than I expected."

He drops kisses on my eyelids and then my lips. "Open your eyes for me, sweetheart."

I do and find him looking down at me, his blue eyes a muted cobalt. Then he takes the rest of me until our bodies are flush. And he holds himself still. I'm lost in the moment, in his tender gaze.

This intense stare down we're having should feel uncomfortable, but it doesn't. It seems like the most natural thing in the world, being studied by this incredible man. His eyes hold mine hostage as he pulls out and slides back in with aching slowness.

"You're like silk around me, Liberty. I think this is the most perfect moment of my life."

I've never cried during sex. Never felt such a pervasive draw to another person that liquid feels compelled to escape my tear ducts. But it happens now. A single droplet spills over my eyelid and makes a track down my temple. Before it can reach my hairline, Riggs's lips kiss it away.

"I know, baby," Riggs whispers. "I feel it too."

With our eyes locked together, we begin to move as one. Our bodies are in perfect sync, hips rolling sensuously as our torsos maintain constant contact. His hands cradle my face, thumbs caressing my cheeks like I'm some kind of treasure.

Our lovemaking is slow and sweet, completely different from our usual frantic fucking, and Riggs seems as lost in the moment as I am. Gone are his filthy utterances, instead replaced by tender affirmations of how beautiful he thinks I am, how perfectly we fit together.

His kisses are the same, loving and leisurely, as we rock against each other. Our tongues meet with gentle strokes and licks that have me wrapping my legs around his waist to hold him more tightly to me.

I'm mesmerized by him, not even thinking about orgasms, but as soon as Riggs wedges a hand beneath my butt and pulls me tightly against him, the new angle shoves pleasure to the forefront of my mind.

"Riggs," I gasp, "come with me."

"Liberty, I think I'm… I'm falling…"

I'm not even able to fully process his words and what they might mean because Riggs reaches the depths of me in one smooth roll of his hips. We cling together and ride the waves of satisfaction as our mutual moans fill each other's mouths.

Maybe it's the slow pace, but our climaxes seem to drag on forever as Riggs thrusts in and out of me, emptying himself as my fingernails dig half-moons into the damp flesh of his back.

He kisses across my face and down my neck, soft pecks and gentle sucks, and I revel in his undivided attention. Tugging my arms until I unwind them, Riggs links our fingers together above my head as he returns his mouth to mine.

With lazy sweeps of his tongue, he worships me, holds my hands to the bed, and steals my entire heart.

"I can't believe I'm meeting you in person," the woman gushes. She's short and curvy, with an adorable spiky haircut.

Riggs flashes her his sexy smile and signs the three books she's brought with her. His handsome face graces the cover of each one.

Then he places a bookmark—one of *my* bookmarks—on top of the stack before handing it back. "Thank you for stopping by. I want you to make sure to check out this book by Libby Cox," he tells her with a wink. "It's so hot, it even made me blush."

"I will," she says, nodding fervently.

I use the woman's phone to snap a picture of them together, and she drops a ten-dollar bill into the donation jar I set up on the table. The next woman in line approaches.

"Hi, Riggs."

And he starts the whole thing over again. He's been doing

this all day long… handing out my bookmarks to every person who has stopped by his table. He's fucking promoting *my books*, and I want to kiss the hell out of him each time he does it.

"Where did you get those bookmarks?" I ask when there's a slight lull.

He gives me a chagrined smile and shrugs. "I got one of each of your bookmarks from your stash at your house and had a local printer make some for me this week. I hope you don't mind."

"Mind? Heck no, I don't mind, but I certainly didn't expect you to do that."

"It's the least I could do since you agreed to come with me." He strokes a hand down my arm and wraps his pinky around mine. "How much have we gotten in donations today?"

"Over three thousand dollars," I tell him excitedly. "I can barely zip the locking money bag."

"That was such a good idea, babe. What about the silent auctions?"

I giggle as I check the sign-up sheet on the table. "The highest bids are almost two thousand on each one."

He rolls his eyes. "I can't believe women are willing to pay that much to remove my tie and unbutton my shirt."

"If you'd agree to let them take off your pants, we could quadruple the bids," I point out.

Riggs levels me with a flat stare. "You're pushing it, woman. And how did I let you talk me into the second one?"

"My irresistible sexual prowess?"

The event coordinator, Kat Bancroft, approaches with a smile. "How's it going, Mr. Romero?" she asks.

"Very well, Kat. Thanks for agreeing to let us do this."

"Oh, we're more than happy to. The room is buzzing about it." She checks the time on her phone. "I'll send the photographer over, and you can get started."

Twenty minutes later, a crowd surrounds us as they await the announcement. Riggs smiles and addresses them.

"First of all, thank you to everyone who has donated money for the children's home. The kids will be moved to a new house very soon, and every donation you've made will go directly to helping with that. You are truly making their lives better."

Everyone applauds, and he gestures at me. "The gorgeous Libby Cox will be accepting any last minute donations. She can take cash, credit cards, or PayPal."

Kat, the coordinator, steps forward and takes over. "Okay, let's move on to the main events. First of all, who gets to undress Riggs Romero?"

The crowd of mostly women cheers loudly.

I hand Kat the silent auction sheet, and she glances at the name at the bottom. "It looks like the highest bidder is… Greg Waller."

Riggs's eyes widen for a second, and then he laughs in that good-natured way he has.

A thin man who appears to be in his late twenties shoves his way through the crowd and literally sprints to Riggs, pure excitement brimming his brown eyes.

Riggs grins cheerfully and removes his jacket before spreading his arms open wide. "Do your worst, Mr. Waller."

I turn on some burlesque music, and the crowd hoots and hollers as Greg unties Riggs's red tie and swings it over his head like a lasso. Then he wraps it around his forehead like a headband before his fingers unbutton the crisp white shirt Riggs is wearing. Everyone claps and yells as the photographer snaps a ton of pictures.

Riggs poses for a few more photos with Greg, both men grinning widely before Greg walks over to give me his credit card. "That was so much fun," he chirps. "Well worth the eighteen hundred dollars."

I run his card quickly through the Square reader so I don't miss the next event, which I think was a genius idea on my part. Last time I checked, the bid was a little over two-thousand dollars, but I've seen a few more women write down bids since then.

Kat picks up the next auction sheet and raises her voice to be heard over the buzz of chatter. "All right, everyone. It's time for our final event. Who gets to spray oil on our handsome model?"

The crowd grows raucous, whistling and catcalling as Riggs removes his shirt. *Dear god!* The man looks like a sculpture with his navy pants and bare torso.

"I think every person in the room is standing in a puddle of their own drool," Greg tells me, checking out Riggs's hard, chiseled pecs and abs.

"We need a cleanup on aisle two," I jokingly intone in my best grocery store announcer voice.

Kat looks down at the sheet. "The highest bid is—wow—three thousand dollars!" There's a collective gasp in the room and then more cheering. When everyone finally quiets, she says, with much fanfare, "The lucky lady who gets to spray oil all over Riggs Romero is… Melinda Pratt."

"That's me." The crowd parts, and a tiny woman with dark skin and a curly white hairdo marches to the front with a huge smile on her face. She's got to be at least eighty years old.

Riggs bends to say something to her, and she laughs before taking the spray bottle filled with oil. To much delight from the crowd, she sprays him down and then rubs the oil all over his torso. She's quite… thorough.

Once Melinda is done, my handsome boyfriend bends and places a sweet kiss on her cheek, and the lady's face flushes. God, I adore him. He's such a good sport.

After cleaning her hands with a towel provided by Kat, Melinda walks over to me and whips out her credit card.

"Thank you so much, Ms. Pratt," I tell her as I punch in the amount. "Did you have fun?"

She has a bit of a midwestern accent when she replies, "Honey, I haven't had that much fun since the pigs ate my sister." We share a laugh, and her face turns serious. "I grew up in one of those homes. The folks that worked there did their best, but the place was obviously lacking in funds."

I hand her card back to her. "Well, I think it's lovely that you're in a position to give back."

Melinda's shoulders straighten and her chin lifts. "I was adopted by a wonderful family when I was thirteen and then went on to become a pediatrician. Practiced for almost forty years."

My eyes fill with tears. "So you pulled yourself up by the bootstraps."

"That I did, missy," she says before glancing over her shoulder at Riggs, who was chatting amiably with some fans. "Is he your boyfriend?"

"He is," I confirm.

Melinda turns back to me with a sly grin. "You're a lucky woman. He seems like a fine man."

I press my lips together and nod, overwhelmed with emotion as Riggs meets my eyes and gives me a wink. "He sure is."

CHAPTER 24
Riggs

It's been a week since Libby and I returned from New York, and I'm fucking gone for this woman. She didn't worm her way under my skin. No, she dove in and implanted herself there.

I park in front of our usual pub and sit in my truck for a few minutes, remembering last Sunday, our last day in New York before we'd taken a late flight back to Florida. We'd spent the entire day walking around downtown, shopping and holding hands. I'd kissed her every time the mood struck me, which was surprisingly frequent.

Reaching for my phone, I smiled at the lock screen photo, one of Libby and me in front of the huge Christmas tree at Rockefeller Center. Her eyes are bright and her smile brilliant in the pic. And me? Fuck, I look like a lovesick puppy, gazing down at her in her jeans, boots, red sweater, and black peacoat.

She is absolutely the most stunning woman I've ever seen, and as I get to know her better, she only gets more attractive to me. Her heart is as big as her home state of Texas, and that's the most beautiful thing about her.

Stowing my phone in my pocket, I climb out of my truck and

enter the pub to find Ty sitting in a green vinyl booth. "What's up, Mills?" I ask, sliding in across from him.

"Romero," he says with a grin. "Salazar will be a few minutes late."

Yes, we're those guys who call each other by their last names, but we actually have a good reason. When we met in our college dorm as suitemates, the fourth member of our group was, oddly enough, also named Tyson. So to avoid confusion, the last names thing was born.

We order our beers, and by the time the waitress drops off our drinks, Salazar arrives. "How's it going with New Erica?" he asks Mills.

Our friend's face softens. "I told her about the whole dick tattoo mix-up, and she was very understanding."

"She didn't freak out?"

"Nope." He glances around the room and lowers his voice. "She said she's going to imagine that I got it for her because she realized she has a bit of a stalker kink. We've been… exploring that with some role playing."

"Sounds hot," Salazar says before turning to me. "Romero, weren't you on the cover of a stalker book once?"

"I was." I pull up a pic on my phone and hand it over.

Salazar rubs one side of his chest as they stare at the photo of me dressed all in black with my blue eyes narrowed at the camera. "Damn, son. You're looking all sinister and shit. Would it make you uncomfortable if I told you this pic makes my nipples hard?"

He looks up at me, and I stare at him, deadpan. "Extremely uncomfortable. Don't speak of your nipples again." The asshole smirks at me.

Though my back is to the door, I know the second she enters the bar without even turning around. Since Libby and I have been dating for a couple weeks now, and it's obviously serious, we decided to tell our friends and families about our relationship. We're supposed to tell Salazar and Mills tonight.

Libby told me she has a plan and asked me to just roll with it. I have no idea what that plan entails, but from the wicked smile on her face when she said it, I'm sure it's going to be entertaining.

She's getting closer, my gut tells me as Salazar's eyes fix over my shoulder. Then he grins and says, "Look who's here. It's Libbidy Bibbidy."

Her goofy laugh reaches my ears, and my heart does a stomping River Dance in my chest when I look up at her standing beside our table. She's wearing jeans, a white sweater, and an adorable hot-pink Santa hat.

"Hi, Tyson, Penn." Then our eyes meet, and she says, "Riggs, correct?" I want to tell her she should know my name because she spent last night screaming it into the mattress, but I nod instead, playing along with whatever her scheme is.

"Nice to see you, Libby. Would you like to sit down?"

"That would be great." I stand and allow her to scoot into the inside of the booth before I sit again. *What the hell is she up to?*

When the server comes by, Libby orders a beer, and we all make polite chit chat for a few minutes. Then she props her chin in her hand, looks up at me, and purrs, "Riggs, would you like to go out some time?"

Salazar and Mills jerk their eyes between us as I pretend to think about it. "Hmm, we could probably make that happen."

She smiles sweetly. "How is your penis situation?"

I bite the inside of my cheek hard to keep from barking out a laugh. Mills chokes on something, and our other friend pounds him on the back.

"I'd like to say it's strong. I haven't had any complaints," I assure her.

Libby gives me a stern look. "I don't want to get involved with you only to find out you have a sub-par peen. I can't tell you how many times that's happened to me."

Nodding in understanding, I say, "That's a shame. Penis status transparency is very important."

I feel a hand on my leg. I recognize that hand. I fucking love that hand. "I'd like to know for sure," she tells me, sliding her hand up until it's cupping my cock, which immediately pops up to say hello.

Swear to god, I think I love this woman.

Finally, Mills speaks. "A-are you rubbing his junk?"

She smiles at him. "I am." Giving me a squeeze beneath the table, she says, "Wow, Riggs. You're bigger than Bruce."

"Bruce Willis?" Mills asks. "Because that dude gives off some serious BDE."

For fuck's sake.

Libby giggles. "No, I'm talking about Bruce Banner. That's what I call my vibrator."

Salazar's beer bottle slips from his hand, and he barely catches it before it spills. "Y-you named your vibrator after the Incredible Hulk?"

I'm trying so hard not to laugh. Or moan. Because her hand is still on my goddamn dick.

"Yes," she replies, the picture of nonchalance. "It's green."

"Really?" Salazar drawls. "I thought all vibrators were pink or purple."

Are we seriously sitting here talking about vibrator hues?

"Those are the most popular, but you can definitely find more fun colors if you look," she assures him before turning her attention back to me. "Can we go to your place, Romero?"

"Of course," I tell her, having difficulty meeting her eye because I'm afraid I'll laugh. "I just got a few new board games."

"Dude," I hear Mills say, disappointment evident in his tone.

"Do you have Yahtzee?" she asks brightly. "We could play a couple rounds, and then I could really use a good, solid weinering."

Oh my fuck... this woman...

Mills chokes on his own tongue, and Salazar's eyes look like they're about to pop out of their sockets when I scrunch my face.

"I dunno. That would make me feel kinda cheap, Libby. Picking up a girl in the bar and taking her home for some weinering."

"The fuck?" Mills whispers, and I'm barely holding my hilarity inside.

"What if we were in a relationship?" Libby suggests, and I nod slowly.

"That could work. Do you want to be my girlfriend?"

A smirk plays across her pretty lips. "As long as you're a good kisser."

In response, I wrap my hand around her braid and hold her in place as my lips descend on hers for a very long, very inappropriate kiss.

When we pull apart, Libby's eyes are dreamy, but she says, "That wasn't bad at all, Romero. You've got yourself a girlfriend. Now let's go. I have my strap-on in my purse."

"What?" Mills practically screams, but Salazar's brown eyes narrow into shrewd slits as he points back and forth between us.

"They're fucking with us, Mills. That was no first kiss."

Libby's mischievous smile does mushy things to my insides, and I think I'm fucking falling hard for this woman. When she tries to move her roving hand from my dick, I clamp my fingers around her wrist to hold it there.

"Finish your drink," I tell her in a low voice, "and then we're going back to my place."

The green in her irises sparkles when she gives me a wink and turns back to my shell-shocked friends. "Okay, maybe Riggs and I have been seeing each other." Her fingers drum against my balls, and I'm seriously about to haul this woman out of the bar and fuck her in the backseat of my truck.

"Fuck yeah," Mills says holding up one fist. I give him the obligatory bump and then curl my arm possessively around Libby's shoulders. She leans into me and takes a long pull from her beer.

"I love this," Salazar adds with a genuine smile on his face as he looks between us. "In fact, it's making my nipples tingle." He gives them both a nice pinch.

"That's it," I bark. "We're leaving." I shoot out of the booth before he can do anything else nipple-related and hold out my hand to help Libby stand.

"I guess we're going to play Yahtzee now," she teases, wiggling her fingers at my friends. "Bye, guys."

I give my buddies a cursory nod before placing my hand on Libby's lower back. As we turn, Mills says, "See ya, Libbidy Bibbidy. And Romero, enjoy that strap-on."

I flip them off over my shoulder as I lead my girl from the bar.

I help Nana Viv into my SUV. It's five days till Christmas, and she's looking beautiful in a sage-green pantsuit with a wreath pin on her lapel. I close the door once she's buckled into the front seat and then round the vehicle and climb in.

"Are you excited about seeing the trees in Port Saint Joe, Nana?"

She smiles and claps her hands under her chin. "I am. It's my favorite part of the year. And it's our little tradition, just me and my handsome grandson, looking at all the Christmas trees folks have decorated."

My nerves skyrocket. Maybe this wasn't such a good idea after all. But I steel my spine and say, "Nana, I have a new friend I've been spending time with, and I invited her to go with us. Is that… okay?"

Her sharp blue eyes bore into me. "A friend or a girlfriend?"

"A girlfriend. I know this seems sudden, and I guess it is, but I feel like I've known her forever."

"There's no set timeline for romance. People come into our lives exactly when they're supposed to."

"I know, but Lucinda and I broke up so recently. Libby and I got together after that, so I don't want you to think—"

Nana interrupts me by bopping me on the back of the head. "Oh, stop fretting like I'm some prudish old bat, Riggs." That makes me laugh. "Your grandfather always said he knew I was the one from the first time he saw me, even though I was supposed to marry someone else. I told you our story, so you'll hear no judgment from me."

"Thanks, Nana. I think Libby and I have something very special. I hope you like her."

"What does Ace think about this Libby?"

I chuckle. "He adores her, and she likes him too."

"Then I like her already. You can tell a lot about a person by how animals respond to them. Now, let's go get your new friend."

I needn't have worried about Nana liking Libby. As soon as I lead her from her house, she opens the passenger's side door of my SUV to give my grandmother a warm hug.

"Nana Viv, it's such a pleasure to meet you. I've heard so much about you."

"Only the good parts are true," Nana quips.

Opening the back door for Libby, my eyes can't help but drink her in. She's wearing a festive red top with long sleeves and wide, black upturned cuffs. Her black pants are high-waisted and flared at the bottom, and her ass looks amazing in them.

As soon as I pull onto the street, Nana pulls down her mirror so she can see into the backseat. "Libby, what do you do?"

"I design websites for companies, and I'm also a romance author."

Nana's head tilts in interest. "Do you use a pen name?"

"Yes, ma'am. It's Libby Cox."

My grandmother's eyes widen. "Are you serious? I've read a couple of your books. My granddaughter gave them to me."

What the hell, Silvia? I got my sister hooked on Libby's books, but I had no idea she shared them with our grandma.

Libby's cheeks pinken, no doubt at the thought of Nana reading her steamy novels.

"I didn't realize you read romance books," I say.

"Oh, don't look so scandalized, Riggs. At my age I've seen and done it all."

My face really wants to scrunch up at the thought of my Nana *doing it all*, but I manage to maintain something resembling a neutral expression.

"That's so awesome," Libby tells her. "A lot of my readers are over sixty-five. What's your favorite kind of romance to read?"

"I really like reverse harem," Nana informs her. "All those hands and mouths and… you know." She winks into the mirror at my girlfriend and *dear god, help me!*

"Why don't we listen to some Christmas music?" I break in, pressing a button until José Feliciano is wishing us all a Feliz Navidad.

Because, for fuck's sake, my Navidad will not be very feliz if I can't scrub the thought of Nana reading RH books from my brain.

CHAPTER 25

Riggs

We had a blast at the annual Port Saint Joe Festival of Trees at the Center of the Arts. As we walked around and looked at the festively decorated Christmas trees, Libby, my fucking dream girl, hooked her arm with Nana's. She acted as though they were old friends out for a stroll, but I knew she was lending support because Nana's too stubborn and prideful to use her cane out in public. That simple act of kindness only made me fall harder for Liberty Hill.

Afterward, as was my tradition with Nana, we all had a fancy dinner at The White Marlin, a waterside restaurant on the bay.

"Are you taking me home?" Libby asks after I drop off Nana at her house in Mexico Beach and hop back on Highway 98 toward Port Saint Joe. She sounds disappointed.

Reaching for her hand, I lift it and kiss her knuckles. "No, I wanted to show you something."

"You just like to do the time warp thing, don't you?"

I laugh at that. The change from central to eastern time zone occurs in Mexico Beach. There's even a big photo op chair so people can sit in both time zones at the same time.

"It's a surprise," I tell her, hoping she hasn't already seen it.

I go through a drive-through and order us each a hot cocoa with extra marshmallows, and a few minutes later, I back my SUV into a parking spot.

"Keep your eyes closed," I remind Libby as I open the door for her.

"They're closed, you weirdo. Where are we?"

Leading her to the back of my vehicle, I pop the hatch open and guide her to sit down before pressing a kiss to her lips.

"Keep 'em closed. Let me get the cocoa." After retrieving our drinks, I settle in beside her and cover us with a light blanket. "Okay, you can look now."

"Am I going to see your penis when I open my eyes?"

I chuckle. "No, I'm saving that for when we get back to my house. You can penis-gaze to your heart's content." Focusing on her face, I watch the wonder in her eyes when her lids lift.

"Riggs, it's gorgeous!" she gasps.

My chest swells because I love sharing things with her, making her happy. I finally pull my eyes from her and look beyond the vehicle. The local lighthouse has been draped so it looks like a Christmas tree, the tiny white lights sparkling against the dark backdrop of night.

We snuggle close together and drink our cocoa as we enjoy the beautiful sight in front of us. No words are spoken. We're simply *being*.

Turning my head, I kiss Libby's temple and she looks up at me with stars in her eyes, literally and figuratively. "Thank you, Riggs."

"You're welcome, baby." Our lips brush for a brief second, and my next words whisper against her soft mouth. "I've never felt like this with anyone."

"Me neither."

I kiss her again—more deeply this time—tasting the marshmallow and chocolate on her tongue, but the flavor is nowhere as sweet as the emotions surging through my chest.

And in the soft glow of the lighthouse, I fall madly in love with Liberty Hill.

There are only two days left till Christmas, and today is my last day of work at Mercato. Yes, I'm still going to be involved in the family business as a member of the board of directors, but Silvia is going to step into the VP job until Leo retires.

I feel so fucking light and free as I walk out the door of the office building. My phone pings, and I smile when I see Nana's name.

> Nana Viv: Your girl called to get my lasagna recipe. Let me know how it turns out.

Goddamn, my heart is full right now. And so is my cock. Is it weird that I'm turned on by the thought of Libby cooking my grandma's recipe?

On a whim, I stop and buy a bouquet of daffodils wrapped with a big yellow bow before heading home. I gave Libby a key to my house because she likes writing on my back porch, and I'm happy to find her car parked out front when I arrive.

I enter quietly and hear singing from the kitchen. Leaning against the doorframe, I watch Libby's cute little ass swaying as she browns ground sausage on the stovetop and croons a sultry version of "Santa Baby."

Her blonde ponytail bounces with her movements, and I smile. Libby manages to be sexy and adorable at the same time. Scooping some of the meat onto a saucer, she blows on it before squatting down and setting it on the floor.

"Here ya go, my little nugget." Ace gobbles the snack and

ogles at the woman rubbing his head. "Is that good stuff, buddy?" His tongue lolls out as he grins.

Libby continues her singing as she moves to the sink to wash her hands. While she's drying them, a pop sounds from the stovetop, and she squeals.

"Shit, the sauce!" Rushing to the stove, she attempts to stir something in a large pot, but red splatters plop up from inside and make a huge mess. "Fuck you, stupid sauce," she growls, grabbing the handle and moving the pot from the burner. The odor of burned tomatoes reaches my nose.

"I don't think it's supposed to smell like that." At the sound of my voice, Libby yelps, snagging a knife from the counter and whirling around. "Easy, killer," I say with a laugh, holding my hands out in front of me.

When she realizes it's me, she sets her weapon down. "Dammit, Riggs, you almost gave me a heart attack," she complains before her eyes fall to what's in my hand, and she smiles. "Did you bring me flowers?"

"No, I brought them for that poor sauce you murdered," I tease, striding toward her and handing her the flowers.

Her smile when she buries her nose in them makes me want to buy her every flower in the world, and I can't help but be struck by the difference between Libby and Lucinda. I'd bought my ex a huge bouquet of imported, very expensive white roses once, and she'd complained that it was only two dozen. Libby, on the other hand, has tears in her eyes over a simple bouquet that cost me around forty bucks.

And it's a million percent *not* about the money. I have plenty of that and don't mind spending it on my girl. It's about the enti-tled attitude versus the appreciative one.

Libby's pretty eyes lift to mine, and she flashes me a chagrined smile. "Thank you, Riggs. I love these so much, but I probably don't deserve them since I ruined the sauce." She turns to frown at the mess on the stove, but I cup her chin and force her to look at me.

"Liberty, you could burn every single thing you cook for the rest of our lives, and I'd still want to shower you with flowers."

A blush of pink rises on her cheeks. "But it was Nana's—"

I shush her with a soft kiss on the lips. "I know, and thank you, baby. That's the sweetest thing anyone's ever done for me." I press my mouth to hers once more, just because I fucking love doing it. "And we'll start over and make the sauce together… after…"

"After what?"

"Glad you asked," I say, tossing her easily over my shoulder. She squeals, and I turn off all the burners and stride toward my bedroom. "You have sauce in your hair, so I'm going to clean you up. But first I'm going to get you nice and filthy."

"I don't get this kind of service at the salon."

I smile around the nipple in my mouth as my fingers dig deep into Libby's scalp. Releasing her with a pop, I stand to my full height and guide her beneath the rainfall shower spray.

I purchased all Libby's favorite shower items, and she has her own shelf in my luxurious shower. The smell of her tropical shampoo surrounding us has me hard against her stomach. As soon as she's completely rinsed, she locks her eyes with mine and sinks to her knees.

"Libby, you don't… have… to…" My words falter as my gorgeous girl licks a languorous stripe up the underside of my rigid cock.

"What were you saying?" she asks with faux innocence, just before wrapping her lips around the head of my erection and sucking.

"It wasn't important," I pant. "Please carry on."

Her smile is pure wickedness a second before she takes me to the back of her throat. "Goddammit, your mouth is heaven, Libby," I groan, slamming a hand against the black diagonal shower tiles on the wall.

And it is. She knows the perfect amount of suction I like, and the way she constantly moves her tongue against my aching dick is fucking captivating.

My other hand grips the back of her hair and guides her mouth up and down my length. The woman has no gag reflex, but that doesn't stop me from trying as I push to the back of her throat. She merely hums around me, and a bolt of desire races up my cock.

"Fuck, you're pretty when you're on your knees for me, baby," I tell her, thrusting hard and deep into her warm, welcoming mouth. "You look like an angel, but you suck cock like a dirty little slut."

I watch as one of her hands slips between her spread thighs and moves against her bare pussy. God, I fucking love when she gets so into sucking me off that she has to touch herself.

"That's it, my little angel-slut. Rub one out while my cock is down your throat." It takes less than a minute of my dirty talk and her talented fingers before she's coming, moaning around my erection.

"I'm close," I tell her, my voice a harsh rasp as I guide her head up and down. But she resists my hand and pulls back, releasing me from her mouth. "You need a break, baby?"

She shakes her head and lowers her mouth to my ball sack. With a flicking tongue, she laps at me as her hands grasp my hips. "Put both your hands on the wall, Riggs. I'm about to give you a ballgasm."

I do as she asks, a grin ripping across my face. "I don't know what a ballgasm is, but I'm here for it."

She shows me, sucking one swollen orb and then the other into her mouth, that sweet little tongue massaging my nuts until my knees feel like they're about to fail me. "Libby," I moan, spreading my legs wider as my fingers curl against the damp tiles.

Increasing the intensity of her suction, she slips one hand between my ass cheeks and circles my hole, her eyes turned up to me. I know she's silently asking my permission, and though no one has ever done that to me before, I give her an affirming nod. I'd fucking deny her nothing.

Her finger pressing into my ass feels foreign, but she's gentle with me, her movements slow as her mouth continues to suckle my balls. First one, and then the other. When she pushes into my backside all the way to the knuckle, I can't hold back for another second.

"Fuuuuck," I shout as the first spurt shoots off like a cannon from the end of my dick and lands in her hair. My hands fist against the wall as she moves her mouth upward and clamps her lips around my crown, sucking me completely dry. "Dear god, woman. What are you doing to me?"

My legs tremble and my heart pounds like a bass drum as I look down at the woman smiling up at me, looking awfully damn pleased with herself. *I love her. This sweet, kinky, beautiful woman has stolen my heart, and I don't ever want it back.*

I tug her to her feet and wrap my arms around her before lowering my mouth to hers. I've never had the desire to taste my own release before, but on her tongue, it tastes like sin and lust and love, all rolled into one.

"Let me wash your hair again, baby. I came on your head," I whisper against her lips, and she giggles, surprisingly unperturbed by the thought of it.

"It's like a protein treatment," she tells me. "Maybe we can do that more often. It will save me a lot of money."

Seriously… love her.

"Plus, you said the people at the salon don't suck on your tits," I tease, before going back in for another long kiss.

By the time I've shampooed and conditioned her hair and

then washed every inch of her body—spending an unnecessary but delightful amount of time between her legs—I'm hard again. I've been edging my girl, and she's panting for me.

"Please, Riggs," she says, gripping my dick and jerking me hard. "Fuck me with this big, veiny cock. I need it rough."

That I can do, sweetheart.

I spin her around and slap her ass. "Hands on the wall, Liberty. Don't make me tell you twice."

Hearing the unmistakable command in my voice, she does as she's told, her breaths hitching in and out of her chest. My girl likes when I get nasty with her. And by god, I love giving that to her.

Leaning forward, I rest my throbbing erection against her backside and growl into her ear. "Do you know what the fuck you do to me in this position? Do you have any idea of the depraved thoughts I have about this tight ass?"

"It's yours," she whimpers.

"Good answer, sweetheart," I tell her, grinding against the pillowy cheeks. Taking my cock in my hand, I rub the tip between her wet lips before nudging her clit, causing her to drop her head down and groan.

"Fuck me, Riggs."

"I plan to, baby. First, I want you to arch your back for me." She bends slightly, and I spank her ass. "I said. Arch. Your fuck-ing. Back."

Libby bends forward and juts out her ass, forming the most beautiful curve I've ever seen. Gliding my hand down her spine, I feed an inch of my cock into her. The grip of her pussy is exquisite, and I take her hips in my hands before slamming the rest of the way home.

"Fuck yes, Riggs. Ride my ass like you own it," she cries, pressing her hands into the wall and shoving back against me.

That's what I love about screwing this woman. She's not a passive lover; she fucks like a pretty little beast. I smile to myself.

Except for last night when I had her at my mercy, tied spread eagle on my bed so she couldn't move an inch.

With one hand fisted in her wet hair, I give her exactly what she asked for. I ride her ass with deep, hard strokes, holding her hip so I don't slam her into the wall. The water from overhead sluices between us, magnifying the slap of hips against ass.

"Christ, baby. You take me so well. You're my good girl, aren't you?"

"Yes," she breathes, the word barely audible. "I'm your good, naughty girl."

"So fucking naughty," I tell her, smacking the slick flesh of one butt cheek and then the other, alternating again and again until her skin is is the most beautiful shade of *I got my ass spanked* red.

The slap of my hand on her backside makes her feral, and she rolls her body to grind back onto me. Banding one arm around her waist, I lean forward and press my chest to her back, taking her deeper with each ruthless thrust.

"I've never felt anything better than this sweet, tight cunt. The way you ripple around me when you're about to come all over my cock." I encircle her throat with my hand, giving her a five-finger necklace that has her voice box humming with pleasure against my palm.

"Riggs, I'm so close," she moans, turning her face in search of my lips. I kiss her, and our mouths fuse together as we both near our peak.

"I'm right there with you, baby."

Releasing her neck, I reach for the detachable shower head and flick it on. Starting at her pert breasts, I work the powerful spray down her body until I reach her pussy. As soon as the jet of water touches her clit, Libby's entire body bucks with the most potent orgasm I've ever felt a woman have.

The walls of her pussy clamp down around my cock so tightly, I can barely move, and she screams my name. My body goes into overdrive, fucking her through her climax as I spill my release inside her.

As the last tremor of her sex fades away, Libby's knees buckle, and I drop the shower attachment to hold her up. "I've got you, my beautiful girl," I murmur into her ear.

But in actuality, It's the other way around.

She's got me… hook, line, and sinker.

CHAPTER 26

Libby

It's Christmas Eve, and I just finished some last minute shopping. I got Riggs the cutest boxer briefs with Fish Assassin printed across the butt. And there's a fish on the front directly where his *ahem* will sit.

My fingers drum on the steering wheel as I fret about the size. I mean, he's a big man, so the large will probably fit him, but what if he wears a medium? He does have slim hips.

Shit. I hate returning items after the holidays. All the lines and grumpy-ass people are annoying. Gnawing my bottom lip, I turn on my blinker and head toward Riggs's house. He's at the marina with Joe today, so I'll just dash inside and check his underwear size. I still have time to return them before the store closes at five.

I hop out of the car and use the key Riggs gave me to unlock the front door. Ace skids up excitedly, and I bend to give him a quick neck rub before jogging to the bedroom. Checking the sizes in a couple pairs, I sigh with relief. *Large.* I figured all that cake couldn't be contained in a medium. Not to mention what he's packing in the front.

I'm about to close the drawer when something catches my

eye. "Is that a ring box?" I ask the empty room. It doesn't respond.

Scratching the side of my face, I stare down at it as my heart rate picks up a notch. I recognize the distinctive black and white box as being from an exclusive jeweler that specializes in engagement rings.

Surely he's not… No, of course he's not. We haven't even said *I love you* to each other. And that's when my gaze snags on the paper beneath the box. It's folded so only the words HOLIDAY PROPOSAL are visible.

Shit. I know I'm falling in love with the man, and I'm certain he feels the same, but a proposal after only two months? And we haven't even been a couple for the entire time.

Should I talk to him about it? I'd hate for him to propose only to have me ask for more time. I'd never want to make him feel bad. What if he does it out in public? Oh my fucking god. What is he thinking?

I have to look. I have to see what's on that paper. Maybe it will give me some kind of clue. It's possible that the ring is a family heirloom that he's holding onto, and he's planning to propose next Christmas.

I won't look at the ring though. I want to see it for the first time when he gives it to me. Carefully pulling out the papers, I begin to read.

> *HOLIDAY PROPOSAL*
> *As soon as dessert is served, get down on one knee with our families surrounding us. Say the following:*
> *My dearest Lucinda,*

"Hold on a damn minute. Lucinda?" I snap at the paper. I read that part again before continuing.

> *From the very first time I saw you, I knew you were the one for me. Your beauty is indescribable, but your warm*

heart is what captured my own. The love I have for you burns from within my soul, and I can't wait to spend my life with you.

My lungs have forgotten how to breathe. My heart has forgotten how to beat. My legs have forgotten how to hold me up.

As I sink to my knees, I force myself to read the rest of the elaborately worded proposal. *To her. Not me.*

A warm nose nuzzles my neck, and I wrap an arm around Ace's furry body as he whimpers, trying to give me comfort that I'm not sure is even attainable at this point.

"Is this how he feels about her?" I ask the dog, and he licks my face. "Thank you, nugget. You love me, don't you?" Sweet Ace crowds me until his big body is on my lap, and I bury my face in his fur and dampen it with my tears.

Sitting like that for the longest time, I let the pain pour out of me. I feel more for Riggs after a couple months than I did during the years with Logan. I thought he was my person.

My stomach clenches with nausea at the thought of losing him. He can't possibly want to be with Lucinda. She's not right for him. Because *I'm* right for him.

Wiping my face, I kiss Ace on the head. "I'm okay, buddy. You can let me up now." With a gentle shove, I manage to remove the pooch from my lap and stand. After replacing the letter in Riggs's underwear drawer, I give my fluffernugget one more hug and leave.

My lips press together as I sit in my car and stare at the house I love but will probably never see again.

"Goodbye," I whisper, gritting my teeth against the need to cry again. My breastbone feels like it's sinking into my chest, attempting to crush my heart, and *fuck, this hurts.*

Without thinking, I swipe on a name on my phone and wait.

"Hey, Libs," a voice answers.

Pulling out of the driveway, I don't even look back as I speak. "Gemma, I need you."

Her voice is instantly alert. "What's wrong?"

"You know how I called you, Ava, and JoJo this week and told you about me and Riggs?"

"Yeah," she replies warily. "And we said we're all happy for you."

"It's all blown up in my face, Gem. I think it's over."

On the short drive back to Port Saint Joe, I fill her in on what I found.

"What the fuck? Why are men so goddamn stupid?" she spits, and I hear something in her tone that worries me.

"A-are you and Trey okay?" I ask, momentarily forgetting about my own problems. Trey was Gemma's first BBB client, and much like Riggs and myself, they fell hard for each other.

"No, I don't think Trey is my happily ever after," she sighs sadly, and my broken heart manages to shatter into even more pieces.

"Gemma, no! I thought…"

"I did too," she murmurs.

"Tell me what happened." I pull up in front of my cute little house and grab my purse. By the time I get inside and change into lounge pants and a long-sleeved T-shirt that hangs to my knees, Gemma has spilled her guts.

"So that's it," she says, as I lounge onto my couch.

"Damn, Gem. I'm kinda torn. On one hand, I'm thinking maybe he had a good reason, but on the other hand, I want to put on a boxing glove and punch Trey in the face."

That earns me a watery laugh from my friend. "I'm oscillating between the two as well. Why are all the men with good dicks so deceptive?"

"I don't know whether to laugh or cry at that. What are you going to do?"

"I have no clue. What about you?"

"Same. All I know is that I can't go to the Christmas Eve

party at Nana's tonight. Especially if he's going to propose to Lucinda there. I was thinking, since you're visiting your grandmother in Florida, and you're only about an hour from me…"

"You want to come hang with us?"

"I don't want to intrude."

"You won't be. We've just gotten into our pajamas, and we're about to watch movies and eat enough crappy food to make us bloat. You're welcome to join us, but, hmmm."

My ears perk up at her thoughtful hum. "What are you thinking?"

"I'm thinking this whole thing doesn't sound like Riggs, not from what you've told me. It sounds like he's being pressured or something because that man is completely into you, not his ex."

"What the hell can I do about it? I'm not going to beg a man to love me."

"Fuck no you're not. Look, do you have that hair-styling iron I sent you?"

"The one I thought was a sex toy at first?"

"You should have known I wouldn't send you a sex toy without the appropriate lube."

"In a fuchsia tube?" I ask dryly, and she bursts into laughter.

"Here's what's going to happen, Lubey Libby. We're going to FaceTime so I can help you pick out a spectacular outfit, and then you're going to do your hair and makeup like the sexy vixen you are."

"Okaaaay," I drawl. "Then what?"

"Then you, my friend, are going to be the most kick-ass book girlfriend that's ever lived."

CHAPTER 27

"Where's your new girlfriend?" my mother asks. She's dressed in a green dress that looks lovely with her dark hair. "Nana said she really likes her."

Checking my phone again, I see Libby is around thirty minutes late. The Christmas Eve party is in full swing, and I tug at the collar of my burgundy button-down.

"I texted her, and she said she'd be a few minutes late," I reply.

"She'll be along," Mom says, soothing me with a hand on my arm. "Your father and I can't wait to meet her."

I hear a car door slam outside, and my head jerks toward the front of the mansion like Ace when he hears a cat in the yard. "Maybe that's her." Making my way out to the expansive front porch, a sense of joy infuses me when Libby emerges from her car.

Holy fucking hell. She is stunning. Her blonde hair is styled in long, loose waves, pulled up with a sparkly clip on one side. My eyes run down her body, and all the saliva in my mouth dries up. Libby is wearing a red pantsuit that makes her look like a Christmas siren.

I'm not sure what kind of bra she's wearing, but *goddamn,* that cleavage. The pants fit her slender legs like a glove, and high glittery heels catch the last rays of the sun.

She's wearing more makeup than I've ever seen her wear, with winged eyeliner and glossy red lips. I grin as my girl strides toward me with a… frown?

"Baby, you look gorgeous," I say, trying to take her hand as she stomps up the steps, but she shakes me off.

"You have some nerve, Riggs Romero." She gives me a poke in the chest with a red-painted fingernail.

"I, uh, what?" I ask, confused by her aggression.

"I know," she hisses, her eyes tapering to slits.

"Know what?" I ask, my hand automatically going to the small box in the front pocket of my black gabardine pants. Her gaze zeros in on that movement, and her eyes are so squinty, I can't even see a hint of hazel iris.

"That!" She looks back up at me, and I almost shiver from the furious pinch of her mouth.

Shit, she knows about her Christmas present and is pissed. But why? Because she thinks they're too expensive? Probably. Well, she's just going to have to fucking get used to it. I have money, and I plan to spoil her rotten.

"If we're going to be together, you're just going to have to deal with it, Libby. I—"

Her eyes go saucer-round, and she cuts me off with another jab against my chest. "Deal with it? Oh, noooo, Mr. Romero. I will certainly not *deal with it.* Do you think you're going to marry her and still see me on the side? I'm nobody's side piece."

Okay, I'm completely perplexed at this point. "Marry who?"

Libby throws her hands up in exasperation. "Lucinda! I know all about your little *holiday proposal,*" she grits out. "I found the ring box in your underwear drawer."

Ahhh, things start to clear up in my mind, and I fight a smile at her gross misconception.

"So you were snooping."

"I was not," she snaps indignantly. "I was checking your underwear size for… something. It's not important right now. The point is that I know you don't want to marry Lucinda. You don't even like her. You like me. And I like you, even when you're being an idiot."

"An idiot? Seems you have poor taste in men, Liberty," I say, biting the inside of my cheek to control my face.

"It seems I do, but you've grown on me. Like a wart," she snarks, and I cover my snort with a fake cough. "If you're being pressured to marry Lucinda, I'm here to stand by your side and help you resist the pressure. I know it can be hard standing up to people you love, but I plan to be here to support you."

My heart melts into the consistency of warm oatmeal. I mean, she's completely off base, but she's offering to be something I've never had: a true partner.

Then those pretty eyes narrow again, and she grips my jaw. "But if you still think you're going to propose to Lucinda tonight, you're going to have to do it in front of me. You're going to have to get down on one knee before her, knowing you're breaking my heart in the process. And that's not the kind of man I know you to be, Riggs Romero."

Then she nods with finality, pats my cheek a bit harder than necessary, and marches into the house.

I watch the door close behind her and finally allow my smile to break free. The fucking balls on this woman. The strength and loyalty.

God. Damn. Is it weird that I'm fully hard right now?

After giving my penis a moment to calm down, I follow Libby into the house, only to find her standing with Nana Viv. Their clasped hands are between them, and the grin on my grandmother's face smacks me right in the chest.

How did I ever mistake the tolerant smile she used to have when she saw me and Lucinda together for this… this… purely joyous one?

I'm happy Nana approves, but like she told me, it's no one else's business who I decide to love. And I'm utterly, head-over-heels in love with the sassy woman in the red pantsuit.

The one who adores me. The one who plays peek-a-boo with my dog. The one who can write a sex scene so hot it makes my neck sweat. The one who can bring those scenes to life in my arms.

Heading to the corner of the living room, I motion for the deejay to turn down the Christmas tune he's playing, and I take the microphone. Tapping on it twice, I step onto the small, raised platform and say, "Everyone, can I have your attention please?"

All the furniture has been removed for the party, and the enormous space is filled with almost a hundred people, a mixture of friends and business colleagues. Their chatter dies down as every eye turns toward me. Including Libby's.

Getting through all the formalities, the whole *thank you for coming, we're so grateful, happy holidays* spiel, I allow my eyes to skitter across Libby as I look around the room. She stands with her arms crossed defensively over her chest at the front of the crowd, and her eyes are hazel fire.

Oh, my sweet Libby.

"I have something special I'd like to share with you all tonight," I say, and I can feel the sharpness of her gaze, like she's shooting actual daggers at me. Then I turn to look at her, reveling in the shock on her face when I hold out my hand. "Libby, can you join me, please?"

When she doesn't move, I walk to her and take her hand. "What are you doing, Riggs?" she whispers but allows me to lead her onto the low stage.

"You'll see," I say in a low voice. "Just smile and listen."

Libby bares her teeth, but instead of looking like a smile, it looks more like she may bite off any part of my anatomy I get too close to her mouth.

Speaking into the microphone again, I hold tightly to her hand. "I want to introduce all of you the beautiful Libby Hill." I smile reassuringly down at her and get lost in her eyes. "She's my girlfriend, and I'm absolutely crazy about her."

A series of *awww* noises come from the crowd, and her face softens. I kiss the tip of her nose and manage to pull my gaze away to once again address the guests. "Libby is fairly new to the area, so everyone please make her feel welcome because she's very important to me." Releasing her hand, I wrap my arm around her waist, claiming her as mine. "Except for you, Phillips; you keep your distance."

I look pointedly at Andy Phillips, one of Mercato's food suppliers and a known playboy, as the room lets out a collective chuckle. He lifts his champagne glass in a silent salute of surrender.

"Everyone enjoy the food and drinks, and if you'll excuse me, I need to speak with my girl privately for a moment."

"Really, Romero? I didn't realize you could speak with your d— *owww*!"

Penn's charming remark is cut short when Nana cuffs him upside the head. "Penn Salazar! Where are your manners?"

"Sorry, Nana," he mutters, though he tosses me a wink.

"Come on, sweetheart," I say in a low voice to Libby, guiding her to a door behind us. We make our way through the next room, out into the hallway, and up the curved staircase to the second floor. Once there, I push open the door to an upstairs parlor and open the glass door to the balcony.

Libby and I step out onto the flagstone, and I turn to face her. "Is this okay, or is it too cold?" The temperature this evening is in the fifties.

"I'm fine. Did you bring me up here so you could toss me over the balcony for being an asshat?"

Laughing, I pull her to me. "Never. I just thought we needed a private place to talk. You seemed to have some… misconceptions."

Even in the moonlight, I can see the blush coloring her high cheekbones. "Is that your way of saying I'm a raging bitch who jumped to conclusions?"

"You did jump to conclusions, but you're the farthest thing from a bitch, Libby. You showed up here ready to fight for me, and it was about the hottest thing I've ever seen." I kiss the spot between her eyebrows. "For the record, I never intended on proposing to Lucinda. She stuck that ring in my pocket at Thanksgiving, along with fucking directions on how she wanted the proposal to go. We argued about it and that's when we broke up."

Libby glances down and squinches her eyes shut. "Oh. Well, I feel like a complete idiot."

"Lucinda isn't even here tonight. I called her today as a courtesy to let her know that I'm seeing someone. I didn't want to blindside her. She said she wasn't planning to come anyway. She's dating someone as well, and she's spending the evening with his family."

Libby looks up at me and smiles. "Hopefully he's better suited to her."

I bark out a laugh. "She's going out with the guy who owns the jewelry store where she picked out the engagement ring that wasn't to be. I'm sure he's pretty perfect for her. For the record, the only reason I kept that ring is because I'm trying to figure out what to do with it. I'll probably sell it and donate the money."

Her head tilts in thought. "So what's that box in your pocket?"

I smile. "That's your Christmas present. I wasn't sure what you'd be wearing, so I brought it just in case it would look good with your outfit. Which is smokin', by the way." My eyes roam down and hang up on her rounded cleavage. "I want to fucking motorboat your tits right now."

She giggles and swats my chest. "Stop it, Riggs." Her teeth sink into her bottom lip. "Can I see my present?"

"Of course. I think they'll look gorgeous with what you're

wearing." I pull out the box that's wrapped with yellow paper—Libby's favorite color—and has a tiny, festive green bow on top.

When Libby unwraps the gift and opens the lid of the pale-blue box, the sparkle in her eyes tells me I made a good choice. "Riggs, these are… oh my god, I love them!" she squeals. "They match my shoes!"

"Do you want to put them on?" She nods happily and reaches for the silver studs in her earlobes. I remove one of the new earrings from the box and hold it up, letting the moonlight gleam off the shimmering strands of tiny diamonds that dangle down like streamers.

After she has both of her studs removed, I lean in and kiss each bare earlobe and whisper, "Can I put them on you?" She nods, and I feed one post through the hole and secure it before doing the same to the other. The simple act seems so intimate, and I resist the urge to blurt out that I love her.

But no. I have plans for that revelation.

Libby shakes her head from side to side, making the earrings dance as a smile takes over her lips. "I love these so much, Riggs. Thank you. Rhinestones are my favorite."

"Are they?" I ask with an amused grin, and she picks up on it.

"What are you—Oh my shit! These aren't real diamonds, are they?"

"They are," I reluctantly inform her. When she reaches for one of them, I grip her wrists and stop her.

"Stop it, Riggs."

"Do you like them?"

"They're too expensive."

I tug her closer to me and kiss her forehead. "That's not what I asked, Libby-girl. Do. You. Like. Them?"

"Of course I like them. They're stunning, but—"

"But nothing. If you like them, wear them. It's simple."

"I bought you underwear," she wails. "I mean, I got you some other stuff too, but nothing like diamond earrings."

"It's not a competition, baby. I got you some other stuff too, and not everything is expensive. In fact, my favorite is a four-dollar magnet of the Christmas tree in Rockefeller Center. It's the first place where…" I pause and adjust my words. "It's the first place where I realized how perfect we are together."

Her eyes well up and her voice crackles. "You got me a magnet?"

God, I love this woman so fucking much. She tears up at a damn magnet that costs one-thousand times less than the earrings she's currently wearing.

"I did, because it holds a special memory for us. And these earrings… I immediately thought of you when I saw them. They move like they're full of vibrance and energy, just like you."

"Riggs," she chokes out, throwing her arms around my neck. "Thank you."

"You're welcome, baby. Now sit down." I guide her to a rattan chair and kneel in front of her. "I'm about to prove to you that you're the only woman for me."

Her eyebrows lift. "Oh really?"

I nod, running my hands beneath her suit jacket to search for the button of her pants. "Where the hell…"

"There's a zipper on the side," she says with a smirk, and my fingers immediately locate it.

Locking my eyes with hers in the dim blue moonlight, I say, "Prepare to be claimed, Liberty."

Twenty minutes later, I have three of my woman's orgasms still vibrating against my tongue as I guide her down the steps and back to the party.

"You're looking awfully smug," she comments, holding my hand.

"I'm feeling awfully smug," I admit. "How does it feel to know I'm about to introduce you to my parents with the taste of your sweet cunt in my mouth?"

Her lips curl up into a wicked smile. "You're a pervert, Cobra McSnugglebuns."

"And I've met my match in the very spicy Libby Cocks."

CHAPTER 28

Libby

The tiny sparkles of light wink at me from the Rockefeller Center tree magnet that I've placed at eye level on my refrigerator. Memories of our trip to New York flood my mind, but my reverie is broken by a ping from my phone.

I smile when I see a message from the BBB group text.

JoJo: Happy New Year's Eve, ladies. I need a new kink. I feel like I've worn out the old ones.

Gemma: I wore out my favorite vibrator last week.

Libby: Thank you for that completely irrelevant tidbit, Gem. What kind of kink are we talking here, Jo? Personal life or book kinks?

JoJo: I'm doing quite well with my personal kinks, TYVM. It's for a book.

Ava: Ok, don't judge me, but I read a book recently where the guy liked fucking her feet. Or is that more of a fetish?

Gemma: I think that's a fetish. You always surprise me with your reading choices, Ava. Absolutely no judgment though. You do you, boo.

Ava: I read a holiday romance about an elf last week. Who knew pointy ears could be so hot?

Libby: Since we're not being judgy, I read one at Easter about a Cadbury Creme Egg that hatched a very well-hung Easter Bunny.

JoJo: I feel as though there's a cream joke in there somewhere, but I can't quite place it.

Libby: Oh there were plenty in the book. It wasn't very good, but it made me laugh.

Gemma: Since it was Easter-themed, please tell me there was a penis-related "he is risen" line.

Libby: I can confirm.

JoJo: Can we get back to the kinks?

Gemma: I've got one that's literally pure gold... golden shower.

JoJo: No.

Gemma: Brown shower?

Ava: Oooh, I know someone who knows someone who dated a guy that had a glass table fetish.

Libby: WTF is that?

Ava: Where he lies beneath a glass table and the woman lays on top and... relieves herself.

JoJo: FFS, no bodily waste whatsoever. I can't bring myself to write about peeing or dropping a deuce in a sexual manner.

Gemma: Can we go back to the fact that Ava "knows someone who knows someone who dated a guy?" Sounds a lot like "asking for a friend."

Ava: I can assure you that is not my thing. I couldn't even bring myself to pee in the toilet in front of Zach, and we were married.

JoJo: Hellooooo? Control your ADD brains and help me with kinks.

Ava: Pacifier play.

JoJo: Is that like that baby/mommy thing Gemma was talking about in Colorado?

Ava: No, the penis is the pacifier.

JoJo: Ah, gotcha. I'll look it up and do some research.

Libby: You could do breeding kink. Kinda hot when he's so obsessed that all he can think about is putting a baby in her.

JoJo: Another good possibility. This guy is kinda stalker-y, so it might work.

Gemma: Role play could be really fun. An endless supply of options.

Libby: In the same thread, he could have a clothing kink. Like he insists she wear fishnet stockings and garter belts. I dated a guy like that once. I broke up with him when he wanted me to sleep in fucking stockings.

JoJo: Adding it to the list. Lots of different ways that could go. Maybe he only wants her to wear satin panties or the color blue.

Gemma: Orrrrr…

Gemma: The color gold.

JoJo: I'm out.

Libby: Hope y'all have a Happy New Year!

Ava: You too.

Gemma: HNY

I'm cackling out loud when I hear a knock on my front door.

"Hey, handsome," I say when I open the door and find Riggs standing there in his graphite-gray sweater. With one hand stuffed casually into the pocket of his black pants, he looks like a damn model. Well, technically, he is.

"Happy New Year's Eve," he says, holding out the yellow roses he has in his other hand.

"Riggs, you've got to stop spoiling me."

"Nope." He presses a firm kiss on my lips. "It's my right as a book boyfriend to do what-the-fuck-ever I want."

My grin is so big it almost hurts my face as I take the flowers and lead him into the kitchen. "Well, thank you. It's sweet of you, but you didn't have to. You bought me so many clothes for Christmas."

"This looks cute on you, by the way," he says, taking in the slim navy pants and yellow sweater with blue and yellow trim around the V-neck. Soft brown Sperry loafers complete the look. "Very yacht-like."

"Are we really going on a yacht tonight?" I ask, putting the flowers in a glass vase and adding water.

"Yep. I'm thinking of buying it, and I want you to help me decide."

I blink rapidly and shake my head. "I don't know anything about yachts, Riggs. I've never even been to a party on a boat."

His smile is soft as he winds a lock of my hair around his index finger. "I know, but I'm not buying this to be a party vessel. It's mainly just for us to enjoy, so I want you to let me know if you like it."

"Just for us?" I question, unsure if I've heard him correctly.

"During our first meeting, we talked about what would make us happy, and you said you wanted to be out on a boat with your computer so you could write. Words and water, remember?"

Curling my arms around his waist, I bury my face in his neck and inhale his fresh scent. He smells like expensive sunshine.

"I remember. I can't believe you do though."

His arms tighten around me, binding me to his hard body. "I remember everything about you, Libby-girl. Everything."

Dear god, I am so fucking in love with this big, beautiful man. I only hope that maybe one day he'll feel the same.

"What do you think?" Riggs asks.

"It's beautiful," I assure him. "I love all the wood and recessed lighting inside. It's fancy without being opulent, if that makes sense. Makes it feel cozy."

"That was my thought as well. It's big but not obnoxiously so, which is what I like about it. I want you to be comfortable here." He wraps an arm around my shoulders as we stand on the deck and look around. He anchored the boat about a mile offshore before giving me the tour. "It can be a place for just the two of us."

"I'm a fan of the master bedroom," I tell him with a coy smile, and he cops a feel of my boob and squeezes.

"You're going to be even more of a fan once we christen it tonight."

"Make it good, and I'll write yacht sex into my next book," I promise.

Riggs chuckles. "Challenge accepted, Miss Hill. Now let's have dinner while the sun sets."

"This has been the perfect night," I sigh, cuddling into Riggs. We're sharing a luxurious lounge bed on the upper deck, simply enjoying the sounds of the water lapping against the sides of the boat.

We'd had a divine dinner of seared scallops and roasted vegetables as we watched the sun descend until it was gone. Then we'd cruised around for a few hours with me sitting on Riggs's lap. He even let me take the helm and work the controls for a while, and I managed not to run into anything, which was pretty easy, given that we were on open water.

He rolls toward me and presses his palm against my cheek. "I'm feeling so fucking lucky right now."

"Why?"

"Because this is your idea of a perfect New Year's Eve night. No wild parties or fancy restaurants. Just you and me out here on the water together."

I smile and turn my head a little to kiss his palm. "I can't think of anything more romantic."

Riggs leans up on one elbow, his thumb tracing my cheekbone as he looms over me. "You mean so much to me, Libby. I know it's only been a little over two months, but I can't ever imagine being with anyone else."

"Me neither," I say, my voice scraping up my throat with a soft rasp.

"You've become my everything. My sunrise and my sunset."

"That seems like a lot of pressure, being both," I say, and he chuckles.

"And yet you do it so effortlessly. You're my sunrise because you bring light to every day. And you're my sunset because you make me feel secure in knowing I'll get to see the sun again tomorrow. You give me hope, Libby, and…"

He pauses as the sound of fireworks begins in the distance. And then, as the old year bleeds into the new, Riggs finishes his statement.

"I love you, Liberty Hill. I'm so goddamn in love with you, I can't see straight."

As the fireworks sparkle in the sky, I feel like my heart is bursting with the same vibrance and light. *He loves me? He freaking loves me?* My eyelids are heavy with tears that want to escape.

"Riggs, I… I've never been happier than I am with you." His lips crook up into a smile that makes it difficult for me to breathe. I suck in a deep breath and sink my fingers into his hair as I exhale. "I love you too."

It wasn't nearly as poetic an expression of love as his sunrise/sunset analogy, but he doesn't seem to mind my simple words. His lips crash into mine, and we share the happiest kiss in the history of love.

His soft laugh dusts across my lips. "I can't even kiss you properly because I can't stop smiling."

"Same," I say against the curve of his mouth as his hand lowers to my hip and drags me beneath him. My legs automatically wrap around his waist, and the feel of the man I love on top of me makes me blissfully dizzy.

We make out to the soundtrack of lapping water and fireworks, and I'm positive my heart has never been so full.

Eventually, we end up naked on the lounge bed, and Riggs rolls back on top of me. The chilly bite of the night air is warded off by his big, warm body covering mine.

"If this is a dream, I don't want to wake up," I whisper as he notches the head of his erection against my center.

"This is real, Liberty. The realest thing I've ever had." And he slides in deep, his hands buried in my hair. "This is love."

His blue eyes are darker than usual, lit only by the intermittent kaleidoscope flashes in the air above us. My eyes feel swollen with tears, and one escapes as Riggs begins to move.

"Am I hurting you?" he asks, brow furrowing with concern.

"No, you're loving me," I reply, lifting my head to press a kiss to his firm lips. "You're mine."

"I love when you steal my book-boyfriend lines," he whispers, rolling his hips to tunnel impossibly deeper inside me, and I smile.

I don't think I ever smiled during sex before I met Riggs. It was always a mixed mass of concentration and striving for pleasure. But with the man currently on top of me, sex is effortless, like it's something made especially for us to do.

"Do you want me to tell you to shut the fuck up and take this pussy like a good boy?"

His responding grin is so motherfucking cocky, I almost come on the spot. "I'm pretty sure I'm already taking this pussy exactly how she needs to be taken," he growls.

Yeah, the man can growl out filth like a champ. I'm talking Olympic gold-medal worthy rasps that have me tightening around him.

"Ahhh, that's my good girl," he croons. "Come for me. Come for the man who loves you more than all the stars in the sky and all the fish in the sea."

That mixture of dirty and incredibly sweet pushes me over the brink of need and directly into a soul-bending orgasm.

"Riggs!" I call to the night sky.

"Yes, baby. Let me feel you squeeze around me. Show me how I make you feel, Libby."

And I do. I come undone in his arms, digging my heels into his butt as he continues to pump into me, thrusting through my orgasm with long, slow strokes that extend the climax way beyond what should be humanly possible. I cry out his name over and over while he makes love to me, out on the water we both love with the twinkling stars our only witnesses.

A few minutes later, we find our final releases together with our lips melded and our hearts fused.

Riggs Romero loves me. And I love him. And life can't get any better than this.

We sit naked on the huge bed in the bedroom—or the *cabin*, as Riggs informed me. I've also learned that the kitchen is the *galley*, and the bathroom is the *head*. And yes, I made blow job jokes when he told me that.

"I can't believe you made me a diploma from Book Boyfriend University," he says, staring at the official-looking document with a huge grin on his face. "And I graduated summa cum laude."

"Only the highest honors for my man," I tell him, leaning forward for a kiss.

"Are you going to do this for all your clients?"

I nod. "I think so. It's a cute idea. But you're the only one who will be receiving a report card."

He glances at the ivory cardstock resting on the nightstand and chuckles that low, deep laugh that never fails to tighten my nipples to hard points. "Probably a good idea since you included some very naughty and… inventive categories."

"You're also the only one that will be getting these," I sing, pulling a clear plastic bag from the drawer.

Riggs's eyes light up, and his voice goes an octave higher in excitement. "I get gold stars?"

"Yep," I say, popping the P, pulling out a huge metallic star and affixing it to his chest, directly over his heart. "This is my favorite part of you."

A mischievous grin rips across his face as he reclines and lifts his hips, waggling his magnificent dick at me. "And what's your second-favorite part, Libby-girl?"

For the next thirty minutes we laugh and kiss as we cover each other with shiny gold stars. "I can't believe you put fifteen of them on my ass," I say with a giggle once we've emptied the bag.

Riggs pulls me into his arms and gives me a light swat on the butt. "You, my dear, have a fifteen-star ass. Highly recommend."

"I'm glad you added me to your cart," I tell him cheekily, and he thumbs the star over my left nipple.

"I'm buying this yacht," he says suddenly.

"Okay," I say, my heart swelling with happiness.

"This is the first place we said those three little words to each other, so I guess I'm buying the memory for us."

"That's sweet, Riggs. If I had another star, I would put it on your chest."

He plasters our sparkle-covered bodies together and kisses the tip of my nose. "I want to spend my days with you out here on the water. I can do paperwork and marketing for the marina, and you can write to your heart's content."

"Words and water," I say dreamily, and Riggs gently holds the side of my face, his blue eyes shining with adoration.

"Words and water," he repeats. "And love, Libby-girl. Always love."

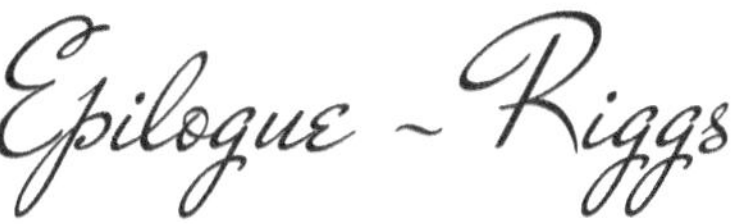

Epilogue ~ Riggs

ONE YEAR LATER

"You get everything set up?" I whisper to Darryl as Libby chats with Joe. The old guy retired a few months ago and turned everything over to me, but he still comes to the marina almost every day. He can't help himself, claiming his blood is fifty percent salt water.

"All done," Darryl says, glancing up at me from the flounder he's cleaning.

"And you put the thing on the… you know, *the thing?*"

"The thing is on the thing," he confirms, looking over his shoulder and smiling as Joe waves his hands animatedly as Libby nods along. "She's a good woman, Riggs."

"The best," I say on an exhale of pure nervousness. "I think we're going to head out now."

"Good luck, and Happy New Year's Eve."

"Thanks. Same to you." I stroll over to the bench where Joe is explaining to Libby that Vienna sausages are actually made from chopped up aliens.

"That's fascinating," she says. "I guess I thought aliens would taste more… gamey."

"Huh. Never thought about that," Joe says, scratching his scraggly beard.

"Sorry to interrupt, but we'd better get out on the water if we don't want to miss the sunset."

The smile she shines up at me is luminous and still has the power to stop my heart, even after being together a little over a year. I'm not sure this feeling will ever go away.

Thirty minutes later, I drop the anchor and take in a deep breath of salty air. Walking up behind Libby, I curl my arms around her and kiss the back of her neck.

"Darryl said the flounder were biting today. I thought we'd do a little fishing."

Little rivers of wrinkles appear on her forehead when she turns to face me. "But we're all dressed up," she says, indicating her sparkly gold top, black leather pants, and sexy matching jacket, as well as my dress pants, white shirt, and blazer.

Shit, I didn't think about that.

"Just for a few minutes. I'll handle the bait so you don't mess up your pretty clothes."

Her face is coated in confusion at my insistence. "O-kayyy."

"Just stand over there, and I'll get everything set up."

Giving me another perplexed look, she does as I ask while I go to the cabinet and find the fishing rod. I check to make sure the *thing is on the thing* and attempt to swallow my nerves.

Here we fucking go.

I hand Libby the rod and keep my eyes trained on her face, waiting for the moment she sees *the thing*. She turns toward the water and grips the pole.

"You might want to check the rigging and make sure it's to your liking," I suggest, and she blows me a kiss over her shoulder.

"It's okay, I trust you."

And then to my horror, she rears back, ready to cast.

"Libby, stop!" I yell, and she startles, letting out a little yelp.

"Shit, did I hook your ass again?" she screeches, and like a slow-motion flashback, I watch as she pivots, completely releasing her grip on the rod, and it falls into the Gulf of Mexico.

"Fuck!" Without a second thought, I dive into the frigid water and wrap my hand around the handle as it begins to sink. *Thank Christ.*

I resurface to find Libby leaning over the edge of the yacht, her mouth agape at my apparent stupidity. "Riggs Romero, are you insane? That water is freezing."

"I'm aware," I say wryly, feeling the cold in my bones as I swiftly swim aft and climb back onto the boat with my rescued treasure in my grasp. *Holy fucking shit, that was close.*

Libby is there with a towel and immediately begins rubbing my sopping wet hair and face. "You have completely lost your mind," she scolds. "You could have died. A fishing rod is not worth losing your life, Romero."

"It's not the rod," I tell her, my teeth chattering as I strip off my now-hundred-pound jacket. "It's what's on it."

"What do you mean?"

In answer, I hold up the pole and dangle the line directly in front of her face. Her eyes follow like she's being drawn into a stupor by a hypnotist as the engagement ring swings back and forth. Thank god Darryl knows how to tie a proper knot.

"Riggs, that's… oh… that's… and I almost…" Her eyes are wide and filled with dread.

"This isn't exactly how I had this planned," I tell her as I drop to one soggy knee on the deck and grin up at her with lips that I'm sure are quite blue at this point.

Libby covers her mouth with both hands, and I attempt to untie the ring from the end of the fishing line. The task proves impossible with fingers that are trembling from the cold. "Fuck, I can't…"

She lets out a hysterical giggle before turning to the tool cabinet and grabbing a knife. Gripping the ring between her finger and thumb, she cuts it loose before handing it back to me.

"Christ, this is officially the worst proposal ever," I grumble. "I wouldn't blame you at all if you said no."

She smooths my dripping hair back with gentle fingers and smiles down at me. "I won't say no."

Fuck, that makes my hypothermic ass happy. I manage to hold the ring—which has a large yellow diamond surrounded by a double halo of white diamonds—steady as I take her hand.

"I know I've fucked this whole thing up, Lib," I start, but she shushes me with a finger to my icy lips.

"You didn't. This is the best proposal ever because it's unpredictable and funny and a little bit crazy. It's *us*. Plus, I'm the one that freaked out and threw the fishing rod."

I wiggle my eyebrows, which feel like they have icicles dripping from them, but I soldier on. I've got some proposing to do. "That's true, so I hope you'll feel sorry enough for me to say yes."

She laughs as I take her hand and continue. "I had a whole thing I was going to say, but I think my brain is frozen. I'll tell you the rest once I can feel my face again. But I love and adore you more than anything, Lib. I want you to be my wife. My family. Along with the fluffernugget of course." Her smile is brighter than the sun that's starting to set behind her. "Liberty Hill, will you please be my wife?"

"Yes," she rasps, and tears stream down her face as I slide the ring on her finger.

Thank Christ.

I rise, and before I can stop her, Libby throws her arms around me, drenching the front of her clothes. Her mouth feels like fire against my cold one as we seal our engagement with a kiss.

"Let's go get in the shower and warm you up, handsome. Your lips are blue."

"So are my balls," I toss back.

A few minutes later, we're naked beneath the shower spray as Libby rubs her hands all over my body to warm me. Seeing my bride-to-be naked and wet, my penis is the first part of my body to make a full recovery. I nudge it up against her stomach.

She glances down and then back up at me with a cute smirk. "I see Rocket Romero has come out to play."

"He's very excited about the wedding and can't wait to see how many lists you make."

"Oh, I can assure you, my list-making will be epic."

I crowd her against the white tiles and lift her by the ass. Her legs automatically wrap around my waist, exactly where they belong. "You're also going to need a new spreadsheet," I say as my cock finds her entrance.

Libby's lips curl into a smile. "You know I always get wet over new spreadsheets. Tell me more."

"There will be lots of boxes, and you can adjust the sizes and borders."

"Mmm, that sounds hot."

"You can color-coordinate the rows with shading."

Libby rotates her hips, taking the first inch of me. "Now you're talking my language, big boy."

"And the title of it," I say, sliding deep inside my future wife with a groan, "will be…"

"Yes?"

I pump in and out and whisper against her lips.

"Rating the Book Husband."

More From Jade

If you want to know more about Auburn and Gianna from this book—and trust me, you do!—check out my Bouvier Family Saga:

- **Love Without Numbers** on Amazon and Audible
- **Love Without Influence** on Amazon
- **Love Without Demands** on Amazon
- **Love Without Control** on Amazon

My Fierce Protectors Series will have your heart if you love spice, found family, former Navy SEALs, and banter galore. This six-book series is now complete:

- **Dauntless Protector** Grumpy protector X sunshiny nanny
- **Devoted Protector** Breaking all her rules
- **Deadly Protector** Second chance with a side of voyeurism
- **Young Protector** Prequel novella to Deadly
- **Disgruntled Protector** Enemies to lovers
- **Determined Protector** Single parents

- **Damaged Protector** Age gap / forbidden

Highway to Hale Series

- **Hale Yes**
- **Hale No**
- **Hale Damage**
- **All Hale the Queen**

Standalones:

- **The "Kinda" Secret Pineapple Island Swingers' Resort** Hilarious rom-com about a romance author who accidentally books her writing retreat… at a swingers' resort!
- **Delay of Game** Angsty, funny sports romance
- **I Dream of Johnny** Romantasy with a sexy Cajun genie

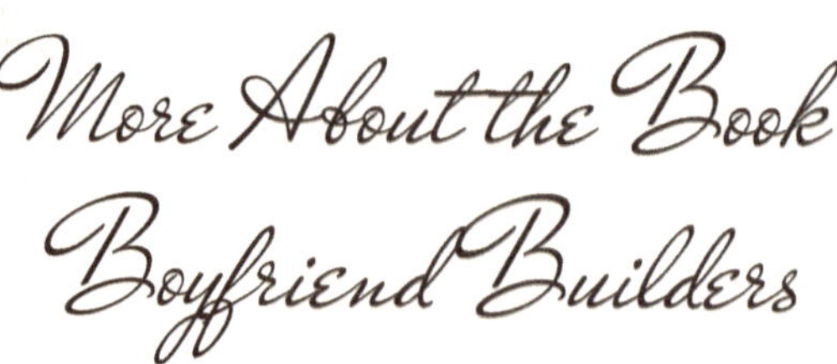

Now you know Libby's story, but you'll definitely want to hear more about her author besties.

- Will **Gemma**'s "plumber" finally open up to her? Will she let him thoroughly clean her pipes? (I'm going to say yes.)
- Can **Ava** finally find a guy who acts like a grown-ass man instead of a boy?
- Will **JoJo** walk away from the red flag guy or will this one be different?

Check out the other BBB titles to find out. You can find them all with the QR code below.

Acknowledgements

- First of all, thank you so much to my **readers**. It means so much that you took a chance on an indie author, and I appreciate the time you took to read **Rating the Book Boyfriend.** I love when readers reach out to me while they're reading, so feel free to do so on my social media platforms.
- **To the fabulous TL Swan:** Thank you so much for your encouragement, advice, and humor. If it weren't for you, my stories would still be collecting virtual cobwebs on my computer.
- **To my beta readers:** You chickies are amazing! Lakshmi, Mindy, Thorunn, Brittany, and Amanda, my days would not be complete without seeing you ladies argue in the comments. I'll keep writing if for no other reason than the hilarity y'all bring. Also, thanks for the "inspirational" Instagram reels you send me. I adore each of you.
- **AK Landow, Carolina Jax, and LA Ferro:** Thank you for being such wonderful and perverted friends. I've loved doing this series with you. You're all amazing authors, and you inspire me every day with your

brilliance. AK, my sister from another mister, my book signing roomie… thanks for hashing out every single detail that goes into publishing a book with me. (But seriously, do you REALLY like the L in this font, or should I switch to another one?)

- **Chrisandra:** You are the most amazing editor in the history of ever. Thank you for the REAL TALK and for your confidence in me and my writing. I'm also so happy to be your fave–but don't worry—I won't tell the others!

- **Chanel, Becca, and Kalie of Good Girls PA services:** Wow! I am so freaking lucky I found you ladies. Thank you for handling business like boss bitches so that I can spend more time writing. Your support means everything to me.

- **To my ARC and Street Teams:** I honestly couldn't do this without you! I love getting to know all of you in the groups, and I just want you to know that I think you're the most amazing, beautiful, fun, book-pimping people on Earth. So keep pimping! Mama's got book covers to pay for.

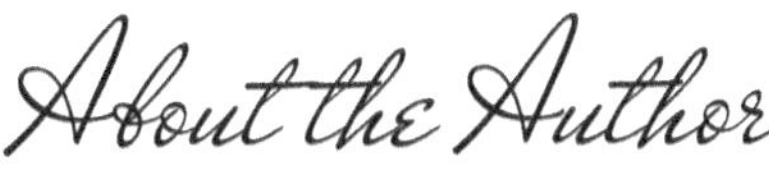

Jade is a Texas author who married her high school sweetheart. They have one semi-grown daughter.

Jade's love of reading all things smutty has turned into a love of writing all things smutty. She enjoys a diverse selection of romance, and this is reflected in her writing style. Be prepared to laugh, cry, cringe, and fan your face, possibly all in a single chapter.

Jade is so excited to share her work with you all and hopes that you enjoy reading the words from her heart.